CYBERKISS

Also by Sally Chapman

Raw Data
Love Bytes

CYBERKISS

Sally Chapman

St. Martin's Press ≈ New York

Design by Basha Zapatka

Library of Congress Cataloging-in-Publication Data

Chapman, Sally
    Cyberkiss / Sally Chapman.—1st ed.
      p.   cm.
    ISBN 0-312-13952-7
     1. Computer industry—California—Santa Clara County—Fiction.
   2. Women detectives—California—Santa Clara County—Fiction.
   3. Santa Clara County (Calif.)—Fiction.   I. Title
PS3553.H295C93   1996
813'.54—dc20   95-39103
                                      CIP

First Edition: March 1996

10 9 8 7 6 5 4 3 2 1

For my brother and Sweetie's father, Lloyd Chapman

Special thanks to Dr. Richard Horuk, Dr. Paul Guttman, Toby Baly, Dan Reese, Joe Valentino, and Mark Pilarski for their assistance with this book.

CYBERKISS

1

Bernie Kowolsky was a textbook example of the species known as Silicon Valley Techno-Dweeb Maximus. You see a thousand like him any day during lunch hour—keyboard jockeys roaming the sun-drenched sidewalks, discussing M-flops and disk capacities while they feed on veggie sandwiches and gulp Jolt Cola.

Before I met Bernie, to me they all looked blandly the same. I guess it's like that with any profession. I had worked in the high tech community long enough to blind me to its inhabitants and each day I looked right through the people who passed by me, assuming I knew who they were without my really knowing them at all, never imagining what fire, what shadows inhabited their souls. To be honest, I don't think I ever looked too deeply into my own soul. But that was all B.B.—Before Bernie.

We met him on a Thursday, a day too sunny and promising to portend the days ahead. It was four in the afternoon. The computer was being serviced and I was frustrated by trying to pay our bills without the aid of technology. Normally I have the computer programmed so it spits out the checks on the tenth of every month, but this month the disk drive threw a temper tantrum. As a result I was having to write the checks by hand, a process I find primitive.

I wasn't making much progress in this effort, mainly because Vic Paoli, my business partner / mi amore, was on top of my desk, balancing on his knees and pointing a camera at me. Whenever I glanced up from our business checkbook I found myself looking directly into Paoli's pelvis, a distraction for even the most self-controlled of women.

Paoli and I were living proof of the old cliché that opposites attract. I was serious-minded and hard working, a natural-born worrier who couldn't sleep at night thinking about our unpaid bills. Paoli's favorite T-shirt said WHAT? ME WORRY? and he was much more concerned with the 49ers' stats than our accounts payable. But before I met him I was a workaholic, tense and sexually repressed. Now I was still a tense workaholic but at least I was having great sex and laughed more.

I was pretty sure he was aiming the camera at my bustline, a feature of mine that I wouldn't consider riveting photo material, especially since I maintain a strict librarian-with-attitude appearance during business hours and all my blouses button up to my chin. I could be a centerfold for *BookWorld*. Paoli never seemed to mind.

"Now give me that look. You know how you raise one eyebrow and pucker your lips. I love that look. It says, Yeah, I'm sexy, but touch me and I'll punch your lights out."

I locked my eyes back onto the checkbook, hoping that if I ignored him he might give up and go back to his desk, but Paoli was persistent. Unfortunately for him I was trying to diet, which always makes me cranky. It crossed my mind that beating him on the head with the checkbook might work off a few calories.

Paoli was supposed to be making phone calls, trying to drum up new clients. Instead he was continuing his folly of producing a glossy color brochure advertising the skills of Data9000 Investigations. I wasn't so keen on it.

"We don't need brochures," I said for the one-hundred-and-twenty-second time, keeping my head down to minimize photo ops. "It's too expensive, too flashy. We're not selling condos in Florida. We're selling computer fraud investigation services. Our business is serious, it's professional, it's—"

Paoli interrupted by reaching over and lifting my chin with his fingers so I had to look at him.

"And you don't think a brochure is serious and professional?" He peered back through the camera lens. "Okay, now toss your hair and lick your lips."

I shot him a look. "No."

"So I guess unbuttoning the top three buttons of your blouse is out of the question?"

I looked at him over my tortoise-shell glasses. "It's outside the time/space continuum as we know it."

He groaned and lowered the camera.

"Don't be a prude, Julie. It wouldn't hurt to show a little skin in the photograph," he said with a smirk that on a day of normal calorie intake I would have found extremely attractive. "Everybody knows that sex sells. People use sex to sell toothpaste, garden hoses, even computers. So why not strut your stuff a little if it'll boost revenue? Come on and give me a couple of buttons. I'm not talking cleavage here. I'm talking just that cute little hollow place at the base of your throat."

I was considering giving him a large gaping hollow place at the base of *his* throat when in the gap between Paoli's thighs I saw a figure in the doorway.

He had all the identifying marks of a computer geek—short, uncombed brown hair, shirt that needed ironing, soiled chinos, Birkenstocks with dark socks, and a nebulous, distracted look in his eyes as if he were receiving psychic transmissions. He looked in his late twenties or early thirties. He also looked scared to death.

It was then I noticed he was carrying a thin black vinyl briefcase with the name of a software company printed on the side, the type they give out as freebies at computer trade shows. My geek suspicions were confirmed.

"Hi. Can we help you?" I asked. Paoli turned his head,

and upon seeing our visitor, climbed down off my desk. I love it when he gets professional.

"I may have a job for you," the man said, his voice hesitant.

Paoli immediately waved him inside with a grand sweep of his arm. "Come right on in," he said happily, approaching our guest and vigorously shaking his trembling hand. Paoli and I had been in business together for only a few months and clients were still a rarity. To be honest, having anyone at all walk into our small office was a rarity, especially anyone using the word "job."

Our prospective client stood there, a look of fear and bewilderment on his face, then he suddenly darted across the room, his body moving in a peculiarly brittle fashion. Staying to one side of the window he pushed his head only far enough to peek out the glass while I watched with apprehension. Something about him didn't bode well.

"Is something wrong?" I asked.

His eyes didn't leave the window. "She may have followed me."

I walked over and took my own look out the glass pane but didn't see anyone. "Who followed you?"

He shook his head. "I'm not sure."

I looked as far around the corner of the parking lot as my neck muscles allowed. "What does she look like?"

"I don't know," he answered.

While our guest stared outside at nothing, I looked at Paoli, tapped my head with my index finger and silently mouthed the word "wacko." Paoli mouthed back "Who cares?," then smiled, held up his hand and rubbed his thumb and index finger together.

We did need money, so I decided to be more open-minded. I had a crazy aunt who heard voices and she was perfectly harmless, even charming sometimes. Besides, Data9000 Investigations was an equal opportunity kind of business and didn't discriminate against those who might be sanity-challenged. I gave our visitor a visual once-over and didn't see any bulges that looked like a knife or gun.

Apparently satisfied that there were no phantoms in the parking lot, he turned back toward us. "I really need your help," he said, his voice thin.

"Lots of people do," Paoli told him, then checked his watch, which he knew perfectly well had stopped running two days earlier. "Let's see, our schedule is pretty packed today, but please have a seat. I think we can spare a few minutes. Julie, are we free for the next half-hour?"

We were free for the next half century, but I checked my calendar anyway, then feigned surprise.

"Why, yes, we have a five o'-clock conference call, but our four o'-clock meeting got delayed so it looks like we're free for the next hour."

The four o'-clock meeting was really our daily trek for frozen yogurt and the five o'-clock conference call was my weekly phone call to my mother. Only a few months before I wouldn't have lowered myself to such petty fibbing, but it was the end of the month and the bills were due.

I gestured toward the two leatherette Deluxe Rental Package chairs that sat in front of our desks. With any luck this client would pay us some money so we could afford the chair he was about to sit in.

"Please, have a seat Mr. . . . ."

"Kowolsky. Bernard Kowolsky." He sat in the chair in front of my desk, twisting sideways in it.

"I'm Julie Blake and this is my partner, Vic Paoli," I said in my best professional voice. Kowolsky smiled weakly. Paoli and I stood next to each other, leaning back against my desk while he looked up at us like a sick dog.

"So, what can we do for you, Mr. Kowolsky?" I asked him, my heart full of hope.

His hands danced in his lap. He examined them a moment, then looked up at me. At first when he opened his mouth to speak the words wouldn't come.

"I'm . . . I'm being stalked," he finally blurted. My hopes for our chair rental payment evaporated faster than a hooker's youth.

"Mr. Kowolsky," I began.

"Call me Bernie."

I smiled politely. "Bernie, you see, Data9000 Investigations specializes in cases of data security and computer fraud."

He sat up in his seat. "But that's why I came to you. I'm being stalked on the Net."

Paoli and I glanced at each other. He was referring to the Internet, an international public computer network. The newsmedia referred to it as the Information Highway. Computer users called it the Net or, jokingly, the InfoBahn or even the Worldwide Information Organism. Call it what you like, basically it's several million computers, large and small, hooked together with phone lines. People from all over the world link into the Net with their computers to send electronic mail, retrieve information and do all kinds of other things.

"How exactly do you mean that, Bernie?" Paoli asked, his arms crossed, speaking slowly, carefully enunciating the words as if Bernie might be a mental patient on an unauthorized field trip.

Bernie fidgeted in his seat, moving left, then right, then finally stabilized. "Have you ever heard of news groups on the Net who focus on special subjects?"

"Sure," Paoli said. "They have discussion groups for all sorts of topics—political views, software, stock tips, whatever."

"We use the Net ourselves," I added, trying to be polite when I was really thinking of ways to get Bernie out of our office.

"Well, there's a group that exchanges messages that are more, well . . ." Bernie pulled his shoulders up to his ears, then relaxed them. "Messages that are, you could say, well, erotic in nature," he said shyly.

I decided to let him stay. It wasn't like we had any real work to do anyhow. Bernie sounded like a nut, but at least his conversation was getting interesting, and I had heard about user groups on the Net that used electronic porno bulletin boards. Rumor was that some of it got pretty kinky and I had always wanted to know more about it but never had the nerve to ask.

But there was something else that drew me to Bernie. He looked so scared, as if he were being chased by demons. Something in his life had beaten him into frightened submission and I was curious to know what it was.

"I'm aware of the erotic groups on the Net" I said, adding quickly, "I've never used the Net for that."

"Yes, well I have," he said, his voice getting squeaky with anxiety. He looked like he was in physical pain. "Only as a joke, of course. At least it started out as a joke. You see, I'd read about ErotikNet in a magazine, and one day about two months ago I was sitting at my desk and needed a break, so I logged into ErotikNet and looked at all the messages."

"A little sex for the head. That sounds harmless enough," Paoli told him. "Like sneaking a peek at a skin magazine. Everybody does that." I made a mental note to check up on Paoli's reading material.

Bernie sat there nervously watching us as if he wasn't sure he wanted to tell the rest, as if he was making the decision whether to stay or bolt out of the office.

"Would you like coffee or water or anything?" Paoli asked, trying to ease the growing tension in the room. Bernie did look a little faint. He shook his head.

I decided he needed some urging. "So, you logged into ErotikNet and looked at the messages. Then what happened?"

Bernie took a deep, shuddering breath. "Well, a few days later I sent a message using an alias. Almost no one uses their own name. You send in a message and it gets lumped in with all the others. You take a look at the messages and then if you want, you can respond to any of them."

Bernie paused and stared down at his groin area, an act I found interesting, considering the direction his story was taking. His face became more pained as each second passed.

"And then?" Paoli asked.

"So the next day I got a few responses. Most of them were pretty predictable, but there was one that really stood out. The user's name was Night Dancer. Night Dancer really had a flair for fantasy," Bernie said with a fleeting smile. "So I responded to her note, and after that we began a conversation—an electronic conversation with our computers."

Bernie stopped talking for a moment.

"So what happened, Bernie?" I asked, egging him on, but Bernie didn't look like he wanted to continue.

"It's like this," he said. Finally ready to spit out the rest of the story, he tried to take a deep breath but it got stuck somewhere around his Adam's apple. He ran his hand through his cropped hair. "Our notes gradually became more personal. More explicit. More graphic." He saw my eyes widen. "To you it may sound sleazy, but I felt like I was more honest and intimate with Night Dancer than I had ever been with anyone."

Paoli shrugged. "Okay, so you had a testosterone surge. Nothing wrong with that. Happens all the time. Why, I have this buddy named Sam back East who—"

I stopped Paoli in midsentence by placing my hand on his arm and applying pressure. I knew what story he was about to tell and it involved some scuba gear and a blonde named Mitzi.

"So how can we help you, Mr. Kowolsky?" I asked.

"Please, call me Bernie. Well, after a few weeks our messages began taking on a sort of sadomasochistic tone, if you know what I mean."

I wasn't sure I did, but I nodded anyway.

Bernie continued. "Night Dancer began threatening me, and eventually she described actually murdering me." He hesitated. "It was quite graphic," he said, uttering the last sentence in a high-pitched stammer.

Bernie closed his eyes and shook all over as he relived the memory. "She described how she would kiss me, and while our lips were together she'd stick a knife in me. A big knife." He held his hands apart to demonstrate how big the knife was supposed to be. It was a big knife.

"She called it 'a date with a Night Dancer.'" At this point his voice broke and his face whitened. He rested a moment while he regained his composure.

"At first I was spooked, but not too worried, because Dancer didn't know who I was. I mean, she only knew me as Whip Boy." Paoli and I exchanged a sideways glance. "But in the message I received yesterday, Dancer described my street and my apartment. I think she's following me." Bernie was visibly shaking again. "Dancer knows where I live. And she wants me dead."

I saw the anxiety on his face and pitied him. The poor guy seemed so terrified. He looked broken, a man who had seen a vision of his own murder and was desperate to survive. My heart went out to him and I wanted to help him, but I didn't see how.

"Bernie, I think this is really a matter for the police," I told him.

He slid to the edge of his chair, his hands clasped in front of him. "But I've gone to the police. I was there this morning. They had me fill out a report."

"Couldn't they run a trace on the communications line? Tracing a computer connection is just like tracing a phone connection," said Paoli.

"A trace is impossible," Bernie replied. "You see, I did all this at the office. There's no way they could run a trace on the communications line without the company knowing. And if my boss found out I was sending these notes during work hours she'd fire me. So there's not much the police can do. I need someone who knows computers, who knows networks. I need you two. You could log on to the Net directly with my ID and figure out where Night Dancer's computer is."

Bernie reached into his pocket, pulled out a check and handed it to Paoli. I peered over at it and saw that the amount was two thousand dollars. It took me a second to catch my breath.

"We charge by the hour, and I don't think—" I said, but Bernie stopped me.

"This would be a retainer. And if you find Night Dancer you keep the whole amount, even if it doesn't take that many hours to find her," he said.

Two thousand dollars was just what we needed to pay the printer for the Data9000 brochures, plus enough left over for two cappuccinos and some doughnuts. I sensed destiny calling.

"How did you find out about us?" I asked him.

"Well, after I left the police station this morning I started phoning up friends, contacts, trying to find out if there was anybody who could help me. I told everyone I had a security problem at the office. A friend of mine at Comtech told me about Data9000. I went to the library and looked up a newspaper article about you. You're the only ones who can help me. I need you to locate Night Dancer. All you have to do is find out who she really is, then give her name to the police."

A pregnant pause filled the office, then Paoli spoke. "Could you excuse us for a moment? My partner and I need to confer."

"Okay, sure," Bernie said.

Paoli took my arm and steered me out the door and into our conference area, which was by the water cooler in the hallway. He shut the office door after him.

"Okay, we stand out here a few minutes like we're discussing it, then go back in and tell Whip Boy we just can't fit him in," Paoli said, keeping his voice low.

"Why?" I asked. Paoli looked at me funny. His blue eyes crinkled at the corners as they narrowed with skepticism, reminding me of how much I adore him. He cocked a thumb toward the office.

"You don't think we should actually work for that guy?"

"I don't see why not."

Paoli put his hands on my shoulders and looked me in the eye.

"Does the term 'fruitcake' mean anything to you—boy meets computer, boy falls for computer, boy has sex with computer? Old Bernie's taking a one-way ride on the Strange Train and I don't like it."

"But Paoli, he's scared to death. You saw him. The poor guy's on the verge of a breakdown. The police apparently can't do anything for him. If we don't help him, who can?"

"How about a team of trained psychiatrists? I can't believe you want to take this case. You're the one who's always talking about how we should be investigating computer fraud for General Motors and Lockheed. And now you want to take on a case for Whip Boy? I can see it in our brochure: 'Data9000 Investigations specializes in computer fraud, software security and cybersex.' Should we get a nine hundred number? And don't forget, we may get that debugging job at Pacific Bank next week. We don't have time for Whip Boy."

"But they're not getting the purchase order approved until next Tuesday. That means we can't start on the job until Wednesday at the earliest. We can have Bernie's problem solved by then."

"Julie, his problem can only be solved with counseling and a handful of Thorazine."

It was time to try a new tack.

"Paoli, is it the sexual nature of this case that's bothering you? Naturally, if you have a problem with that, then—"

Bull's-eye. Paoli pulled his shoulders back and gathered up all his considerable manliness.

"Listen here, sweetheart," he said, jabbing his thumb into his chest. "I can handle the sex part as well as you can. Better than you can. You're a prude. You won't even tell me your bra size."

"Then what's the problem?" I gave him a few seconds to come up with one, then pressed on to the big finish. "And the two thousand dollars will be just enough to pay the design and printing costs for the brochures. I've spent hours going over our finances. We don't have the money to pay for the brochures, Paoli. You want your brochures, don't you?"

I knew he had his heart set on them. He was making plans to send them out to all his friends with his Christmas cards. His body language told me he was softening.

"Well, I never met a dollar I didn't like," he said. "But I think Whip Boy is overestimating our networking skills. Neither one of us specializes in that."

I turned up my palms. "How tough can it be? We're smart. We log on and do a trace from our office. If that doesn't work I'll talk to a few network managers who know the Net. It should be a no-brainer to track this woman down. We'll turn her name over to the police and it's all over." I took his hand and kissed it while I gazed lovingly into his baby blues. "So we help Bernie?"

Paoli sighed. "Okay, but you have to promise me you'll never tell anyone that I worked on a case for someone called Whip Boy."

"I promise." I kissed him, then whispered in his ear. "Thirty-four B."

"What's that?" he asked.

"My bra size."

He chuckled. "I know that. I checked the label months ago." I looked at Paoli with the raised eyebrow / pouty lip look he so admired.

We walked back into the office. Bernie was out of his chair, pacing the room. When he saw us he froze, looking at us hopefully.

"We'll take your case," I told him and his eyes closed with relief. "Let me just get you one of our client forms to fill out."

I found the virgin stack of forms in the file cabinet, pulled one out and handed it to him along with a pen. Putting the form on the edge of my desk, he bent over it and began furiously completing it.

"When can you start?" he asked while he wrote. I looked at Paoli, then back at him.

"Our computer's being serviced right now, and obviously we can't access the Net without it. We get it back on Monday, so I guess we can start then," I said. Bernie's eyes left the form and aimed straight at me, then he put down the pen and rushed up with that weird stiff little walk he had.

"Monday? I can't wait until Monday," Bernie said, losing his few remnants of composure. With a frantic look in his eyes he grabbed my shoulder and began shaking me. "I could be dead by then. Dead, do you hear me? I need your help now. Today. This minute!"

Paoli pulled Bernie away from me. Bernie wasn't a large man, so if the two of them had to duke it out I was sure Paoli would come out the winner, but there was no sense in beating on a client, especially before his check cleared. I gently pushed Paoli out of striking distance and gave Bernie a few comforting pats.

"Now, Bernie, let's not get excited. If we don't have a

computer, we don't have a computer. That's all there is to it."

"No, it's not. There's something we can do. I work for a company called Biotech. I'm the applications manager there."

"I've heard of Biotech," I said. "It's a drug company."

Bernie nodded eagerly. "Yes. You can come to Biotech tomorrow morning and use a computer there. I'll just tell people you're contract programmers I hired. The place is a revolving door for programmers. Nobody will know."

I shook my head. "I don't like that idea, Bernie. It's deceitful and I don't—"

"Please," he pleaded. He grabbed my hands and squeezed. "Please. Just until Monday, then you'll have your computer back. I'm begging you. You could save my life."

What could I say to that? I looked at Paoli. He rolled his eyes, then said okay.

"Fine, we'll work at Biotech."

"Oh God, thank you, thank you." Bernie fumbled through his briefcase and pulled out a stack of papers. "I printed out some of the messages. I thought you should take a look at them." He glanced at the papers in his hand, then uncertainly at us. "They're confidential," he said.

"Naturally. No one will see them but Mr. Paoli and me," I assured him, and Bernie looked at least a little relieved.

Bernie headed out the door, but stopped and looked back at us.

"I feel like I have a new lease on life," he said.

Paoli and I didn't know then that someone intended it to be short term.

2

I like to think of myself as an open-minded person. I'm against censorship, believe in sex education starting with elementary school and hardly flinched at all last year when my gynecologist stuck a mirror between my thighs and insisted I get to know my cervix. But when I read the Net messages between Night Dancer and Bernie-alias-Whip Boy I was reminded of what my best friend, Max, had been telling me for years. I'm basically a prude.

It was more than just the notes I found disquieting. What bothered me most is how wrong my initial impression of our client was. To me Bernie Kowolsky seemed like your basic techno-weenie, and I assumed the erotic notes between him and Night Dancer would be the electronic equivalent of playing doctor—a little network naughtiness and nothing more.

But whether he intended it or not, old Bernie went way past the naughty stage. The notes revealed a bubbling caldron of kinky passion inside him. He wanted sex and he wanted to be tied down while he was having it.

On one hand the idea of it put me off. On the other hand, in a weird way, it made me feel protective of him. He seemed so needy and so exposed. All that vulnerability made me want to put my arms around him and shelter him, although it occurred to me that if I did, he would prefer I do it naked wearing only a leather mask and some stiletto heels.

Paoli and I began reading the messages that night even

though Thursday was a separation night for us. We had recently begun an arrangement in which we stayed apart on Tuesday and Thursday evenings, the objective being the supposed preservation of our independence.

Mind you, this was my idea and not Paoli's. I would never seriously consider dating anyone else, but somehow having a few nights to myself made me feel less nervous about my increasing attachment to him. I had never really been in love until I met Paoli. The emotional roller coaster was new to me, as well as unsettling, and I was struggling to maintain my balance. If Bernie's passion was a bubbling caldron, I was trying to divvy mine up into plastic bags and flash-freeze them so they could be doled out in controlled portions.

Problem was, it didn't work. I didn't like being away from him even for a night, and so far I had always found some transparent excuse to make exceptions to the Tuesday/Thursday rule. This Thursday was no different, and I explained to Paoli that since we were working late on a case there was no logical reason for him to drive all the way home late at night when he would be tired. Knowing what I was doing and expecting it, he grinned and wholeheartedly agreed that late night fatigue could be hazardous on the highway. On the way home we picked up a pizza since there's rarely any food in my house except for granola bars and frozen Lean Cuisines that date back to before the collapse of the Berlin Wall.

I live in a one-level three-bedroom house with a fenced yard, the kind of upper middle class tract house you're supposed to raise a family in, but so far the only thing raised in my house has been my mother's hopes for grandchildren. I originally bought the house when I was the youngest vice-president at International Computers, Inc. and enjoyed a high enough income to need the tax write-off. But in the past year, in an entrepreneurial fever, I quit ICI and Paoli quit his job as a computer specialist for the NSA, and we started Data9000 Investigations. As a result my cashflow had stopped flowing and I had been struggling to keep up my mortgage payments.

In spite of all this, I like my house. It gives me a feeling of stability in a time when my life has been anything but that. When I bought it, it was already painted a friendly gray and had lots of cheery, low-maintenance, drought-tolerant landscaping. It's when you walk inside that you are aware of my personal touch or lack thereof.

· I've never had time for fussing around the house, and if my refrigerator is considered bare and white, my interior decorating coordinates perfectly. I call my decor Neo–Sears Modern, with everything giving off the warm glow of a public restroom. So sue me.

We dropped our coats on a chair, then I changed from my suit into bluejeans and a T-shirt while Paoli traded his shirt and chinos for a sweatsuit.

I grabbed a couple of Diet Cokes, two plates and some paper towels for napkins and brought everything into my living room, which is where we usually eat our meals.

With pizza in one hand and Bernie's ErotikNet messages in the other, we got down to work. After taking a few bites of food to stave off starvation we started reading the notes in the chronological order in which Bernie had them arranged.

As Bernie had said, his relationship with Night Dancer had started out innocently enough, at least by ErotikNet standards. Bernie's first notes had been posted to the general ErotikNet bulletin board, which meant everyone who logged onto ErotikNet could read them, and I found them more pleadingly lonely than erotic. His initial message read:

I am a sensitive, single male who seeks physical and emotional domination by a strong mistress. I've experienced love, but love has seemed shallow compared to the yearning inside me. I want to need someone intensely, feel them deeply. I want to go beyond normal sexual experience but don't know how. My soul hungers for domination. I am a slave searching for his master.

WHIP BOY

When I read the note I felt embarrassed, as if I had rummaged around in Bernie's underwear drawer, yet his words intrigued me and I felt a mixture of interest and pity. We continued through the stack of messages.

Included were several responses he had received from other Net users before he hit pay dirt with Night Dancer. Most of them were replies from college students using university computers and I wondered if the parents knew how their little Muffies and Brads were spending their time. One college student who called himself Bad Daddy suggested that he and Bernie get together, with Bernie to wear diapers and pink plastic panties and be spanked until he was a good boy. Surely Bernie passed up that one.

We flipped through the replies until we came to Night Dancer's. Her reply was several cuts above the rest—more probing, more seductive and darker in tone:

I gaze into the sunless caverns beyond your words and I sense the dark spaces inside you. They are a void, black and velvet. They wait to be filled with dark smoke, white heat and the violence of terrifying pleasure. There are places you need to go, Whip Boy. Places of pain, places of ecstasy. Take my hand. Let me guide you through your secret dreams.

NIGHT DANCER

Paoli chuckled as he read the last few sentences. " 'Dark smoke, white heat and the violence of terrifying pleasure.'

Old Night Dancer is getting ready to boot up Bernie's mainframe." He took a bite of pizza, then wiped a drip of tomato sauce off the Night Dancer message. "Do you have any wine? Reading this stuff makes me want a drink."

I found a half jug of cheap white in the kitchen and hurriedly poured two glasses, anxious to get back to the reading material.

"Let's go to the next one," I said, trying not to sound too eager.

Although I'm thirty-four years old, I've led a sheltered life. During my school years I was the type who won science projects, but never any hearts, and after college and graduate school I was too busy with my career to have much time for men, even when they pursued me. Although I had occasional dates and once even a fiancé, my sex life had the sizzle of Cream of Wheat until I met Paoli, and even with him we hardly whipped each other into sexual submission. I had always suspected that the rest of the world was doing things I knew nothing about.

I gave Paoli his wine, took a few fortifying sips of my own, then we resumed reading Bernie's messages. After Bernie had received Night Dancer's first reply they had begun a private conversation. Instead of posting messages to the general ErotikNet bulletin board where they would be public, their notes were sent directly to each other so no one else saw them.

It was at this point that the exchanges between Whip Boy and Night Dancer became increasingly provocative until after a couple of weeks they broke through the sly references and got down to the sadomasochistic essentials. In one note Bernie described how he wanted to be dominated:

I want to submit to you completely, at least in my fantasies. In a darkened room lit only by a single candle I want you to tie me to the bed with your nylons. I want to feel the burn of your lash, the mark of your heel, the pain of your teeth. I am weak. Make me worthy.

WHIP BOY

As I read these words I stole a glance at Paoli and suddenly felt uncomfortable reading Bernie's messages in front of him. Sure, we regularly saw each other without our clothes, but Paoli and I had known each other less than a year and were still navigating our way through the relationship. I reminded myself that our reading the messages was critical to the case.

"Whoa," Paoli said, looking a little self-conscious himself. "Now we're getting to the good part. Good old Bernie wanted to be chewed on like a steak."

"Don't make fun of him," I said, my protective feelings for Bernie once again rearing their head. "These are his deepest, most secret feelings. What did Night Dancer say to the 'pain of your teeth' part?"

Paoli rifled through the pages. "I think this is it."

Be patient. I will bring you uncommon pleasures of body and mind. You will hear my voice, you will want to submit to me. A part of you will want to resist, but the darker hunger in you cannot resist. I will punish you with my mouth, reward you with my probing fingers. I will invade your most private places, and your face and throat will burn crimson with shame and pleasure. I will fill your empty spaces with the sounds of your screams.

NIGHT DANCER

My eyebrows raised. "That sounds like it would hurt," I said.

"You're telling me. And check this out. In this note he wants to be lashed on the buttocks with a leather whip."

I flipped through the rest of the notes. "Let's find the threatening ones."

"Julie?"

I felt Paoli's hand on mine. "What?"

Paoli leaned over and began kissing my neck. "Reading this stuff is having an effect on me, like I have empty spaces that need to be filled and only you can fill them," he said playfully. Paoli's lips on my neck gave me goosebumps, but I felt we should go through everything Bernie had given us before showing up at Biotech the next morning.

"Let's finish reading the last few notes," I told him, gently pushing him to a safe distance. "Then I promise I'll stuff your empty spaces so full you'll have to rent a storage locker." I held up the note I had in front of me. "Here, this has a direct threat in it."

The time has arrived for your date with the Night Dancer. I come to you, Whip Boy, in darkness. In one hand I hold a rose to caress you, and in the other hand I hold a knife to cut you. You will come to me naked and submissive. I will teach you to enjoy the pain. I will kill you with my love. In the shroud of darkness I promise I will come. Your mouth will open in silent horror but you will not scream. My red lips will devour you. My knife will sink deep within you. I'll taste your blood on my fingertips. I'll experience your pain, and a part of me will die with you.

NIGHT DANCER

Paoli peered over at the paper. "Yes, I would definitely call that one a direct threat."

I looked at the next page in the stack. "Here's the one where she describes Bernie's house."

I know where you live, Whip Boy. I know your little apartment on Carson Avenue. So pristine, so safe. Its shingles are brown as dust and the flowers on your deck red as blood. The flowers need water. Who will take care of them after you're gone, Whip Boy? I look at your house and see your bedroom window on the right side, next to the tree. Look closely at the glass and see the trace of my lips. Will I visit you tonight? Will I come to your bedroom or follow you in the night? You will feel my breath on your neck and know the time has come. I want to touch your blood with my fingertips, taste it on my tongue. Tonight could be the night.

NIGHT DANCER

The doorbell rang and Paoli and I both jumped a foot off the couch.

"I'll get it," I said, laughing, but Paoli grabbed my hand. "No, Julie. Let me."

"Why? Do you think it's Night Dancer at the door?" I said in a mock Boris Karloff voice, but the joke was half-hearted. Night Dancer had me spooked.

We answered the door together and found my best friend Maxine LaCoste standing on my front steps, dressed in bluejeans and a T-shirt and still looking like she had walked off the cover of *Vogue*. Her shoulder-length dark hair was pulled back in a French twist with one silky strand purposely askew in front of her ear. I had always admired her skills at self-decoration. As for me, I had only two styles for my brown hair—ponytail and no ponytail. I checked my watch. It was ten and I wondered what she was doing at my house that late.

"Am I interrupting?" Max asked.

"Nah. We're just sitting around reading pornography," Paoli said.

"Good, I didn't want to bother you."

Max walked past us into the living room and plopped

down onto the couch, throwing her Gucci handbag on the floor with an exaggerated sigh. "I need to talk," she said with her typical dramatic flair. Realizing she was sitting on some papers, Max pulled them out from under her and glanced at them. The glance quickly turned into a stare. "I see your relationship is expanding."

"We're working on a case. Those notes belong to a client," I told her. I tried to take them from her but she pulled them out of my reach. The last thing I wanted was Max pawing through Bernie's private messages like sweaters at a Neiman's sale.

"You shouldn't be reading those," I said, but naturally she ignored me.

"This is work?" she asked as she perused one of them. She tilted her chin up at us, her finger tapping the paper. "You should tell whoever this is that scarves work much better than nylons. Nylons are too stretchy. Of course, I wouldn't use good scarves. The knots ruin them."

It took me a good ten seconds before I realized my mouth was hanging open. That was the great thing about having Max as a friend. She could be irrational, impulsive and annoying, but she was never boring.

"You tie up Hansen?" Paoli asked. Max directed her gaze at him, her expression somber.

"Of course," she replied.

She sounded so matter-of-fact. Was I the only person not into bondage? A nagging little thought bubbled up in the back of my brain, forcing me to briefly speculate on what sort of kinky things Paoli had engaged in before he met me. He had known lots of women. I quickly shook off the thought. It was best I didn't know.

"Our client's been receiving threatening messages on the Internet," I told Max, and she began pressing me for details. I didn't want to give her too much information, but filled her in on the generalities without identifying Bernie.

"I'm sorry, but these printouts are private, Max," I told

her, grabbing them so fast she didn't have time to stop me. She crossed her arms and gave me a curious look.

"I wonder what it is about humans that makes us so fascinated with other people's intimate details?" she said.

"The same thing that makes us look into the Kleenex after we blow our nose. Plain old human curiosity," Paoli replied.

"I wonder," Max said with a devious smile. "I think it's more than curiosity. I think we all have a dark side to us, a side that scares us and thrills us, and we're dying to see if everyone else is as dark and devious as we are."

"Speak for yourself. Max, you know you're welcome in my home any time, but is there something specific you wanted to discuss?" I asked, although I already knew the topic.

Max was engaged to Wayne Hansen, one of Silicon Valley's brilliant, rich, completely eccentric young computer geniuses. Their relationship had always been rocky, but with the wedding only a few days away, Max was having an anxiety attack every eight to ten hours. I was doing my best to be supportive, and I'd been having lunch with her several times a week so I could listen to her anxieties about the upcoming nuptials. What are friends for? And she had heard all my trials and tribulations with Paoli. But at the moment I was too wrapped up in Night Dancer to give Max the proper attention.

"I'm concerned about the wedding," she said. Big news.

"I thought you said at lunch yesterday that you were definitely ready to commit," I told her. Paoli buried his face in the newspaper sports section. He had heard this conversation before.

"No, I mean the wedding itself. I always thought when I got married it would be more traditional. I'm having second thoughts about this Saturn thing."

Wayne Hansen had his heart set on a virtual reality wedding on Saturn and he had hired a team of engineers who had been working on the software for a month. Secretive on the details, Hansen had told Max only that the bride and groom would be set up with full virtual reality datasuits and helmets to experience their wedding on make-believe Saturn. The guests as well as the minister would participate with VR headsets. I thought it was a great idea.

Listening in on our conversation, Paoli peered at us over the top of his newspaper.

"Max, you're marrying a bizarre genius. If you want a traditional wedding, marry a plumber."

I shot him a look.

"Here's an idea," I said to her. "Have the datasuit taken in so it's really tight. It'll look like a catsuit and you'll look wonderful."

Max always liked any opportunity to show off her figure. We discussed the catsuit idea a little longer; placated, she left. I closed the door behind her and sat down on the couch. Paoli put the paper down.

"Don't worry about Max. She'll be fine. Both she and Hansen are crazy in their own way, but I think they'll make a good couple," he said.

"I hope so," I said absent-mindedly, as I looked through more of Bernie's notes.

"Have you ever thought about marriage?" he asked. That one got my attention.

"I was engaged when you met me, remember?"

Paoli knew my engagement to Charles Christian was a sore point with me. Paoli put his face back behind his paper but continued the line of conversation.

"You know, Julie, we've been together almost a year now, and I just want you to know that if you ever want me to make you an honest woman, that I would certainly consider it. Not that I'm ready to jump into anything." He put down the paper again. "But I would want the wedding to be on Atlantis."

His tone was joking but I knew he wasn't, except maybe about the Atlantis part.

"I think outer space would be much more suitable," I said with a laugh intended to hide my nervousness, then tried to change the subject. "Do you want to go through some more of Bernie's notes?"

I could tell I had hurt his feelings by brushing off the marriage conversation. Though he had mentioned marriage in a joking manner, that was just his way of communicating. I knew that and he knew I knew that, but it was a subject I just couldn't deal with. Maybe it was because my engagement to Charles had turned out to be such a disaster. Maybe it was because my father had died when I was little and I had some fear of abandonment in my head. Maybe it was because Paoli referred to women's breasts as "hooters."

We went through a few more of Bernie's notes, then went to bed, which was one place we were usually in perfect sync, but not that night.

I lay there in the dark with Paoli sleeping beside me and thought about Bernie. On the outside Bernie looked like an average guy with average thoughts, but on the inside was part of himself he tried to hide from most of the world. I supposed Max was right. We all have darker sides to ourselves, and it made me wonder about my own. It was a side of me I would soon have to face.

3

Sex is a state of the brain, more of a hungry stirring between the ears than between the legs. Bernie said he had felt more intimate with Night Dancer than he had with anyone, yet his was an intimacy of mind only. Bernie could not see, feel or hear his lover. He wasn't even certain of his lover's gender, yet some sexual need of his had been satisfied through words alone.

The next morning I opened my eyes and saw Paoli's face close to mine, and I wondered what it was that fueled my craving for him. Was it love or lust or self-delusion? I could have happily stayed in bed for hours just looking at him, pondering the meaning of life and love, but I didn't have the time. Instead I crawled out of bed and threw on a terry cloth bathrobe.

I wanted us to get an early start at Biotech, so I gently shook Paoli's shoulder, leaned over, kissed him and told him it was time to get up. He grunted and rolled over.

At six forty-five I brought in a cup of instant coffee and suggested a touch more strongly that he rise to the occasion, but he responded by pulling a pillow over his head. At seven, lacking cymbals or Sousa music, I opened the bedroom window, welcoming in a chilly breeze, then ripped the covers off him, taking a moment to gaze lovingly at his pectorals, perfectly formed from frequent workouts at Gold's Gym.

He turned his handsome baby face in my direction, muttered a few curses, then grabbed my hand and pulled me back into the bed. Laughing, I wrapped my arms around him, buried my face in his neck and breathed in deeply. Paoli has this wonderful aroma about him I call Eau de Testosterone. If Bernie's sexual needs could be satisfied through the brain, perhaps mine could be satisfied through the nose. But of course it's more than just the way he smells that draws me to Paoli. It's the way he walks and talks, the way he eats his lunch and drinks a can of Pepsi, what he whispers to me alone in the dark. Although at that moment bed was an attractive option, I gathered up my self-control and reminded him we had a paying customer who expected work to be performed.

I coaxed him into the shower, then went over to my closet. Contract programmers usually dress casually, so I toned down my usual serious business look, choosing a skirt, a cotton sweater and beige linen blazer. I pulled my hair, still damp, back into a low ponytail, applied my usual minimal makeup and declared myself ready. Paoli wore his usual cotton shirt and chinos topped with a sport coat. He looked great.

Within a few minutes we were in Paoli's weathered orange 1969 Porsche en route to the Hard Drive Cafe for our morning's double cappuccino to go. Using the term "weathered" for Paoli's Porsche is unabashed flattery. "Trashed" and "junkyard bait" are more accurate descriptions, but at least it was running, and Paoli likes to drive it as much as possible. He claims it cleans out the pistons, when I know it's a guy-type hormonal thing.

My foot brushed against something slimy and I made the mistake of looking down.

"Paoli, there are rotting banana peels here on the floor. I'm so glad you're getting your fiber, but I think you may be violating several health codes," I said in a badly calculated attempt to start up a conversation.

Paoli grunted, keeping his eyes on the road. His awakening process takes a good hour and a half, and now that he was fully conscious he had turned aloof. I knew him well enough to guess that his cold shoulder was due to the fact that he had remembered our abbreviated marriage discussion from the night before, and the memory had made him grumpy. I don't think he was really too anxious to tie the knot, but I had insulted him by brushing off the marriage topic, especially when he was the one who had brought it up in the first place. His half-Italian, half-Polish macho background makes him sensitive to that sort of rebuff.

"I have more important things to do than clean the car," he said, sounding miffed.

"Paoli, it's not a matter of just cleaning. You're composting in here."

Paoli refused to continue the conversation further, and I kicked myself for starting it in the first place. Sometimes I have trouble keeping my mouth shut. So what did a few old banana peels matter when you were trying to maintain a relationship?

Paoli still wasn't speaking to me when we walked into the Hard Drive. Its tiny floor space crammed with every conceivable snack food and beverage, the Hard Drive Cafe contained all sustenance required by your average Silicon Valley white collar worker. Paoli and I went there two or three times a day and jokingly referred to it as Conference Room B. As we entered that morning I smelled the familiar aromas of coffee beans and fresh muffins.

The owner, Lydia, was busy polishing her latest acquisition, a state-of-the-art espresso machine. Silicon Valley is filled with people obsessed with technology, and Lydia had recently turned in her old stainless steel machine for an impressive Italian brass model with a dozen dials and functions. When she saw us she looked up and smiled, but as soon as she had the chance to inspect us further, her smile turned circumspect. She always knew when we were bickering, which was frequently.

"The usual?" she asked, and I wasn't sure if she was talking about our order or our argument.

We both nodded.

"So how's business?" she asked. The Data9000 office is in the same small complex as the Hard Drive, and Lydia is always interested in how her customers are faring financially, even more so since she invested in the new espresso machine. Double cappuccinos provide a nice profit margin. Lydia knew our revenue stream was meager, and she liked to hand out advice the same way she liked to hand out coffee, although the advice was free of charge. She had been Paoli's co-conspirator in the Data9000 brochure scheme.

"Business is okay," I told her, exaggerating wildly. That appeased her somewhat, but as she steamed the milk, Lydia kept eyeing us.

"You're a cute couple. Such beautiful babies you'd make." She gave me a meaningful glance and patted her tummy. "And it's not too soon to start."

Gee, thanks. Just the information I needed verbalized. I grimaced inside while freezing the smile on my face. Why is it that at thirty-four years old everybody acts like your uterus has an expiration date stamped on it?

Paoli had the good taste not to say anything, but he and Lydia shared a glance that made me suspect they had already discussed the subject.

After Lydia bagged our muffins, we snapped to-go lids on the coffees and drove the fifteen minutes to the Biotech office in Mountain View, eating our muffins so we didn't have to talk.

Once a sleepy country town, Mountain View had gone high tech and was now the home of numerous computer and software manufacturers. Biotech was in a moderate-size office building that looked like it had been designed by Darth Vader with a black glass facade and sharp edges.

We brushed the muffin crumbs off our clothes and walked into the lobby, a small spare area decorated only with a potted plant. Hanging prominently on the wall was a large framed photograph of a middle-aged man. I walked over to it and read the brass plaque on the bottom of the frame, which said BENJAMIN MORSE, CEO AND PRESIDENT.

A reception desk that looked like a space ship's command central sat in the middle of the room, but it was empty. Personal computers and voicemail had already eliminated a large percentage of the secretarial workforce, but there was also a new trend toward eliminating receptionists. Instead of an actual human to greet us, a sign instructed us politely but firmly to look up the phone extension of the person we needed, then call him or her directly, which we did.

Within sixty seconds Bernie burst through the door, looking like all his circuits were about to blow, his face contorted with anxiety. And it was only eight-thirty in the morning. His slacks had a smudge of dirt above the knee and his shirt needed ironing, the clothes of a man who had too many unpleasant things on his mind to be concerned with grooming.

"Thank God you're here. I got another one."

"Another message from Night Dancer?" Paoli asked. Bernie's head bobbed up and down.

"I saved it. I can show it to you."

We followed Bernie as he walked with rapid, brittle steps through a doorway and down several halls. Biotech's interior had a high-priced, smooth simplicity well suited to an organization preoccupied with science. The walls were a light gray, the trim a soothing pale green; the natural wood doors, spaced at regular intervals, led to small, expensively furnished offices. But even during those first moments I noticed an unsettling coldness about Biotech. Enter an average company early in the morning and you normally see employees chatting in the hallways, heading for coffee, telling the jokes they heard the night before. Such social niceties are a waste of corporate time, but when I was a manager

I never discouraged it. It's a necessary ritual and the resulting camaraderie makes a workplace friendlier and more livable.

But none of this social interaction went on at Biotech. There was an odd silence in the halls, and the people who passed by us didn't smile or say good morning. An aura of apprehension hung in the air.

I stopped at the ladies' room and noticed a red metal box fixed outside the door that read DECONTAMINATION KIT on the cover and it crossed my mind that the toilet seats must be really clean. I knew that Biotech manufactured pharmaceuticals, so the presence of a decontamination kit was probably standard, but still, the whole place gave me the willies.

When we reached Bernie's office a tall, thin blond man in his thirties stopped us outside the doorway. Obviously going for a throwback sixties look, he was wearing a white peasant shirt and black jeans with leather clogs. His nose was prominent, he had a bug-eyed expression, and he was at least a foot taller than Bernie. As he stooped over Bernie to speak to him, he reminded me of a big blond vulture.

"I worked on the data collection module at home last night until real late. I think I've got it almost finished," he said in a voice as lean and bony as he was. The emphasis he put on the words "real late" made me assume he was looking for brownie points. I noticed a tiny hole in his left ear where an earring would dangle during non-working hours.

Having more life-and-death issues on his mind, Bernie gave him only a cursory glance.

"Yeah, sure, George, that's great," he said distractedly. George's attention now turned to me and Paoli, and he stood there looking at us, waiting for an introduction. Finding he wasn't going to get one from Bernie, he initiated it himself.

"I'm George Hunsacker." He said it as if we ought to be

impressed and he made a point of crossing his arms to forestall any disease-spreading hand contact. That bothered me, especially after seeing the decontamination kit on the wall. Were there germs floating around the hallways I should be worried about?

Bernie looked flustered for a second, then got his thoughts in order. I guess he assumed he could slip us in and out of Biotech without anyone noticing or asking questions. Apparently he was wrong.

"Oh, of course, this is Vic Paoli and Julie Blake. They're going to be working on the patient statistics program."

Bernie muttered the words without conviction, but George seemed to buy it. His previous mild interest in us ripened into wariness as he looked us over more closely.

"You two are BBS's?" he asked.

I gave him a puzzled look. "I'm sorry, what's a BBS?"

He placed a hand on one hip. "Basic bit slinger. A programmer," he said testily.

I laughed. "I guess we are."

"Well, nice to meet you." He stared at us a moment then suddenly turned and clomped off, his clogs thumping down the hallway. Bernie rolled his eyes, hurriedly ushered us into his office and shut the door.

Bernie's office was moderately large with the typical potted plant and view of the parking lot afforded a midlevel manager. Glancing about me I saw very little that was personal in the room—no knickknacks, no photos of friends or family. I noticed a plaque on the wall honoring him for his volunteer work at an AIDS center, but everything else in his office was work-related. I felt sorry for him, because the lack of personal items revealed a lack of a personal life, a void he had probably tried to fill with ErotikNet.

Although the room was filled with printouts and manuals, they were stacked neatly, and his desk was clear except for his computer, the bearer of bad tidings. We gathered around it while Bernie retrieved the message. I put on my glasses. The words soon glowed in black print against a vivid blue screen:

Ready for our date, Whip Boy? I'm planning what I'll wear. Black leather, I think, and gloves, so my fingerprints won't show on the knife. When it cuts you, Whip Boy. When it cuts you.

\ \ \   NIGHT DANCER

Seeing the note again seem to heighten Bernie's nervousness. I couldn't blame him. The words were chilling. I put my hand on his arm, a small gesture of comfort, wanting to remind him we were there to help him.

Paoli put his hands on Bernie's desk, leaning his body forward so his face was close to the computer screen. "Why the slash marks?" he asked, still looking at Night Dancer's note.

"I'm guessing because, you know, slash, slash, slash. Like with a knife," I said, and it struck me I was being insensitive to our client. "Sorry, Bernie. I didn't mean to upset you. I really—"

"It's okay," he mumbled.

"Bernie, are all the computers here at Biotech connected to the Net?" asked Paoli.

"Yeah, most of them. We use the Net for E-mail and for research, but the newsgroup facilities are masked off so employees can't use them. You have to know special commands to get to them."

"And who would know those special commands?"

"Anybody in the computer department. Anybody who cared enough to ask around and find out what the command was," Bernie answered. He reached for a mug of water on his desk and I could see his hand was quivering.

"I'll be honest with you," I said. "I don't think this

Night Dancer person really intends to hurt you, because first of all, what's her motive? She doesn't have one. Second, if she wanted to kill you, why wouldn't she just go ahead and do it? Why broadcast her intentions and give you time to call the police?"

"She could be a nut case," Paoli said. I made a face at him. What Bernie needed now was optimism. I returned my attention to our client.

"If we're going to help you solve this problem, Bernie, we have to jump into it head first," I said, trying to sound upbeat and goal-oriented. "All Net messages get routed through the network, so Night Dancer's note had to pass through another computer before it reached yours. The first thing we have to do is find out what computer that was."

"But how are you going to do that? There's no return address on the note," Bernie said.

He was right. Most messages sent over computer networks show a mandatory return address so you could identify the sender. The note from Night Dancer didn't have any usable identification except the word "anonymous." I glanced at Bernie's computer sitting innocently on his desk and it occurred to me that the computer itself could tell us who sent the note, if only it could speak. Although I don't talk about it in mixed company, deep down I've always suspected that computers have souls and minds and that they know things we simple humans will never comprehend.

I gave Bernie a reassuring pat. "Don't worry, we'll figure it out. Is there someplace we can work?"

Bernie looked like he was in a trance but my voice snapped him back. At that moment I felt sure that he was thinking about more than just Night Dancer. He seemed like a guy running from a pack of wolves, with Night Dancer being only one of the predators.

"Yes, I have an office for you. It's around the corner."

We followed him down the hall into a small bullpen of

desks separated by partitions. Past the bullpen and in the far corner was our temporary office, already set up with two workstations. As we put our briefcase on the desks I could hear Bernie breathing, the air coming in quick gasps.

"If anybody asks you, you're working on the patient statistics program, okay?" he said, his voice hushed.

"No problem," I told him. He looked so upset, I wanted to console him. "Look, we'll figure this out. We'll find Night Dancer. It'll be all right. I promise."

"You don't have to worry about me. I'm okay. It's just that there's so much going on now. The Night Dancer thing, and then I've got some work issues." He managed to smile. "Call me if you need anything."

"We'll need your log-on ID," Paoli said. Bernie scribbled it down for us before he left.

We settled in, unloading our notebooks and networking manuals from our briefcases. When we were properly arranged, Paoli logged onto the Net with Bernie's ID. We were about to scroll through a list of Internet computers when we were interrupted by a knock on the door. It opened, and I saw George and a companion standing there. Paoli and I didn't have time for chitchat, but if we were going to pass ourselves off as programmers I supposed we had to be sociable.

"Hello," George said. "This is Abdul." Abdul smiled halfheartedly. He was about five foot seven with a dark complexion and deep brown, pained eyes. "We both work on the operations programs. Accounts receivable, payables." George moved a little farther inside the office, a meaningful invasion of our space. "I don't want to interrupt or anything, but when I see a VID I like to check it out."

"A VID?" I asked.

"Very interesting development. I mean, why would Bernie hire outsiders to do the patient program?"

"We could have done the program ourselves. We're

perfectly competent," Abdul said, the bitterness in his voice easily detectable.

So that was it. Abdul and George were ticked off that Bernie had hired outside programmers. Performing regular maintenance on standard programs gets pretty boring, so I could understand their pique. Finally an interesting project comes along and the company hires outsiders to do it.

"Listen, I think the company hired us just to keep their costs down. Paoli and I work cheap," I told them.

"Bargain basement prices," Paoli added. "And the company doesn't have to shell out for benefits."

George walked around the small office, examining it as if he were the health inspector. Abdul stayed near the door.

"Well, the company is trying to keep costs down. We're going public soon and I guess they're trying to make the company financials look as strong as possible. Still, you never know when a VID can turn into a CIP," George said as he checked the view from our window.

"Translation, please," Paoli said.

George turned to Paoli and raised an eyebrow. "Career interruption potential. I'm due for a promotion. Past due, actually, and it concerns me when Bernie starts bringing in outsiders."

I wondered if the upcoming stock offering accounted for the strain I noticed around Biotech, but normally the prospect of a company's stock going public would inject excitement in the air, not anxiety. My corporate instincts told me that something must be going wrong.

"Hope you own some stock," Paoli said cheerfully. "Public stock offerings can make you big money."

George lifted his shoulders a couple of inches. "I've scraped together some, but most of the stock is held by upper management or people who got in on the ground floor. They don't let the bucks drift down to the lower rungs, if you know what I mean."

George pushed my networking manual aside and sat

down on the desk, apparently ready for a long chat. "Let me give you some advice. Keep your heads down or before you know it you could be uninstalled."

"Huh?" Paoli asked.

"You could get fired. They love to go on firing sprees," Abdul said, still holding up the doorway. "They decide they don't like your face and you're history. This place can be pretty screwed up."

So that was it. The reason for the bleak atmosphere was that people were scared of losing their jobs. But that seemed strange for a company that was supposedly doing so well. There had to be more to it and I was curious about what it was.

"So why do you work here? I mean, if it's so screwed up?" I asked Abdul.

"Things used to be a lot better. Last year when the company came out with Alphaphrine everybody was happy."

"Alphaphrine?" I asked.

"A drug for AIDS patients. It eases pulmonary symptoms. It's been a big moneymaker and Biotech got a lot of publicity from it, but in the past month it's gotten weird here."

"How's that?" I asked.

Abdul paused. "Just weird, that's all."

He didn't seem anxious to elaborate. I was about to push him on it when a pretty girl appeared in the doorway. She started to come inside but stopped when she saw George and Abdul. Small and fragile, her hair a soft wavy brown, she wore black tights, a long bluejean skirt and a red scoop-neck blouse. I could feel the vibrations in the office change upon her arrival. George looked annoyed at the interruption in the corporate gossipfest, but Abdul's formerly hard expression softened like pudding as adoration emanated from his pores.

"I just saw Jennifer and she asked me to find you. She wants to see you both in her office," she said to George and

Abdul, her voice so soft it was barely audible.

"This is Gloria Reynolds," George said to us, having obviously named himself social director. "Gloria, this is Vic and Julie."

She smiled. We smiled. George looked sulky and Abdul just stared at her. I thought I could see little hearts pounding in his eyes, like an old cartoon, but Gloria seemed oblivious to it. She turned and left without saying anything more.

"The Banshee has called. Gotta run," George said, sliding off the desk.

"Who's Jennifer?" I asked.

"Bernie's boss. And we work for Bernie. I saw Jennifer in the parking lot and she looked a little haggard. She's probably in the throws of BDA and we're the ones to suffer."

"On my planet, called Earth, we communicate using complete words. What's BDA?" Paoli asked.

"Bad date aftermath. Jennifer's social life is less than successful, if you get what I'm saying. We figured she had a date after work yesterday because she was wearing her slut suit."

"The tight black one with the big slit up the skirt," Abdul said dryly.

"I suppose things didn't go well," George said. He and Abdul started to leave, then George stopped and turned back to us. "I've had my eye on this office. Bernie told me I could have it at the end of the quarter," he said, tossing it at us like a shovelful of manure.

With that declaration, George and Abdul abruptly left us. Poor Jennifer, I thought, having her staff gossip about her personal life behind her back. But I pushed Jennifer out of my mind as Paoli and I got back to work. We spent the next hour going through all the Night Dancer notes, searching for a usable return address, but came up with nothing.

"So what's our next step? If we don't know how the mes-

sage was routed, how are we going to locate Night Dancer?"
I asked Paoli.

"Not feeling as cocky as usual, are we?" Paoli said with a
wry smile. "Fortunately for you, my dear, I'm not out of
ideas yet. There are several computers that set up anonymous IDs for Net users. They call them re-mailers."

"Why would someone want an anonymous ID?"

"Lots of reasons. They have newsgroups on the Net for
victims of sexual abuse, or for alcoholics or people going
through tough divorces. They're computer-based support
groups. People don't want their names and locations to
show up on the screen, so they get all their E-mail routed
through a computer that gives them anonymous IDs."

"So we need to find out how you get one."

"Exactly. I'm going to take a look at the Net self-help
bulletin boards. There should be instructions there on how
to get anonymous IDs, and that will help me figure out
where those computers are located. Then I'll contact their
systems administrators and see if there's any way Night
Dancer could be coming through the Net that way."

Just then Bernie showed up looking a little better than he
had an hour earlier, his hair combed and his breathing
easier.

"My boss, Jennifer, wants to see you. You mind? I told
her I had hired two temporary programmers."

It sounded as if Jennifer preferred to get all her staff issues settled early in the day. I wasn't sure about what we
would say to her since we weren't who we were supposed
to be, but I was curious to see what someone looked like in
the throws of BDA, especially when I figured I had been
there a few times myself.

"Sure, that's fine, but if she asks us what methodology
we're using for the patient program we might have a little
problem," Paoli said.

"She won't. I've already talked to her about the program, and I'll be with you. I'll cover for you if she asks for details."

"But Bernie, what are you going to say to her in a couple of days when we're gone?" I asked him. "Won't she be curious about what happened to us?"

"I've already thought about that. I'm going to say you left because you found out we did animal testing."

"Do you? Do animal testing?" I asked.

"Any company like ours has to," he said hurriedly, obviously not wanting to discuss it. "Come on, we better go."

I didn't like the idea of animal testing, but then, I was working for Bernie, not Biotech. We followed Bernie down the hall and stopped behind him at an open door. Talking on the phone, Jennifer Bailey looked up at us and waved us in.

"Thanks for taking the time to drop by. I wanted to meet you," she told us after she hung up.

She didn't look like a banshee or a BDA victim, just tired and overworked. Jennifer Bailey was in her midthirties, blond and attractive, although the puffy look about her eyes and slight downward droop to her mouth made her look like she needed a vacation. The stack of work on her desk told me she wouldn't be getting one soon. Her office was filled with papers—reports, bound documents, printouts. Originally the computer revolution was supposed to convert us to a paperless society, but the opposite has happened. Computers have made so much data available so easily and quickly that companies have to deal with ten times the paper they did before. They are drowning in information, and, in my opinion, much of it of no real use. So much for progress.

I could only see her from the waist up, but she was wearing a well-cut taupe suit with a sheer blouse that I thought was too sexy for the office. I hoped she would wear the slut suit while we were there so I could check it out.

She gestured for us to sit. There were only two chairs, so Paoli and I sat while Bernie remained standing. Once everyone was arranged she offered us coffee, which we accepted, and she went and got it herself instead of sending an underling to do it for her. I liked that.

Her office was simple, but unlike Bernie's it was dotted with personal items—coffee mugs, a couple of office joke toys, photos of people who looked like family. I didn't notice photos of any children.

She gave us our coffee, sat down and leaned forward, seeming to relax a little.

"We're not a large company and I like to know everyone working on the premises. Even though you're contract employees, you're still one of us while you're here."

I liked her. When I was at my old job at ICI I had a hundred people working under me, and I'm sure some of them thought I was a banshee, too. You can't have everybody liking you when you're in management.

"Thanks. We like to make sure we fit into the landscape," Paoli said with a grin, and she returned the smile.

Was it my imagination or did her expression brighten when her eyes rested on Paoli? If the woman suffered from BDA I assumed she was single. For my peace of mind I decided that twinkle in her eyes was gastrointestinal distress. I wanted to give her the benefit of the doubt. She reminded me of me—the kind of woman who's tied to her job, works too many hours and is uncomfortable in her control top pantyhose. We could probably be good friends except for the fact I was in her company under false pretenses and she was flirting with my boyfriend.

"I'd like to know more about Biotech," I told her. "I've always been interested in biochemistry."

"I could give you a quick tour of the lab, if you like," Bernie said. The expression on Jennifer's face turned stiff.

"That's out of the question. The patient program is already behind schedule," she said. I got the impression her concern went deeper than the schedule, but it wasn't any of my business.

Bernie checked his watch. "Then we better get back to work. I have a meeting in fifteen minutes."

We said our goodbyes and left her office.

"I don't care what she says. I'll take you on a quick tour of the lab right now," he said as soon as we got out of earshot.

"Won't that make Jennifer angry?" I asked.

"She'll never know."

Bernie seemed to perk up at the chance to show off Biotech's lab, but I wasn't sure, given his previous mental state, if we should take the time away from locating Night Dancer.

"Look, Bernie, we don't have to do this. We can get right back to the Internet."

He shook his head. "This will only take a few minutes, and, you know, sometimes I think I'm overreacting to this whole Night Dancer thing. I mean, why would anyone want to kill me? It's ridiculous. I'm not saying I don't want you to find Night Dancer. I do. But I don't want to get so weird about this that you can't take ten minutes off."

"We'll make it five," I said with a smile, and Bernie smiled back.

"Besides, I'd like to show you the lab. Biotech is small, but we've established a reputation for cutting-edge technology. Our growth potential is huge," he said as he led us outside the main office and across the parking lot to a smaller building.

"What sort of drugs do you specialize in?" Paoli asked as we walked.

"We started out working with mostly antivirals, then our big breakthrough came with Alphaphrine. That came out last year. We're working on an AIDS vaccine, like a lot of companies, but we're branching out as well."

The outside door was locked and Bernie inserted his

Biotech badge into a card reader. The entry door clicked open.

Paoli gave Bernie a curious look. "Is it normal for someone in the computer department to have access to the lab? Seems like access would be restricted."

"It is, but I work on the computers in the lab area when they have a problem, so they gave me card access to the offices," Bernie said. He used the badge to open two more doors and we found ourselves in a hallway outside a glass wall looking into the laboratory.

"You can't actually go inside this laboratory. It's a level P2 security," Bernie said.

"What does that mean?" Paoli asked.

"We deal with some bacteria, so we have restrictions on who can enter the actual lab. But you can see a lot from here."

I could feel excitement rising in me as I looked through the glass. I loved learning about new technology, and in this lab I had entered a whole new world. The room was filled with glass beakers and microscopes and half a dozen machines I had never seen before.

Several white-coated employees busied themselves over dishes and vials, and lining the walls were glass tanks that looked like some sort of incubators. I saw one of the lab technicians working on something in one of the tanks, his arms and hands stuck into gloves attached to two holes in the glass. I realized that the tanks were used to isolate the lab technicians from the substances they worked with.

"What's that thing?" I asked Bernie, pointing to an odd-looking machine that looked like an old clothes washer.

"That's an incubator shaker. It grows bacteria. And that equipment over there is the centrifuge. It separates cells from liquid. Come this way."

Bernie led us through a door into an office area separated from the lab by another glass wall. A largish blond woman sat at a desk in a far corner. Bernie walked us over to her.

"This is Moira, Franz Kaufman's assistant. Is Franz around?" he asked. Moira, a frisky-looking forty, wore heavy makeup and her bleached blond hair was a mass of curls. Her dangly earrings were coated with rhinestones. She didn't look like she fit in with the general Biotech ambiance.

"Over there," she said. She pointed to a man in the corner who was looking over a technician's shoulder, his back to us. I noticed Bernie's mouth tighten.

"He's the scientific director of molecular biology. He's also an ass. We better get out of here," Bernie said.

But before we could exit, Kaufman turned in our direction, and you could almost see his sphincter tightening as his angry eyes came at us. He walked in our direction with a long, aggressive stride.

He was a physically imposing man, tall and husky with lightish hair and a hastily trimmed mustache. Behind his smudged glasses were pale gray eyes that would have been knockouts if he wore contact lenses.

"What are you doing in here?" he asked, speaking in an irritated German accent.

"They're new programmers. They're going to be working here at Biotech for a while and I wanted them to see the lab. Sorry if it's a problem, Franz." Bernie spat the last sentence with especially sarcastic emphasis on *Franz*.

Kaufman responded with an unattractive grunt I didn't think meant, So pleased to meet you, welcome to my laboratory.

"This is not a peep show, Kowolsky. I don't like outsiders," he muttered without looking at us, then turned and walked off. Bernie looked after him, his face turbulent.

"His social skills are a little rough," Bernie said.

Paoli chuckled. "Like gravel." Just then the beeper on Bernie's belt went off. He checked it.

"Damn, I've got to go. Screw Kaufman. Let me find someone to show you around." Bernie took us back into the hallway, then walked off and came back with a white-coated lab assistant. "This is Leonard. He'll answer any questions you have. Gotta run. I'll check in on you this afternoon," Bernie said, then left.

Leonard was a pale-skinned redhead, his face thin, his cheeks hollow. He waved an arm toward the lab. "This is basically it," he said in a bored voice. "You're looking at the main lab. There are smaller versions in the adjacent wing, but this is where most of the research is done."

"Bernie said Biotech is having a big success with Alphaphrine," Paoli said.

Leonard smirked. "Success? You might say that. There are problems with it."

"What kind of problems?" I asked. Leonard shushed me.

"We don't talk about these things," he said, his tone mocking. "Biotech is like a dysfunctional family. We don't discuss problems out in the open. We just seethe internally until our cells mutate."

Paoli and I both smiled. "So what else are you working on?" Paoli asked.

Leonard leaned closer to us, crossed his arms and lowered his voice, although I don't think he really cared who overheard our conversation.

"Biotech likes to get its name in the newspaper and on television, so we work on high-profile diseases, like AIDS, some cancers. Diseases like diabetes, MS—they take millions of lives, but they don't get as much press coverage, so we don't bother. And now we're moving into designer diseases. You know what our latest project is?" Paoli and I just looked at him. "Have you heard of the flesh-eating virus?"

"Of course," I told him. "It's been in the news."

"Well, it's not really a virus at all. It's a bacterium and it affects a tiny portion of the population, but we're taking resources off the AIDS vaccine and putting them on it because it's a newsmaker. God, how I love science. Listen, I've got to get back to work now. I'm going to have to walk you out."

"I have a question," I said quickly. "People seem so edgy here. We'd like to know what's going on, just so we don't step on anyone's toes. You know, say the wrong thing. We really need this job."

Leonard thought about it a second, then led us through the door into a small foyer where we were alone.

"Alphaphrine is causing some side effects that weren't detected during the trials. It's got everybody worried. If they don't fix it quick, it could hurt the public offering. There are a few people here at Biotech who stand to make small fortunes off their stock going public. Too bad I'm not one of them. But the lab rates are already working on a fix and it's looking good," Leonard said. He put his hand on the doorknob to go back inside. "Enjoy." With that Leonard disappeared down the hallway, the door closing behind him.

Paoli and I stepped out into the sunshine.

"Is there something about this place that gives you the creeps?" Paoli asked.

"Not at all," I fibbed. I felt the same way he did, but I was afraid if we both verbalized our apprehensions we might be tempted to back off the case, and we needed the money. The best thing to do was to quickly locate Night Dancer and get out of Biotech as fast as possible. I noticed I had my arms wrapped around myself, feeling a chill even though the temperature was a comfortable eighty degrees.

4

*B*ingo. Got some responses to the E-mails I sent out," Paoli said happily, leaning back in his chair, his fingers laced behind his head. It was just after lunch and we were back in the office. We had been there only ten minutes, but George had already walked by twice, looking gloomily at us through the glass wall, silently reminding us that we were usurping his territory.

I looked over Paoli's shoulder at the computer screen. "So did anyone claim Night Dancer?"

Paoli scrolled through the messages, stopping on the third one.

"Pay dirt. The systems administrator for a mainframe at the University of Wisconsin says she'll confirm that she has Night Dancer on her system and give us a phone number and address if she receives a copy of the police report." Paoli raised his fist and gave a silent cheer. "We're good, aren't we? We're really good. We'll have this little case slam-dunked by tonight."

I leaned back against Paoli's desk, arms and ankles crossed, and tried not to look smug.

"And you didn't even want to take this case, remember?"

But he was too busy patting himself on the back to hear me.

"Yes, once again, Data9000 comes to the rescue, and wham, two thousand big ones in the old bank account. You know, I'm thinking of a jingle, in case we want to do radio advertising. It's so much cheaper than TV and you hit all those commuters." Paoli stood up and began shimmying around the room, wiggling his fingers in the air. "Got a looter in your computer? Call Data9000. Have a fiend on your screen? Call Data9000."

I checked to make sure our door was closed, although anyone passing by could see through the glass wall that Paoli was dancing. I could always say he was having some sort of seizure, but it didn't matter anyway since it looked like we'd be leaving Biotech sooner than I expected. The freedom of having our own business sometimes brought out Paoli's childlike nature. I guess there wasn't much shimmying at the National Security Agency, where he used to work. Paoli finally sat down, and I got on the phone to Bernie, told him what we had learned and that he needed to fax a copy of the police report to the systems administrator in Wisconsin.

"That's great," Bernie said without much enthusiasm. I expected him to sound more relieved. "I'll call the police right away. The sooner this is over the better. I've been so nuts, I've gotten behind at work, which brings me to a question."

"What is it?"

"We don't have anyone here at Biotech to troubleshoot personal computers, at least not anymore, so when someone has a problem I help out as long as it's minor. Jennifer doesn't like it because she says it takes my time away from my real duties, but someone has to do it."

"I can understand that."

"Well, Gloria—she's Benjamin Morse's assistant—"

"Who's Benjamin Morse?" I asked.

"President of Biotech." He sounded surprised that I didn't know, and then I remembered the photo in the lobby. "Anyway, Gloria needs help. Her word processing software isn't installed properly. It's a small problem, I'm sure, but she can't handle it herself. Could you help her out? I wouldn't ask you to do this, but Jennifer is the one who suggested I call you, and I have to make things look legit, at least until we get Night Dancer's name and you're out of here."

Helping someone with their PC software wasn't exactly my idea of a hot project, but he sounded like he needed help, and if Jennifer was really in the throws of BDA I supposed we needed to keep her pacified. Paoli and I had some time on our hands until the police report got faxed to Wisconsin, and I thought we should do our best to earn the exorbitant amount Bernie was paying us.

"No problem," I told him. "Where does Gloria sit?"

"Second floor, east corner. Thanks a lot, Julie. I really appreciate it. There's just one more thing." I could hear him take a breath. "Gloria and I date."

"And?"

"And Gloria doesn't know anything about my messages to Night Dancer, so please make sure—"

"Don't worry. I won't say anything."

Bernie thanked me and we hung up. So, old Bernie was dating one woman and two-timing her electronically with another. Was that considered cheating? I made a mental note to ask Max for her opinion.

I told Paoli about my exciting assignment. I could easily handle the task alone, but it would be more enjoyable with him around, so I talked him into coming with me. After some good-natured grumbling we went upstairs to the second floor. I was surprised when we found her. I hadn't made the connection when Bernie gave me her name, but it was the girl we had met that morning, the one who had whipped Abdul's hormones into cheese dip.

Looking at her and knowing she was Bernie's girlfriend, I wondered if Bernie perceived her as missing some essential sexuality and if that was why he had turned to ErotikNet. But who could figure out what illogic lurks in the minds of men? Maybe he had asked her to do something kinky like wear a hockey mask and yell "foul!" while they had sex, and she had refused. Some people are comfortable with kinkiness and some aren't. I'm in the latter category.

The door to Benjamin Morse's office was closed and Gloria's desk was right outside. Sitting in front of her personal computer, she looked intently at the screen while she rubbed cream on her hands. She sensed our presence and looked up at us with her big fawn eyes.

"Bernie sent us over to help you with your software," I told her.

"Oh yeah, thanks. Here it is." She pointed to her computer as if we might have trouble identifying it. "Do you need to sit down?"

"If we could," I said. She got up, taking a stack of files with her and moved to a chair in the small waiting area next to her desk. Paoli motioned for me to take the chair while he leaned against the credenza. "So what's the glitch?" I asked.

Gloria told me about her difficulties with the latest version of her software, and Paoli and I immediately got to work. It was a snap since all we had to do was reinstall the program, but when we were halfway through the job we were interrupted by loud voices coming out of Benjamin Morse's office. I heard a man and a woman.

I tried to pretend I didn't hear the argument, but Paoli didn't share my sense of etiquette. He turned to Gloria.

"Should we send in a referee?" he joked, but Gloria didn't laugh.

"Sorry. This is unusual." She looked at her boss's door with worried eyes. "Excuse me a minute while I go to the ladies' room. I'll be right back." She got up and headed down the hallway.

Just then the door to Morse's office snapped open and Jennifer Bailey stomped out, her skin flushed from her head to her chest. I don't think she even noticed Paoli and me as she swept past us. A few seconds later Morse stepped out of his office. Since I was sitting in Gloria's chair his eyes landed on me first.

Morse wasn't as good-looking as his photograph, but he wasn't too bad, either. He was on the short side, but well built with a strong face and a head of thick black hair some men would kill for. He wore the crisp monogrammed shirt and the type of horn-rim Armani glasses that I used to admire but now silently denigrate. When you're in love with a man who wears Boston Celtics socks you find that your tastes change.

"Who the hell are you? What do you think you're doing?" he yelled, then angrily looked around. "Gloria!"

Paoli leaned lazily back against the credenza, regarding Morse with distaste. "Ooh, that's good," he said calmly. "Now let's see you do an orangutan."

Morse glared at him, opening his mouth to say something I was sure Paoli would make him regret, but luckily at that moment Gloria resurfaced. Seeing the look on her boss's face she approached him like a cowering dog.

"They're fixing some software for me, Mr. Morse. They'll be done soon. Can I do something to help you?"

Morse looked down at her, still heated and blustery. "Have you finished the revisions on the financial report?"

Gloria's face turned pale and her fingers twisted together. "You said you didn't need it until tomorrow morning."

"Well, I need it now." He said the words petulantly, like a spoiled child demanding a toy. I didn't care for the man at all.

"Give me an hour," she said, her voice meek. I felt sorry for her, having to scurry around like a slave for a jerk like Morse, but if she stuck up for herself he would probably fire her. He seemed like that kind of person. Morse slithered back into his office.

"Fun guy," Paoli said after Morse slammed his door shut.

"He's usually not this way. There have been some problems around here and he's just feeling the pressure," Gloria said as she rifled through some papers, probably looking for the financial report. I found her loyalty admirable but I could see the strain on her face.

"What kind of problems?" I asked, interested in getting her version of the Biotech gossip. Something had set off Morse and whatever it was, it had had an equally strong effect on Jennifer Bailey.

She didn't look at me. "I really can't talk about it."

I remembered what Leonard had told us, that at Biotech they didn't talk about their dirty laundry. Paoli and I finished up the software installation so Gloria could get back to work, and when we were done her gratitude was sincere. I scribbled something down on a piece of paper and handed it to her.

"What's this?" she asked, looking at it.

"An employment agency that specializes in executive secretaries. It never hurts to keep your options open."

She looked at me, her face serious. Paoli ended the awkward moment.

"Bernie said the two of you date. He's a nice guy," he said. Her stern expression melted into a smile.

"Yes, we go out," she said shyly with a trace of a blush. "I haven't seen enough of him lately." My female radar picked up strong signals that she was crazy about him. Lucky Bernie. She was pretty and nice, and there he was cruising the Info Super-highway for a cheap pickup when all along Ms. Right was in his own backyard. I thought maybe I should have a sisterly chat with him, but on the other hand, I had never had a relationship that lasted longer than a car loan and was really in no position to be passing out advice.

We said our goodbyes and left Gloria to finish up the revisions for Monster Morse. Once we were out in the hallway and out of Gloria's earshot, Paoli whispered to me.

"The reason Gloria hasn't seen enough of Bernie lately is because he's too busy wanking himself in cyberspace."

I tapped my finger against my temple. "Wanking. Now there's an interesting word to look up in the thesaurus," I said as we walked down the hallway toward the stairs.

"You don't need to look it up. I picked up dozens of synonyms in the Boy Scouts. There's—"

I put my hand over his mouth. "Never mind. Let's go back to the office and see if George left any nose prints on the glass."

"I have a better idea. Let's see if Bernie's sent that fax off to the guy in Wisconsin," said Paoli.

"Great, but there's one thing I need to do first. I want to find out more about these problems Biotech is having."

Paoli frowned. "Why?"

"Just curiosity about the corporate culture. Bernie said today that there was something with his work that was bothering him. And the atmosphere around here is so tense. It makes me want to know more about what's going on."

"That's funny. It makes me want to know less."

"Oh, come on, let's go talk to George. It won't take long and he seems like a good place to get the gossip."

Paoli spent the next few minutes letting me know that swapping chitchat with George was not his idea of enjoying himself, but he acquiesced and we walked over to George's cubicle where we found him hunched over his workstation, typing. His cubicle was a mess, piled high with printouts and manuals and old paper cups filled with aged coffee. The only organized thing I saw was a pyramid of empty Mountain Dew cans stacked on top of the file cabinet.

George stopped his work and swiveled his chair around to look at us.

"How are you coming along with the patient program?" he asked in a tone that made me think he hoped it wasn't going well.

"Good, but sometime I'd like to get some input from you on our program design. I've heard you're the best programmer here," I said, hoping flattery would warm him up.

Paoli gave me a quizzical look, then caught on. "Oh yeah, everyone mentions it. How you're the best."

A self-satisfied smile crept onto George's face as he sucked up the compliments. "I guess it is a GAF." He smiled patronizingly. "Generally accepted fact. I don't have time this afternoon, but maybe I could help you on Monday."

"That would be very kind of you. We didn't get much done today because Bernie asked us to help Gloria with a software problem and it took a while. Besides, it was hard to get anything done with Morse and Jennifer shouting in the next room," I said.

George had returned his attention to his keyboard and had begun typing, but when he heard my last sentence his fingers froze in the air. He twisted his neck to look at me. "Shouting?" he asked.

"Like two cats in a burlap bag," said Paoli. "Makes you wonder what it was about."

George looked puzzled. "Jennifer and Morse? That's hard to figure. Usually they meld nicely, mainly because she's such an ass kisser."

"Do you have any idea what it could be about?" I asked.

George shrugged. "Probably has to do with the Alphaphrine report. That's got upper management biting their nails, and I've heard that they've accused the Applications Department of screwing up the patient stats."

"Bernie told me a little about it, but no real details," I said, fibbing. Bernie hadn't mentioned it.

"Well, if he wouldn't give you details, then you won't get them from me." I could tell he was getting suspicious about our nosiness. "Shouldn't you get back to your little program?"

We thanked him for his time and left.

"You bombed out on that one. I'm surprised at you, Julie. You usually manage to wheedle whatever information you want from people," Paoli said when we were back in our office.

"I know George is the type who loves to talk, but remember, he doesn't like us. We horned in on his project, not to mention his office. I'm sure I could get plenty out of him if we were going to be here a few days."

"But luckily we're not. This could be the quickest two grand we'll ever make. What do you say we go out to dinner tonight in San Francisco to celebrate? We can go to Fior d'Italia in North Beach."

"Hmm, sounds wonderful."

There was a knock at the door and Bernie walked in, closing the door behind him. It crossed my mind that Biotech was just that kind of place, where everybody keeps their doors shut.

"I got the police report and faxed it to the number you gave me," he said. "How long do you think it will take to get a name?"

"Maybe this afternoon. Of course it's almost three now, which means it's after working hours in Wisconsin. The systems administrator may have gone home for the day," Paoli said. "But I'm sure we'll get it first thing Monday morning."

"Listen, Bernie, we can't keep the whole two thousand dollars, not for a day and a half of work. I deposited your check last night but I'll come up with a bill and reimburse you," I said, noticing Paoli shudder at the word *reimburse*.

"No, you keep it. That was the deal."

His voice sounded strained. Bernie had seemed more relaxed a few hours earlier. Now he was acting jittery.

"Is something wrong?" I asked him.

"It's just something here at work. Something weird. Actually I'd like to talk to you about it, maybe get some advice."

"Have a seat," Paoli said.

"No, not here. I can't talk about it here. Besides, our staff meeting's in five minutes. Could I meet you at your office tonight?"

I saw Paoli give me a pleading look asking me to tell Bernie no, but how could we turn him down when the man had paid us two thousand dollars for only a day and a half's work? I saw our dinner at Fior d'Italia fly out the window.

"Of course. What time?"

Bernie looked relieved. "How about nine? I know it's late but I have to work late, then I'm running an errand."

"Nine's fine," I told him.

Bernie left and Paoli glowered at me.

"Julie, did you have to agree to meet him tonight? We could have talked to him tomorrow."

But tomorrow would have been too late.

5

By six o'clock the systems administrator in Wisconsin still hadn't called. We were disappointed, but it was Friday and we knew it was useless to wait any longer. When I told Bernie over the phone that we wouldn't be finding out Night Dancer's identity until probably Monday morning, he didn't seem overly concerned. In fact, he didn't even seem to hear me, he sounded so distracted. I asked him what was troubling him, and he told me again that he couldn't discuss it at Biotech and that we would talk about it at our office that night.

Paoli and I were packing up to leave when Bernie suddenly appeared. I thought maybe he had decided to have our discussion right then, but it turned out he had something else on his mind, and he directed it at Paoli.

"I hate to ask you this when you're getting ready to leave for the day, but Jennifer wants to talk to you, Vic, about the patient program. Morse is giving her a hard time about the whole project and she's got to get an applications status report to him first thing Monday. She needs some information so she can get started on it tonight," he said. "I tried to think up an excuse to get you out of it, but she was insistent. There just wasn't any way I could think of to get you out of it."

Paoli stopped what he was doing, his eyes curious. "Listen, Bernie, from what I'm hearing, this patient program is pretty important," Paoli said. "Jennifer's going to be expecting a finished program pretty soon. Who's really working on it?"

"I've been doing some work on it in my spare time. I'll get it done. Vic, if you could just meet with Jennifer tonight, play along, and then on Monday we'll have Night Dancer's name and your job will be finished."

"But why just Vic? Why not both of us?" I asked.

"Because this morning she asked me who the lead programmer was on the project and I just gave her Vic's name without thinking."

"It's my strong chin," Paoli joked, to which I responded with a mock sneer. Bernie continued.

"When I told her that, I didn't think it mattered. I'm really sorry about this. I tried to help her myself but she specifically asked for you, Vic." He focused his imploring expression on Paoli. "Would you mind stopping in? She said it wouldn't take more than half an hour."

An entire half-hour? I thought of several things two people could get done in a half-hour and I didn't like any of them. That nagging suspicion crept up on me again that her interest in my beloved was more than professional.

"No problem. Take the car, Julie. I can catch a cab and meet you at the office when I'm done," Paoli said with his usual good nature.

What could I do, lock him in his room? Relationships are based on trust and I was certain that if Jennifer threw herself at him, Paoli would respond with the appropriate rebuke. Half certain, anyway.

Once when I was fourteen I overheard my mother telling my Aunt Melinda that men could never be trusted. Even though the Rational Adult in me knew it was ridiculous, my mother's statement remained filed away in the back of my brain, to be occasionally dusted off and reexamined. I stared at Paoli and wondered how trustworthy he really was. My Rational Adult felt confident of him, but my Inner Fourteen-Year-Old wasn't nearly so sure.

Paoli and I agreed to meet later at the Data9000 office. I checked our voicemail, then grabbed my things and walked out. One of our messages was the service shop saying our computer was ready early, so I swung by on the way back to the office and picked it up. During the drive I pushed several imagined Paoli/Jennifer scenarios out of my mind and filled the mental void with thoughts about Bernie, but my head remained stuck on the male/female paradigm.

Take Bernie, for example. Here was a fairly normal guy dating a pretty girl like Gloria, a girl who obviously adored him, yet he was getting his sexual thrills from some anonymous weirdo via cybersex. I like computers as much as anybody, but I had never looked at mine as a sex object. What was the attraction?

I hooked up the computer as soon as I got back to the office. After the cables were installed and the power supply connected, I flipped the switch and the computer hummed to life. I patted its central processing unit to welcome it home. Everything was working fine, so I reestablished the Internet connection in case Paoli and I wanted to do some network digging over the weekend.

Next I started a new computer file for Bernie's case, named it KOWOLSKY and logged in the hours we had put in that day. In spite of what Bernie had said, I intended to send him a bill with a summary of the actual hours we'd worked along with a refund of what we hadn't earned. After logging the hours I was about to get started on compiling the mailing list for our new brochure when a little voice whispered in my ear. It told me to log onto ErotikNet.

I hit a few keys on the keyboard, stopped, told myself that I had work to do, that reading erotic messages from strangers was stupid, a waste of time, and, after hearing Bernie's Night Dancer story, potentially not good for my health. Turning my attention to my file drawer I looked for the Chamber of Commerce listing of local businesses, but my attention snapped right back to the keyboard and the next thing I knew my fingers were scrolling through the list of Net newsgroups.

Okay, so I wanted to know what it was about ErotikNet that rang Bernie's chimes. It would help me understand the background of the Kowolsky case better, so in a sense my interest was strictly professional. At least that's what I told myself.

To my astonishment the sexual newsgroups were numerous. I found Bernie's favorite—*alt.sex.ErotikNet*, but there were a dozen others, including *alt.sex.bondage*, *alt.sex.bestiality*, *alt.sex.necrophilia*. My mouth hung open as I read the list.

I hit a few keys and got to ErotikNet. The first screen that came up was a list of the subject lines for all the currently posted messages. The subjects themselves were laughably offensive—"Slave Desperate for Master," "SWF Wants Manhandling," and "Seeking Toilet Slave."

I scrolled down the list, chided myself for wasting valuable time and was getting ready to log off when I saw something that caught my eye. Different from the other message titles, this one was brief and heartfelt. It said "I'm Lonely." My Rational Adult told me to log off and do something constructive with my time, but my pesky little fingers had a mind of their own. The message soon appeared on the screen:

> I pass my nights alone, sitting in my apartment waiting for something that never happens. I don't know why I'm so alone. I only know I ache. I want to connect to someone. Can anyone out there hear me?
>
>   ALONE ON PLUTO

I read it, looked at the words a moment, then moved my finger to hit the Delete key. But I stopped.

I remembered when I was in my first year of college. I

spent all my time in classrooms or studying in the library and was much too nerdy and quiet to ever be asked out on a date. On Saturday evenings I would see the other girls in the dorm getting ready to go out, and though I tried to tell myself I didn't care, I did. I cared a lot. Sometimes late at night I would feel so heartsick and alone that I would sit in bed in the dark, eat barbecue potato chips and Moon Pies and cry for hours. But I lived through it, and probably so would Pluto. I reminded myself that I had work to do.

My Rational Adult again instructed my fingers to log off the computer, but my naughty fingers hit the Reply key instead. They began typing:

Hi there, Pluto. Someone out there heard you. I've been very alone before and I know how it hurts. But I found out that you have to look into yourself to fill the voids within you. I have a wonderful lover, but I find I still feel alone sometimes. Alone within myself. That may sound strange, but it's true. And to be perfectly honest, sometimes it scares me a little.

I typed JULIE at the end of the note, then quickly deleted my name. Thinking a moment, I typed in the words VIRTUAL VENUS, then hit the Send key and smiled to myself. I had always wanted an alias.

A half-hour later I was busy working on the mailing list when Paoli walked in carrying several brown paper bags.

"I thought it would take you longer. How did it go with Jennifer?" I asked, feigning mild interest when I really wanted him to strip his clothes off so I could check for bruises.

Paoli put the bags on his desk and I could smell the wonderful odors of Szechuan.

"For your information, she didn't make a pass at me."

"Don't be ridiculous. The idea never occurred to me," I said, keeping my eyes glued to the computer screen.

"Yeah, right," he said, grinning. "Anyway, I faked it pretty well, but after about twenty minutes she got a phone call, then jumped up and left. Go figure." He shrugged. "I got some takeout from Fung Lo's—two orders of hot and spicy shrimp with a side of snow peas. Be nice and I'll let you have some. You got the computer back?" Paoli asked as he took the cartons out of the bags.

"Yes, and it works just fine," I said, neglecting to mention the little note I had sent to Alone on Pluto. I had a right to my privacy, didn't I? And if he knew, he would never let me live it down.

We ate our Szechuan, then afterward Paoli helped me type in the rest of the company names and addresses for our new mailing list. When we were finished, he asked me for the time.

"Nine-fifteen."

"So where's Whip Boy?" he asked with annoyance.

"I guess he got tied up."

I hadn't intended the joke, but that just made it funnier. When we stopped laughing I called Bernie's office to make sure he wasn't still there, since in the computer business people work all hours, but Bernie didn't answer. I got his home phone number off his client information sheet and tried him there, but again, no answer. By ten-fifteen it was apparent that Bernie wasn't going to make it, so we decided to head for home.

"We missed our celebration dinner, but that doesn't mean we can't celebrate," Paoli said, his lips on my ear. We were walking to the parking lot, an exercise made delightfully difficult by the fact that Paoli had his hands all over me.

"Can we wait until we get home?" I asked, even though I wasn't that interested in waiting.

"No we can't, my love. My empty spaces need filling and they need filling now. Punish me with your mouth or any other body part you have handy."

I laughed as Paoli grabbed me, bent me backward and planted a kiss on me that made my corpuscles dance the mambo. Dropping my briefcase to the ground, I kissed him back and things started to get interesting. We were close to the car, and Paoli pushed me toward it in order to brace us against the fender, but we stumbled on something.

"What's that?" I mumbled, our lips still locked. We pulled away from each other and looked at our feet. I'm not sure which one of us screamed first. Probably me, because when I looked down I saw the bloody corpse of Bernie Kowolsky.

6

I pressed my face into Paoli's chest, but couldn't help turning and looking again. A lump rose in my throat and tears in my eyes as I saw the body slumped at my feet. Bernie Kowolsky–alias–Whip Boy looked stone dead.

My insides turned to oatmeal. When could it have happened? And how? We didn't hear anything. I had just spoken to him a few hours earlier. Who would want to hurt him?

I realized with shame that I had never really taken the Night Dancer threats seriously. My insides clenched as I remembered my promise to him that everything would be okay. So much for Julie Blake's promises.

The parking lot wasn't lighted and it was hard to see through the pitch darkness, but I could make out Bernie sitting on the pavement, his back against the door of the Porsche, a dark stain across his white shirt. Something was smeared across his cheek and I assumed it was blood. I put my purse on the ground and moved toward Bernie but felt Paoli grab my arm to stop me.

"No, Julie, don't get any closer."

Paoli's voice sounded thin and anxious. I turned to him and saw his face twisted with revulsion as he looked at Bernie.

"I'm just going to check his pulse," I said.

"His pulse? Are you nuts? You might as well check and see if he'd like a Coke. Julie, the guy's dead. Murdered. Get any closer to him and you could disturb evidence."

I started to argue but I could hear Paoli making a little squeaking noise in the back of his throat and I knew he was terribly upset. I reached for his hand and squeezed it.

"Are you okay?"

"I'm doing better than Bernie."

"Who isn't?" I muttered. I took another look at the dark smear on Bernie's face.

"Lipstick," I said.

"You look fine, Julie. This is no time—"

"I mean on Bernie. Someone has smeared red lipstick on his face." I reached forward and touched my finger to his wrist.

"Oh jeezus, I'm going to puke," Paoli said, dropping my hand and stepping backward.

The night air was cool, but Bernie's flesh felt warm. "He may be still alive. We have to call an ambulance right away," I said. "You wait here with him. I'll make the call."

But when I turned I found Paoli sitting on the pavement, his head down and his hand over his mouth. He's never at his best around the recently deceased. I'm not any braver, but I have a stronger stomach.

"You better come with me," I told him. I didn't want to leave Bernie alone, but I had to make the call and I couldn't leave Paoli there in his shaky condition. And if I sent Paoli to make the call I couldn't be sure he wouldn't faint before he reached the phone.

Paoli got up and we walked back toward the office. The cool air seemed to revive him. He used his key to unlock the front door, then we went to our office and flipped on the light. I called 911 while Paoli rummaged through the back of his file cabinet. I knew he was looking for his stash of canned margaritas.

I described the situation to the dispatcher. She said an ambulance and the police would be on their way. Paoli, having found his last precious can, was busy shaking it. He then popped the top and took a quick gulp.

"I have to go back out to Bernie. You can wait here," I said.

He shook his head, his mouth full of margarita. He swallowed. "No, I'm fine now. We'll go back out together." He sounded much better, although I noticed he was taking his margarita with him.

No conversation passed between us as we walked back out to the parking lot, but when we got close to the Porsche Paoli stopped in his tracks.

"Listen, if you changed your mind—" I began, but Paoli interrupted me by pointing to the space next to the Porsche where Bernie was lying. Or where he had been lying. Bernie was gone.

Frantically I ran around to the other side of the car, then to the front, but still no Bernie.

"I don't get this. He was here. We both saw him. The blood," I said, my voice getting shrill. Now it was my turn to get hysterical. Paoli put his arm around me and tried to calm me down.

"It's okay, Julie. Take a few deep breaths. There's an explanation for this."

"Like what? An alien abduction? What the hell are you talking about? Bernie was sitting there with blood all over him. He was dead!"

"Julie, listen to me. You said yourself that he might still be alive."

"No," I said, shaking my head, trying to comprehend what had happened. "He couldn't have just walked away. It doesn't make sense—"

Just then we heard sirens. It had to be either the ambulance or the police, and there we were, embarrassingly without a body. Seeing the expression on my face, Paoli handed me the rest of the margarita and I downed it in one gulp. An ambulance pulled into the parking lot, followed by a squad car. The paramedics leaped out and ran toward us, ready to save a life. More sirens cut through the night. The two paramedics, both male, asked us the whereabouts of the victim.

As Paoli explained the situation to them, a squad car pulled up and two policemen walked over and listened to the story. The general response in the group was surprise mixed with annoyance topped off with a hefty helping of disbelief. Nobody looked happy and I couldn't blame them. Just then a second police car arrived. I saw two more policemen get out, but was too wrapped up in the current conversation to take much notice of the new arrivals until I heard a familiar voice behind me.

"Well, Ms. Blake, we meet again."

Turning, I saw Lieutenant Dalton looking at me with the type of leering grin I always imagined was used by cheesy car salesman. I had met him seven months earlier when I was working at my old corporate job at ICI. One of my employees had been murdered and Dalton had been assigned to the case. I noticed he was wearing his usual well-cut sports jacket and slacks with suspenders, and I was sure that if the light were better I would see tiny monograms on his cuffs. He probably had monograms on his underwear although I wasn't interested in checking. His aftershave wafted toward me.

"I think there's been a murder," I said, not wanting to waste time with niceties.

The smile left Dalton's face. "Where's the body?" he asked, the question followed by a pregnant moment of silence.

"It's gone. The dead guy walked off," one of the officers said, his tone dry.

"Yeah, maybe he had an appointment with death," the other one responded, and they both chuckled.

"There's been a complication," Paoli said. Recognizing Paoli, Dalton nodded. They had also met during the ICI case.

I started to talk, but Dalton cut me off. He pulled the two police officers aside, and after a brief conversation the officers walked back to the squad car, leaving Dalton behind. I was relieved. Dalton was no quiz kid, but at least he knew Paoli and me and wouldn't be as quick as the others to assume we were hallucinating.

Dalton came back over to us. "They're going to search the area and see if they can find your friend." Dalton's voice was smooth and unpolicelike. He got out his notepad and a pen.

"He was a client," Paoli told him.

"I heard you two started your own business. Congratulations," he said with sincerity. "Now, could you explain to me what happened here?"

"We just told the other officers," Paoli said.

"Please tell it again."

So we told him, sometimes taking turns, sometimes both talking at once as we spit out the general facts about how we found Bernie and how he strangely disappeared.

Although Dalton usually annoyed me, he listened to our story without looking at us like we were crazy, which I appreciated.

"Did you check his pulse?" Dalton asked. The question threw me.

"I felt his skin and it was warm," I answered.

His eyes lingered on me a moment then moved to Paoli. "What were you doing during all this?" he asked him.

"Checking the area to see if anyone was around," Paoli answered, sounding very manly, apparently feeling the full benefit of his margarita. I let the fib pass. Paoli couldn't help it if he had a weak stomach.

Dalton got a flashlight out of the squad car and shined it on the pavement next to the Porsche. The light illuminated a small puddle of something dark.

"See? It's blood," I said eagerly, relieved to have some corroboration for our story. "That's where Bernie was slumped."

Dalton leaned down and touched it, rubbing the stuff between his fingers.

"It's definitely blood all right," he said, standing up. He shined the flashlight around the puddle. "It looks smeared, like someone was dragged through it. I've got to call in the evidence guys." He pointed a finger at us. "Don't go anywhere."

Standing by the Porsche, Paoli and I watched him walk to his squad car. I wrapped my arms around myself, not sure if the chill I felt came from the outside or inside. I soon felt Paoli's arm reach across my shoulders.

"It's just like Night Dancer's threat, isn't it?" I said. "Her note said she would stick the knife into him while she kissed him. That's why she smeared the lipstick on Bernie's face."

"Why do we keep assuming it was a she?" he asked. I opened my mouth to answer, then realized I didn't have an answer. Not a good one, anyway. Why had I assumed Night Dancer was female? Bernie had used the feminine pronoun, but it was equally possible that Night Dancer was male. Bernie couldn't have known for sure since he'd only known Night Dancer through the computer. Full of our own thoughts, Paoli and I didn't talk for a few minutes, but he finally broke the silence.

"Has it ever occurred to you that our business isn't turning out quite the way we expected?" Paoli's tone was contemplative.

"What do you mean?"

"I'm not saying that the way it's turning out is a bad thing. I'm just saying it's different from our original plan."

"But we're only a few months into it, Paoli. I'm sure we'll build up a regular corporate clientele. We're probably going to get that security project for Pacific Bank. That fits into our game plan, doesn't it?"

Pausing a moment, Paoli gazed out at nothing. "It's just that I thought we'd be working with computers. Call me naive, but I hadn't figured on finding dead people."

He had a point, but life has an annoying way of not turning out the way you plan. We hadn't planned to find corpses. Bernie hadn't planned to become one.

Dalton returned, and while we waited for the crime scene specialists we filled Dalton in on the specifics of the Internet threats and about our work at Biotech. I knew that Dalton was computer literate, and he grasped the facts quickly.

"I use the Internet myself. I'm in the True Crime chat group," he said with pride, edging in closer to us. "Listen, I'd like to talk to you guys later about what interface you're using. I'm thinking of switching my software and upgrading my monitor so I can download graphics. Do you download graphics?"

I guess being a policeman turns you a little cold about death. As for me, I couldn't discuss graphics capabilities when I was standing next to a puddle of blood. I'm funny that way. I politely steered the conversation back to the subject of Bernie, and Paoli explained about the systems administrator in Wisconsin who was supposed to call with Night Dancer's name and address.

"So you're telling me this Night Dancer person is from Wisconsin and that he or she flew all the way here to kill Kowolsky?" Dalton asked.

"No. Whoever it was routed their E-mail through the computer in Wisconsin, that's all. Night Dancer could live anywhere," I explained.

Dalton wanted the phone number of the Wisconsin systems administrator, and Paoli said it was on the desk at Biotech. Dalton told him to hang on to it in case he needed it, then had me go back to the office and get Bernie's client information sheet and write down Bernie's address and phone number. Dalton said he would go by Bernie's house that night, and if necessary check it again the next day.

"You two can go now, but we'll need you to come by the

station tomorrow so we can get your statements."

"That's it?" I asked.

Dalton gave me a questioning look. "You were expecting dinner and flowers?"

I stepped closer to him. "I'm not quite ready to leave yet, that's all. Not without getting your opinion on what happened. Something very strange occurred here. Our client was sitting there dead one minute and the next he was gone. Where did he go? I thought you might have some ideas. I mean, maybe this sort of thing has happened before. Maybe there's a procedure you follow in cases like this, maybe—"

"Ah yes, Julie," Paoli interrupted, acting awfully cocky for a guy who had almost fainted only an hour earlier. "The disappearing corpse procedure. That's in the police manual, isn't it, Lieutenant Dalton?" Paoli said.

Dalton shook his head and sighed. "Look, the way I see it, it can only be one of three things. One, your friend managed to get up and walk away, in which case we'll find him on the streets or in the hospital. Two, he's dead and whoever killed him decided not to leave the body. Maybe you interrupted the killer right after he had done the deed. When he saw you coming he hid, then took the body away after you left. If your friend turns up missing, then we'll pursue it."

"Why would someone take the body?" I asked.

"To hide evidence, probably. If Kowolsky was knifed, it could be that the attacker hadn't planned on his victim fighting back. After it happened he realized that there might be skin under the victim's fingernails, or fibers left on his clothing."

"What's the third possibility?" Paoli asked.

"Your client could be playing a bad joke on you. He pretends to be dead, scares you shitless, then walks away."

Paoli didn't look convinced. "Why would he do something like that? And besides, there's blood on the ground."

"We don't know whose blood it is or if it's even human. It could be part of the joke for all we know. You see him on Monday and everybody gets a laugh. It's happened before. There are a lot of weird people around these days."

"It was no joke. I saw Bernie and it was real," I said.

"I'm just giving you the possibilities, okay? You two go home. I'll see you at the station tomorrow. By the way, you'll need to leave your car here. You can get it tomorrow." With that Dalton walked back to his car.

I didn't want to leave. I wanted to do something, take action, make something happen. I felt close to Bernie. Even though he was a man, even though he had a sadomasochistic fantasy life, for some reason I related to him. Why, I didn't know. What I did know is that I had failed him. He had asked for my help and I had let him get killed, and now I wasn't about to say *Que sera sera* and go home.

I ran over to the squad car where Dalton was just picking up the car phone.

"I can help you with this case," I said, panting from the sprint. Dalton, sitting in the car with the door open, looked exasperated.

"Listen, Julie, I remember your kind of help real well from our little experience at ICI. You like to carry out your own game plan and not let anyone else in on it, and you think you can run things better than the police. I like you, Julie, you know I do, but I'm telling you to go home and leave this to me."

Paoli walked up next to me. "What's going on?" he asked. I didn't answer him. I had to get through to Dalton.

"This situation is different. I won't get in the way," I said to Dalton, but he didn't seem persuaded. "Okay, how about this? I'm assuming you'll be going to Biotech to ask some questions about Bernie."

"If he doesn't show up for work on Monday, you're assuming right."

"Paoli and I are going to be there too. We're going to go

there Monday and act like we don't know anything about what happened." I felt a nudge in my ribs, looked at Paoli and saw his eyebrows go up. "I think we can find out what happened to Bernie as long as you don't let on to anyone at Biotech the real reason Bernie hired us. They have to think we're there as contract programmers."

Dalton grimaced. "Even if Kowolsky turns up missing and we do go to Biotech, I can't play games like that."

"It'll only be for a day or two. We can find out things you couldn't, and any information we get we'll turn over to you as soon as we get it. You'll solve the case. You'll get the credit."

"But you just told me that you were going to get the identity of Night Dancer from the person in Wisconsin. What do you think you're going to investigate?"

"If Bernie doesn't turn up on Monday, plenty. Of course, maybe Bernie will turn up on Monday in perfect health and this will all turn out to be a joke. Maybe we'll get the identity of Night Dancer and that will wrap it up, but if it turns out that it's more complicated than that you know you can use us."

"What's in this for you?" Dalton asked. Paoli crossed his arms and glared at me, also wanting to know the answer to that question.

"Bernie paid us to identify Night Dancer. I think we have an obligation to carry it out."

Dalton considered it a moment. I decided he needed some urging.

"I'll give you any information we get as soon as we get it. You know us. We're licensed investigators. It's not like we just walked in off the street. All I'm asking is that you don't tell anyone at Biotech who we really are. Just for a couple of days. You'll solve the case twice as fast. You'll look like a hero."

I knew Dalton well enough to figure he'd go for something that would advance his career. I could see his wheels turning. Finally he spoke.

"You do know how to deal with weird technical types, and I'll admit that policemen don't. Okay, if Kowolsky turns up missing and we investigate, I'll see what I can do. If I do have to go to Biotech I'll avoid telling them you found Kowolsky, but if I find out you're not cooperating with me or getting involved in things you shouldn't, I'll make sure you regret it. That's a promise."

"You have nothing to worry about."

I used Dalton's pen and scribbled down our phone number at Biotech, the Data9000 office and at home. Dalton said goodbye then started his car and drove off. When I looked at Paoli his mouth was open and his eyes were wide with astonishment.

"I can't believe you said what you just said. I had a bad feeling about this case from the start, but no, it was your idea to get involved, and look what happened," he said with irritation as we walked back to the office to call a cab. "Furthermore, there's no justification for us to ever go back to Biotech again."

"What are you talking about?"

He knocked on my head like it was a door. "Oh, Ju-lee. Hello in there. I agree with you that our client is dead. Gone. His power supply permanently disconnected. He will not be checking the status of his case. That means he will not be asking for progress reports. You cashed the check, right?"

"Yes, I did."

"Then no problem."

"Wrong. There is a problem."

I stopped walking. Paoli walked on a few feet then stopped, turning toward me and looking angry.

"The problem is that Bernie Kowolsky paid us to identify Night Dancer. If we don't complete the job we would have to return the money," I said.

"I don't like it when you use terms like 'return the money.'"

"Paoli, we have an ethical and moral obligation to do the job we were paid to do. That means we show up at Biotech Monday morning just like it's any other day, if only to get the information from the systems administrator and give it to Lieutenant Dalton."

It was dark enough that I couldn't see what color Paoli's face was, but I was certain it was bright pink. I started walking briskly toward the office, Paoli at my side.

"Lieutenant Dalton can get the information himself," he said through gritted teeth.

I didn't want an argument but there was no way I was going to back down. When we stopped at the door, Paoli used his keys to open it and I seized the opportunity to soften my approach.

"Listen, sweetheart, let's go to Biotech and wrap things up. Please."

There was a moment of silence. I put my palms against his chest.

"Just for Monday?" he asked.

"Whatever you say."

I heard him make a *hmph* sound as he opened the door. While Paoli called a cab I waited in the hallway. Both Paoli and Dalton thought that on Monday they would learn the identity of Night Dancer and the case would be closed, or maybe that Bernie would traipse in and the whole thing would turn out to be a joke.

But I knew differently. Bernie was dead, I was certain, and his murder was planned out too carefully for Night Dancer to allow herself or himself to be traced that easily. Bernie had ended up as roadkill on the Information Superhighway, and in my gut I knew the Kowolsky case had just begun.

7

On Friday Biotech hadn't been a cheery place to walk into, but as Paoli and I crossed its portals Monday morning it felt downright eerie. We put up a good pretense—smiled a good morning to the people in the hallways, waved pleasant hellos to George and Abdul. It was hard since we still felt sick over what had happened to Bernie, and our hearts and minds had been consumed with it since Friday night. We had gone to the police department and made a statement, and we spoke to Dalton on Saturday and Sunday, but there was no news about Bernie. He hadn't turned up at a hospital or at his house.

After we reached our office the smiles dropped from our faces, and as soon as I put down my briefcase I dug my Maalox out of my purse and took a big swallow straight from the bottle. Paoli calls it my Breakfast of Champions. Since I had quit my job at ICI my ulcer had quieted down considerably, but Friday night's events had left my stomach ablaze. I put the bottle on the desk to keep it handy.

Paoli got on the phone with the systems administrator in Wisconsin. While they spoke I stared blankly at the top of my desk, thinking about Bernie and about what I could have done to prevent what had happened. Images of him swirled around my head. The last time I saw him he had looked so anxious. He had wanted to talk to us about something, something he didn't feel comfortable discussing at Biotech. Maybe I should have pressed him on it, insisted we talk about it then and there. Later on Friday he said he had an errand to run after work. Was it connected to his murder?

Paoli hung up the phone. "The systems person in Wisconsin called the police half an hour ago and gave them Night Dancer's name."

The news snapped me back to the present.

"Who was it?"

"She wouldn't tell me. She was completely immune to my manly charm."

"I guess there had to be at least one," I said, trying to make a joke, but my heart wasn't in it.

Paoli put a call into Dalton, but he was out. The woman who answered said Dalton would return the call, but I didn't feel like waiting. I felt like running through the halls, grabbing people by their collars and demanding information from them, any information they had about Bernie, but I couldn't. For the time being Paoli and I had to sit in our little office and pretend to be programmers.

Over the weekend I had managed to convince the right side of my brain that Bernie wasn't really dead, and now I found myself dialing Bernie's extension every fifteen minutes hoping he would answer, but he didn't.

Around ten, too fidgety to sit any longer, I walked through the bullpen and asked Abdul if he had seen Bernie. He said no, adding that Bernie had missed an important staff meeting that morning.

I checked my watch. Ten-fifteen. That was late enough to convince Dalton that Bernie wasn't going to show up for work. I went back to our office, sat down and again dialed Dalton's number, but Paoli popped in from the hallway and yanked the receiver from my hand.

"Don't waste your energy. I just saw Dalton in the hallway," Paoli said excitedly, hanging up the phone. He dashed to the door and peered down the hallway. "He just went up the elevator, probably to Morse's office. We've got to talk to him."

I jumped out of my chair. "Something must have happened. Maybe they found him," I said. Paoli nodded in agreement.

"Why don't I stake out Morse's office and you hang out in the lobby and watch his car? That way we'll be sure to catch him."

Paoli and I were about to head out to the lobby when we heard a knock at the door. It was Jennifer Bailey. She didn't look good and it was more than just BDA.

"I need to talk to you." She walked in, closing the door behind her. I could immediately smell her heavy perfume, a smell of sweet cinnamon. It only took one glance to know she had just received bad news. Her blond hair was perfectly coiffed, her makeup in place, yet there was a sense of dishevelment about her—everything in order on the outside, but on the inside everything looking like a Picasso painting during his cubist period. I felt sorry for her. I had been in her shoes at my old ICI job when one of my employees had been murdered. I wished I could tell her about it, let her know how I got through it, but I couldn't compromise my assumed identity.

Jennifer crossed her arms and leaned against my desk, her eyes resting on her shoes as if she was trying to decide what to say and how to say it. She finally looked up at us.

"I'm talking to everyone who was being supervised by Bernie because this situation will directly affect projects."

As she said it, everything inside me tightened up. Her verb tense told the story. Everyone who *was* being supervised by Bernie.

"What is it?" I asked, trying my best to sound like I didn't know what she was about to say.

She took a deep breath before answering. "Something might have happened to Bernie."

"An accident?" Paoli asked.

"Something like that," she said with enough hesitancy in her voice to indicate she didn't know many details.

"The police came and asked to see his personnel file."

"Why the personnel file?" I asked.

"They wanted to check his blood type."

"You keep that information on people here?" Paoli asked.

Jennifer nodded. "We had a blood drive four years ago to set up a blood bank for employees. In case someone was injured and needed blood right away, they could get the blood from our company blood bank and feel secure that it had been tested properly."

I felt a thud in my stomach. I tried inhaling deeply a few times but it just made it worse. In the back of my mind I was still hoping Bernie was alive, that it was all a joke gone too far. Bernie would walk in, I would rake him over the coals for causing so much trouble, but no one would be dead.

A few things began falling into place. Apparently Dalton had already received test results on the blood next to the Porsche. That must have been what made him rush over to Biotech this morning. He had called the personnel department and found out that the blood by the Porsche matched Bernie's.

"I don't know how I'm going to tell everyone," Jennifer said, her voice quivering. At first I thought she was going to cry, but she closed her eyes a moment and pulled herself together. When she was ready, she opened them again and continued talking. "I need you to keep working on the patient program. I know it'll be hard without Bernie since he's the one who came up with the project design, but I'll help you all I can. It's an important application for the company and we have to keep making progress. Will you stay?"

"Of course," I told her, my mind running a hundred miles an hour. "But we may need additional help here. I think we should hire another programmer to work with us."

Paoli and I weren't going to have time to simultaneously

work on her program and investigate Bernie's murder. If we hired an extra programmer I figured we could get him to do most of the software work, but Jennifer didn't buy into my scheme.

"That's impossible," she said without taking time to even consider my request. "We're cutting down on expenses this quarter. You'll have to make out with just the two of you. Can I count on you?"

I hid my disappointment with a cooperative Girl Scout smile. "Sure."

"One more thing. All the departments are turning in quarterly budgets tomorrow. I'll have to do Bernie's figures myself, so I'll need an estimate on the number of hours it will take to complete the patient program. This is a terrible time to be worrying about budgets, but around here the quarterly budget reviews are critical. The numbers have to be in by nine tomorrow morning."

"We'll take care of it," Paoli said.

"Good." She stood up. "We can talk more about the program later." After opening the door she turned back toward us. "Thanks for your help. We'll all need to pull together the next few days."

"We're team players," Paoli said too brightly, but she didn't catch his sarcasm. She tossed him a smile that on a normal day would have irked me.

"I have one more favor to ask. There's a Lieutenant Dalton here from the police and he's asking some questions about Bernie. Since you two spent some time with Bernie on Friday, he'd like to talk to you."

Paoli told her we'd be glad to meet with Dalton, then she left.

"It doesn't look good for Bernie," Paoli said as soon as Jennifer was safely down the hall.

That was an understatement. I put my head in my hands and soon felt Paoli's touch on my shoulders.

"Julie, it's not your fault. It's not mine. It just happened.

Let's go find some coffee. Some caffeine might make you feel better."

I doubted it, but I went anyway. Paoli and I had been so rattled that morning we hadn't stopped at the Hard Drive for our usual caffeine dose and I was probably undergoing withdrawal. With my stomach's acid condition, coffee was the last thing I needed, but at that moment I found that small office suffocating and I welcomed the excuse to get out of it. We went down the hall to partake of the office coffee pot and when we returned, Lieutenant Dalton, looking disheartened, was sitting in my chair, leaning back with one leg crossed over his knee. He was wearing a somber dark blue suit. I closed the door.

"What happened?" were the first words out of my mouth. "You matched his blood?"

"More than that."

"Then you found him. Was he in a hospital?"

"We found him, but not in the hospital."

Paoli and I exchanged a glance.

"Where then?" Paoli asked.

"There's an incinerator here at Biotech behind the lab area. They use it to dispose of lab animals, then they bag up the ashes and send them to a toxic waste facility in San Jose. They do their incinerating early, before dawn." I closed my eyes. I had a sick feeling I knew what he was about to say. "We got a call around six this morning. When they were bagging the ashes they found some human bones."

"Bernie?" I asked.

"Looks like it."

I remained standing, but Paoli sighed wearily and sat down. Even though he had protested staying on Bernie's case, I could tell Dalton's news had affected him.

"How could you tell if the body was incinerated? You haven't had time to get dental records," I said.

Dalton shook his head. "There wasn't enough left for dental records, but we found a gym card with Kowolsky's name on it and a couple of receipts on the ground near the incinerator. We're guessing they fell out of his pocket. It was dark. Whoever carried him didn't see them."

"And you checked Bernie's blood type? We heard that from Jennifer," Paoli said, sitting forward in his chair, his hands pressed together in front of him.

"The lab did the work on the blood by your car on Sunday. They haven't been able to do all the tests, but it looks like a match. We called the Human Resources Department here first thing this morning to maybe get the name of his doctor, then we found out they had all his blood information on file. And they had more than just the blood type. It was detailed enough to make us certain the blood on the pavement was Kowolsky's."

He reached into his shirt pocket and got his notebook. "You'll be interested in this," Dalton said, his voice a little cheerier. "We got Night Dancer's name." He flipped through a couple of pages. "His name is Syd Pascucci and the address is in Lodi."

"I guess Bernie's secret admirer was a man after all," I said.

"Who can explain love?" Paoli replied without smiling. "Well, I guess the case is solved. You arrest Mr. Pascucci and we can all go home."

Dalton slowly shook his head. "Sorry. We already ran the name and address through the computer. No such person exists."

"You're kidding," I said, although I knew he wasn't.

"There's no Syd Pascucci we can locate in California, and the address is a fake. Somebody subscribed to the Wisconsin Internet service using false information."

"You could still locate Night Dancer by putting a trace on Bernie's computer's communications line," I said.

"Not anymore," Paoli said. "That has to happen in real time, and I doubt there will be any more communications from Night Dancer."

Paoli and I were silent a moment while we absorbed the information. A thought started bouncing around my head and it must have showed on my face.

"What are you thinking?" Paoli asked.

"I just realized that whoever Night Dancer is, he set up his Internet service knowing that he didn't want to be traced. He didn't start the communication with Bernie and then suddenly get carried away by homicidal urges. He planned from the beginning to be untraceable."

"But Internet services cost money. So where were the service bills sent?" Paoli asked Dalton.

"He paid three months in advance with cash. There were a couple of start-up brochures that were sent to the fake address and returned, but since the service was paid for and the folks in Wisconsin never received any calls requesting assistance, nobody worried about it," Dalton said.

"How long ago was Night Dancer's service set up?" I asked.

Dalton checked his notes. "On June second."

I looked at my Daytimer. "That's seven weeks ago. Bernie told us he first logged on to Erotiknet in May. So Bernie starts using Erotiknet around eight weeks ago. Night Dancer starts using it about a week later and only pays for a few months. Night Dancer had it all planned."

"The dates could be a coincidence," Dalton said. "Maybe they both started using the Net at the same time."

"I doubt it."

A dull squeak filled the office as Dalton swiveled back and forth in his chair. There was something on his mind. "Are the two of you going to quit your job here?"

"No, not yet," I said. Out of the corner of my eye I caught Paoli's annoyed look.

"Then what we talked about Friday night, about you staying here a few days to see what you can find out. I'd like to keep that deal with you."

Paoli's ears perked up. "Why doesn't the police department hire us as consultants to help identify Night Dancer? We can work on the technical aspects of network identification, work with the Internet people."

"Sorry, but I can't do it. Our budget's too tight. And I want to be clear that I'm not asking you to stay here. But since you've said you're sticking around anyway, I'd like access to any information you pick up."

I sensed Dalton's awkwardness and I understood it. He wasn't the type for unorthodox approaches, but he needed us. "It's okay. We'll do everything we can to help you."

I could see those little wheels in Dalton's head turning again. It looked like it hurt.

"Is there any way someone here at Biotech could know the real reason Bernie hired you?" he asked.

"No," I answered. "He didn't tell anyone. Why?"

"It's just that if someone knew what you were really investigating, you two could be in trouble yourselves. Just be careful. There's a possibility it could be dangerous around here."

With that surprising pronouncement, Dalton stood up, but we weren't about to let him leave.

"So you think someone here at Biotech killed him?" Paoli asked.

"It makes sense. It's not generally known outside the company that Biotech had an incinerator. Somebody put Kowolsky in a plastic bag, the kind used for animal disposal, so they had to know where the bags were kept and they had to have an access card to get inside to get them. They threw him directly in the incinerator. That's where we found the gym card and the receipts. The furnace wasn't turned up high enough to consume a body that large. That's why they found some bones."

We all looked at each other uneasily. Dalton reached for the door.

"I have a lot of work to do. Call me if you find out anything."

We assured him we would and he left.

It was a horrible way for Bernie's life to end. He didn't deserve it. Nobody did. I felt like crying, but I wasn't going to allow myself the luxury because I didn't have time if I was going to find Bernie's killer.

I hit the top of my desk with my fist. "Let's get to work. First we need to circulate around the office," I told Paoli. "Interview everyone we can get our hands on."

Still sitting, he held up his finger. "Uh, Julie, sweetheart, let's talk about this a minute. I know you want to do your best by Bernie, but I distinctly heard Dalton use the word 'dangerous.' Dangerous is not what we signed up for. Re-munerative is what we signed up for. Profitable, fast money is what we signed up for."

I sat down at my desk. "Don't be silly. We're not in any danger because no one at Biotech knows why Bernie hired us. He didn't tell anyone, I'm sure of it. He was way too paranoid about someone finding out about his erotic notes." I searched the desk drawers for a Biotech phone book or an employee list.

"I'm not convinced, Julie. There's probably a murderer walking these halls and it makes me very nervous around the water fountain."

I stopped rummaging around and looked at him. "We can't be completely sure it was a Biotech employee."

"Are you crazy?" He jumped up from his chair and held up his thumb. "One, we know the killer knew about Bio-tech's incinerator and where the bags were kept. That points to an employee." His index finger shot up. "Two, because of the lipstick on Bernie's face we know the mur-der is connected to the Night Dancer notes, and it's un-likely that one Net user could physically locate another Net user who was using an anonymous ID. That also points to a Biotech employee. Someone around here knew Bernie was sending the notes to Erotiknet."

"But how would anyone here know about his notes to

Erotiknet unless they were looking over his shoulder? And I doubt Bernie was sending porno notes unless he knew he was alone. How about this? Maybe someone who worked directly with the computer in Wisconsin got Bernie's name and address that way. The killer could have used Bernie's access card to get into the building and get the incinerator bags."

Paoli threw me a patronizing look. "Possible but unlikely. Face it, our killer is much closer to home. Maybe within spitting distance. You know it. I know it."

He was right, of course. The most likely explanation was that somebody at Biotech had a motive to kill Bernie and used his correspondence with Night Dancer as a cover for the murder.

"So the murderer had to know about the notes between Whip Boy and Night Dancer, but maybe he or she found out without the help of a computer. We know Bernie printed the notes out. Maybe someone found the printed copies."

"You're leaving out the obvious, that somebody here at Biotech actually is Night Dancer," Paoli said. "In which case, my money's on Gloria."

"Gloria? She's a mouse."

"Yeah, well, you thought Bernie was a cuddly lamb until you read about how he wanted to be tied up and kissed where it hurt." Paoli paced around the office as he talked. "Here's the scenario. Gloria's nuts for Bernie, but she finds out he was doing his S and M stuff on the Net."

"How?"

"Maybe Bernie was so fascinated with his S and M messages that he wanted to read them over and over. He wasn't content logging on to his computer when no one was looking and just sneaking a peek. He wanted to hold the messages in his hands, get touchy feely with them. Take them to the men's room, if you know what I'm getting at. So he prints them out. Maybe multiple copies. I mean, after a while they probably got sticky and he needed a fresh set."

I cringed. "Okay, I'm with you so far."

Paoli sat on the edge of his desk. "But Gloria is sneaking a look through his stuff one day. Women do that, I hear. You know, prowl through their boyfriend's underwear drawers to see what they're hiding."

"Don't be absurd." I had only looked through Paoli's drawers once and hated myself afterward. I found mostly gum wrappers and smelly socks anyway.

"Maybe you wouldn't do it, but it happens. Anyway, Gloria finds the messages and she's jealous, so she decides to get back at him. She logs onto the Net as Night Dancer. After all, she's been dating the guy, she's read the messages and knows what would appeal to him. Her trick works and Bernie goes for the bait." Paoli's voice built up steam as he continued. "But as Bernie gets more and more carried away with Night Dancer, Gloria gets more and more ticked off about it, and finally out of jealousy she kills him."

I scrunched up my face. "Sounds far-fetched, and she doesn't seem the type. Besides, she's too small to handle Bernie's body afterward."

"She didn't actually lift him. Remember, Dalton said the blood in the parking lot looked like someone had been dragged through it. She only had to drag him, then push him into her car."

"Dalton said the incinerator bags were put in a bin. Wouldn't she have to lift it then?"

He shrugged. "Maybe she works out with weights. I see girls at the gym who are five feet tall but could beat me in arm wrestling. Well, maybe not beat me, but still, they're strong."

"I'm not buying your Gloria theory, but I suppose it's the only motive we have so far."

"Yeah, well, here's another little problem, and this one's closer to home. How do we write this damn patient program? We don't have the time to do it and we don't really have the knowledge. Jennifer is going to want progress reports."

"We'll hire someone on the side to do it. How about Joshua? He's doing contract work, isn't he?" I asked.

Joshua had worked for me when I was at ICI. I immediately called him at home and left a message on his machine. When I hung up, Paoli looked pensive as he shot rubber bands against the wall. I took his hand and pulled him to a standing position.

"We need a plan for the rest of this afternoon," I said. "I suggest a two-pronged approach. You get on the phone with your Internet contacts and see if there's any way Night Dancer could have physically located Bernie using Net information. If there is, maybe we can use the same methodology to locate the real Night Dancer."

Paoli gave me a suspicious look. "And what's your prong?"

"I'm going to tackle the nontechnical angle. Since Jennifer has talked to everyone working for Bernie, I'm sure the corporate grapevine is busy. Maybe I can talk to a few people and find something out."

"How come you get the gossip job and I get the boring network job?" Paoli asked.

"Because you know networking better than I do. Besides, you're getting the better end of the deal. You know I prefer technical conversation to gossip any day." That wasn't quite true, but it mollified Paoli.

As I walked down the hallway I passed each office wondering if its occupant was Bernie's murderer. Although I had displayed admirable bravado with Paoli, I didn't really feel safe. What if Bernie told someone he had hired us? If Night Dancer was willing to kill once, he might be willing to kill again to avoid being found out.

I shook off the thought and headed upstairs. I decided to start with Gloria since she was currently our only suspect with a motive. I went over to her desk and found it empty, but when I started back toward the elevator, the doors opened and Gloria stepped out. She looked awful, her face pale with no makeup, her hair unwashed.

"Gloria, I heard about Bernie," I said to her. She just looked at me blankly, then her small body began to shudder and the tears came.

"I can't believe he's dead. At first they made it sound like there was some sort of accident, but Angie in Personnel told me he was murdered."

The files she held fell to the floor and I put my arms around her. I'm not the type of person who goes around hugging people I don't know well, especially people who might be murderers, but Gloria looked so vulnerable I couldn't help myself. She didn't look at all like a killer, but while my arms were around her I used the opportunity to lightly pat one of her biceps to check out Paoli's gym theory. If the girl had any muscles there, I sure couldn't feel them.

She pulled away from me, embarrassed, and stooped down and tried to pick up the papers. I knelt down to help her because her hands were shaking so badly that most of the papers she picked up fell right back out of her hands. Finally she gave up and just let them all drop to the floor.

"I'm sorry," she blurted, still crying.

"You don't have to be sorry. Here, let me help you."

"I'm going home. I just had to get these things for Mr. Morse."

"You're in no shape to drive."

"I'll be okay."

I scooped up the rest of the papers and handed them to her.

"How about a cup of coffee or some tea before you leave? Give yourself a chance to calm down." She didn't say anything. I retrieved the papers from her. "Here, I'll put these on your desk and we can have a cup together. There's a deli next door, isn't there?"

I admit that I had ulterior motives in asking her to have coffee with me, but the truth was that the woman was in no condition to operate a car.

I put the papers on her desk and we walked toward the building exit. It was when we rounded the corner to the side door that I noticed Abdul behind us. Once we were outside the building he was still about ten yards behind, and I just figured he was going for a decent cup of coffee. The office brew was more suited to a car's crankcase than a coffee cup.

When Gloria and I arrived at the deli I settled her into a chair, went to the counter and returned with two hot teas. Abdul sat at a table on the other side of the room. I noticed Gloria glance once at Abdul. It seemed to me she was trying hard to ignore him.

"Who would want to kill Bernie?" she asked me once I sat down. Good question. I wished I had an answer.

"Gloria, was Bernie having any problems that you know of here at work? You know, any arguments, rivalries?"

She had been staring into her tea, fingering her hair, but when she realized what I was implying, she looked up at me, her eyes wild.

"Like you think someone at work killed him? No. That's crazy. No one here could have done it. We're a family here."

A dysfunctional one, perhaps. I took another approach.

"Did Bernie say anything odd lately or act differently?"

She bit her lip, her finger mindlessly toying with the edge of the cup. "He seemed nervous, I guess. Sort of edgy."

"When was this?"

"Last week." She opened her mouth to say more but stopped herself.

"Gloria, what is it?"

She paused, then spoke. "Just that it happened once before. About a month ago he seemed upset, that's all. It was probably just the work load." She pushed her tea away from her. "I should get back to my desk and get my things."

"Just stay a little longer, please."

For the past five minutes I had been thinking of how I could tell Gloria about Bernie's cyberfling with Night Dancer. I felt she would talk more freely about him if she thought I was more than just a casual acquaintance of his, and I wanted to bring up his Whip Boy notes and gauge her reaction. I kept reminding myself that Gloria could very likely be a murderer.

On the other hand, if she were innocent, the poor girl had just found out that her boyfriend had been murdered. Was it fair to lay on her the fact that he was asking to be tied up with silk scarves by an anonymous woman who was in reality probably a man? I took a sip of tea and went with my instincts.

"Gloria, I want to tell you the truth about something but I want it to be kept in confidence. Can you do that?" I began. Her eyes fixed on me. She knew something was coming and that she might not like it.

"Bernie told Paoli and me something about his private life. Something he wanted kept secret."

She gave me a quizzical look and swallowed hard.

"You know what the Internet is?" I asked. She nodded. "Well, Bernie was having a problem with someone he was communicating with on the Net."

"What kind of problem?"

"Someone was threatening him." I searched her face for signs of panic, but she just looked innocent and defenseless. "There could be a connection between the threats and his murder. I've told the police."

All of a sudden her eyes turned dark and I could hear her breathing quicken.

"I have to go."

At first I was too dumbfounded to say anything. Gloria pushed her chair back noisily and stood up.

"Let me drive you home," I said.

"No. I can take care of myself."

Just then she bent over and started coughing—a deep hacking cough that sounded like she had rocks and glue in her lungs. It hit me that she wasn't pale because of shock over Bernie. The woman was sick. Still coughing, she turned and stumbled out.

I jumped up, knocking my chair over, but didn't stop to upright it. I ran after her.

"Gloria! Are you all right?" I said as I got close to her. "Can I drive you home? You don't look well."

I felt an arm on my shoulder shoving me out of the way.

"I'll take care of her."

I turned and saw Abdul looking fretful. He stepped close to her, pushing himself between us. It was an aggressive act, Abdul showing me that she was his property. But the property had different ideas.

"Keep away from me! Just keep the hell away!" she yelled at him, the coughing fit now over, although she still looked awful. "I don't want you near me."

Abdul stood there staring at us, looking hurt and angry, but most of all stunned. Finally he turned and stalked back into the building.

"Gloria, what's going on? Are you having a problem with Abdul?"

"No, it's nothing. I have to go home now. I don't feel well."

"Do you know something about Bernie's murder?" I asked her. "If you do, you have to tell somebody."

"I'm not telling you."

"Then please tell the police. Gloria, this is a murder."

She looked at me as if I were very, very stupid. I sure felt stupid. She turned away and I let her go. I didn't see that I had any choice. But one thing was clear. Gloria knew something about Bernie's death, and whatever it was, I had to find out.

8

I walked back down the pathway and inside the building to our office, anxious to tell Paoli what had just happened with Gloria, but he was gone. I was out in the hall trying to decide where to look for him when George walked up with his long, determined stride. He seemed more hunched over that day, as if Bernie's death weighed on him. He stopped only inches from me and peered directly down, the way you'd look at something in a hole. It made me nervous, and I backed away a foot.

"Some of the programmers are going to lunch," he said. "Since Bernie is NLB we wanted to have sort of a memorial for him."

"NLB?" I wondered why the guy couldn't speak with complete words.

"No longer breathing. Want to come?"

Angie in Personnel must have had a sore finger from all the phone calls, but I knew from experience you couldn't keep secrets in the office, especially when the secrets dealt with personal issues. And murder was about as up front and personal as you could get.

"Sure, but I'd like to find Paoli first. Have you seen him?"

"No, but he's invited too." George pointed down the hallway with a long bony finger. "I have to get my van now. Just meet us in front of the building in five minutes."

I searched up and down the hall, then took a run by the coffee pot, but still couldn't find Paoli. I didn't want to leave without him, especially when I knew he hated to miss a meal, but Paoli was quite capable of fending for himself, and I couldn't pass up the data-gathering opportunity of lunch with the locals. I left him a note saying what I was doing, then made my way to the Biotech lobby.

When I arrived I found Abdul waiting there along with three others—two youngish males and a woman. The woman surprised me because George said it would be a group of programmers, and programmers are usually youngish, in their late twenties or early thirties. This woman looked a determined sixty, her gray hair untouched by dye, her clothes matronly, her shoes the squeaky crepe-soled kind. Not that I'm being critical of her lack of adornment. On the contrary, I admired her for it. It's just that I was used to women like my mother who try every lotion and potion to hide their age.

Abdul acted sulky, probably embarrassed that I had witnessed his scene with Gloria, but I smiled reassuringly at him. After I introduced myself to everyone, we climbed into George's battered Volkswagen van, me in the back seat along with a short, plump systems programmer named Justin. Not exactly on the cutting edge of style, or at least style on my planet, Justin sported a Prince Valiant haircut. I knew he was staring at me even though his blue-lensed sunglasses obscured his eyes. I glanced at Justin, then around the van I was riding in, and for a second I thought I might be trapped inside a Beatles' Sergeant Pepper album. In tune with his general fashion sense, George's van was a throwback to the sixties, complete with NO NUKES stickers, a peace symbol on the dashboard and love beads hanging from the rearview mirror. I did some quick arithmetic and estimated that George was in elementary school during the sixties. Go figure.

The other guy was named Julio, and the woman, Lorene. No one said much, which was okay by me since the music was too loud to talk anyway. We just sat there listening to an old Jimi Hendrix tape blaring on George's stereo while Justin bobbed his head and slapped his thighs to the rhythm.

It was past noon and I was starved and in the mood for some good Chinese food. "So where are we going?" I yelled over the music.

No one paid any attention to me, then Lorene finally spoke up. "Bernie's favorite lunch spot," she replied without enthusiasm.

"Which is?" I asked, but she offered no reply.

Okay, maybe it was a secret. I could accept that. I sat back and listened to Hendrix singing "Are You Experienced?" and a few moments later we pulled into the parking lot of Chuck E. Cheese. Looking out the window, I hoped we were stopping for a flat tire, but my hopes dwindled as George pulled the van into a parking space. This was Bernie's favorite lunch spot? Chuck E. Cheese was a pizza parlor and video game arcade that catered to hyperactive children.

As soon as we passed its threshold my ears were bombarded with loud music, the ping-pings and boing-boing sounds of video games and the squeals of children doped on sugar. From my vantage point I could see at least two kids' birthday parties, which accounted for the decibel level, but there were a surprising number of adult programmer types lurking around.

"So this was Bernie's favorite place?" I asked Abdul, wanting confirmation of what I considered questionable data.

He nodded. "Bernie was hot on it. He was the high scorer on Road Warrior. We're going to have a tournament in his honor. Want to play?"

"Uh, sure," I said, then regretted it. Playing Road Warrior was not what I had planned on. When George said it was a memorial lunch for Bernie I pictured us all sitting in a quiet restaurant sharing touching anecdotes, not zapping electronic images on a screen.

We passed through a large birthday party of noisy toddlers, who were screaming "Barney, Barney," at the adult-sized purple furry animal that bounced around in front of them.

The restaurant seemed as big as a football stadium and twice as noisy as we pushed our way to the large video arcade in the back. It must have had a hundred games, mostly video games but some small-scale carnival games as well.

"Road Warrior is over here," said Abdul, pointing to the left wall. "George is going to order the pizzas before we start. We should probably go vegetarian with triple cheese. That was Bernie's favorite." Everyone agreed.

"There's six of us so we'll break up into two teams," Abdul said. Lorene looked petulant.

"I'm not playing. It's a ridiculous game. I never played with Bernie and I don't see why I should do it now," she said, and it crossed my mind she should up her estrogen dose. She excused herself to a nearby table.

How tough could it be to play a silly video game? I assured the guys they could count me in. We raised our hands, high-fived and headed for Road Warrior. I paused when I saw what the game actually entailed and silently chided myself for the low-estrogen slur I had mentally hurled at Lorene. As it turned out, the woman had high standards.

Road Warrior was a stationary motorcycle set up on a pedestal in front of a large video screen. The current player, about twelve, was sitting on the motorcycle, leaning over the handlebars, riding for his life as he crashed through the make-believe obstacles on the screen in front of him.

"Watch. We'll get rid of that kid," Justin whispered to me. Justin, Julio and Abdul walked over to the child, talking in loud and intimidating voices until the poor kid left.

Nice guys. Then they each took turns at the game, getting on the motorcycle, turning the handlebars, revving the pretend engine as they jumped walls and rivers or crashed into unsuspecting, blurry-looking pedestrians. When a collision occurred the motorcycle image on the screen burst into flames. I saw Lorene sitting quietly at the table and wished I was with her.

George came back from ordering pizza and took his turn on the motorbike. When his game was over they all looked at me.

"Your turn, Julie," George said. My smile froze on my face, hiding the grimace inside.

I didn't want to do it. It looked idiotic, immature, demeaning, and besides, I was wearing a skirt. But I, Julie Blake, graduate of MIT and Stanford and former president of the National Association of Women in Business was not the type to back away from a challenge. I needed information from these guys and the only way I would get it was if they thought I was one of them. I hiked up my skirt and straddled the motorcycle.

It wasn't bad once I got the hang of using the handlebars. I never quite mastered braking, but being a quick study I rapidly ascertained that braking was for sissies anyway. In spite of a couple of hairy crashes, I managed to end up with a score the girls at the Association would have been proud of. When I finished I got applause from the guys, although it may have been because my skirt was hiked over my thighs. So much for dignity.

Justin was up next, confidently hoisting his plumpness on the motorcycle and revving the engine.

"He's an expert," I commented to George and Abdul as we watched Justin jump safely over three police barricades at breakneck speed.

"I think he comes here at night by himself and practices. Very childish," Abdul said sourly. "He was always determined to beat Bernie."

"But he never did. No one ever beat Bernie," George added.

I noticed an irritating smugness in his voice and apparently so did Abdul because his eyes flickered and his cheeks flushed at George's remark.

"But somebody finally did beat him, didn't they?" Abdul said, his tone acidic.

George just looked down his nose at him with amusement. "But it wasn't you. Or was it?"

Abdul went stiff. He opened his mouth to say something, but decided against it. "I'm going for a cigarette," he said, then stomped off.

"What was that about?" I asked.

George leaned over and whispered in my ear. "Abdul hated Bernie."

I couldn't hide my surprise. "Then why's he here for Bernie's memorial lunch?"

George turned up his palms. "Who knows? Peer pressure, maybe. Guilt, perhaps. Abdul tried to pretend like he got along with Bernie. Of course, he had to since Bernie was his boss. But I know he hated him."

I hoped George couldn't see my ears pricking up. "Why?"

George smirked. "Abdul was infatuated with Gloria. He still is. He and Gloria were living together when she broke it off to date Bernie."

"Gloria left Abdul to date his boss?"

"This all happened a year ago and Bernie wasn't his boss then. The promotion came a few months later, which just made it that much worse for Abdul." George leaned over and again whispered. "Abdul got very tense. I often thought he was quite capable of violence."

My eyes fixed on him. "Do you think he could have been involved in what happened to Bernie?"

George shrugged. "You mean Bernie's murder? It *was* a murder."

"How do you know?"

He let out a shrill little laugh. "Everyone knows. The police had to get his next of kin information from Personnel, and this morning they were all over the incineration bin. Someone must have dumped his body there."

"And you think Abdul could have done it?"

"It's possible," he said, smiling deviously. He was enjoying the conversation a little too much for my taste. "It seems likely that someone at the company did it. Who else would know about the incinerator? The company likes to keep it secret because the whole animal testing issue is so nasty. The police should check Abdul's alibi, but then, they don't have any reason to, do they? They haven't talked to me yet."

"When they do talk to you, will you tell them about Abdul and Gloria?"

He put his hand over his heart. "It's my civic duty, don't you think?"

What I thought was that Lieutenant Dalton would find out about it long before George told him since I planned to tell him that afternoon.

The tournament ended with Justin the winner, and a few minutes later our pizzas were ready. Abdul returned and we found a large table and shared the three pizzas and a pitcher of beer. We made a few toasts to Bernie, Lorene shed a few tears, but the conversation was mostly limited to chatter about the latest computer hardware. I probed and prodded as much as I dared, but nobody gave any other clues that would help me uncover Bernie's murderer.

It was after two by the time we finished lunch and headed back to Biotech. When I got to the office Paoli was sitting at his desk just hanging up the phone.

"Out with the guys? Should I be jealous?" he joked.

"It was the guys plus Lorene."

"Who's Lorene?"

"A programmer." I closed the door so we could talk in

private. "Listen, I got some information from George that could be important. Abdul had a vendetta against Bernie. It turns out Bernie stole Gloria from him."

Paoli turned over one hand. "Well, it's always love or money."

"But there's more. I had tea with Gloria today and I told her that Bernie was being threatened on the Internet. I left out the Whip Boy details."

Paoli frowned. "Do you think that was smart?"

"Smart or not, it got a reaction. She seemed ignorant about the Net, but when I mentioned that the threats could be connected to Bernie's murder Gloria looked like she'd gotten an electric shock. She jumped up and ran out."

"So she knows something?"

"She's got to."

"Then let's go find her and put the press on."

"Can't. She went home, but we can try first thing tomorrow morning. If she comes in, that is. She looked sick. I guess we could try her at home. What about you? Did you find out anything from the Internet people?"

"You think I'm sitting here on my duff? I've been on the phone with a guy at Sun Microsystems. He told me it's very tough to trace an anonymous Net user using only your networking skills, but it could be done if you were a UNIX guru. And we're not talking a casual UNIX user. We're talking someone who could get inside the internals and do a little outpatient surgery."

UNIX is a complex operating system that runs most of the Net. If computer people tend to be a little odd, UNIX experts are often off the bizarro meter. For a long time UNIX had only been used by academics and scientists. It was currently gaining a stronghold in the commercial business world, but heavy duty UNIX geeks were still on the fringes of polite computer society. Imagine you're at a family wedding and think of the UNIX guys as the weird uncles nobody wants to sit next to.

We got on a conference call with Lieutenant Dalton, who was on his car phone. We told him about the Abdul/Bernie connection, then Paoli suggested the police go through the Biotech personnel files and see if anyone had a strong UNIX background.

Never ones to stand on the sidelines, Paoli and I decided to have our own chat with Abdul. The game plan was to ask for some advice on the patient program, then work the conversation to the subject of Bernie and gauge Abdul's reaction. We meandered to his cubicle but he wasn't there. I muttered a mild expletive.

"Don't get discouraged so fast. When I first met Abdul I thought I smelled cigarette smoke on his clothes," Paoli said.

"You're right. He smoked at lunch."

"So, since he's a smoker he could be in that courtyard near the deli. I've noticed that's where the smokers go."

And that's where we found him. No companies allowed smoking inside buildings anymore, and you could always find a group of smokers huddled in courtyards and patios. Abdul looked lonely sitting on the steps puffing away as he stared at nothing. Abdul was a handsome young man, his skin the color of caramel, his eyes dark and brooding, and I wondered what was going on in his head.

Paoli and I sat down beside him. He looked at us, startled at first, then relaxed. Paoli kicked off the conversation by asking him some questions about the data collection module of the patient program, and Abdul responded with interest, flattered we were asking his advice. He and Paoli chatted for a few minutes. I noticed that Abdul's cigarette was getting short and I didn't want to waste an opportunity.

"George was awfully rude to you today," I said, butting into the conversation.

"It doesn't mean anything," Abdul replied as he gazed at a couple walking by, their arms linked. "It's just his personality."

"That doesn't excuse it. You handled it well, though." I paused, then dropped my first bomb. "It must have been hard for you having to work with Bernie after what happened with Gloria."

Abdul's head snapped toward me. "Who told you about that?"

"George did after you left."

"He shouldn't have said anything. It's nobody's business." Abdul threw his cigarette down, stubbed it out with his foot and pulled another one out of his pocket. "It all happened a long time ago."

"A year's not that long," I said. "You can still hurt after a year when it comes to something like that."

I still remember the way he looked at me, his eyes bright with rancor.

"What do you know about hurt?" he said. "You're a good-looking white American. All doors open to you. Me, I'm an outsider."

"Even insiders get hurt sometimes."

A smirk crept over his face. "Things are harder when your skin is a different color."

"Is that why you think Gloria left you for Bernie? Because you're Indian?"

"Why don't you screw off?"

"Are you still that angry over what happened?"

He stood up and I knew I had put my foot in it. "What is this? Why are you asking me these questions, analyzing me? You think I killed Bernie? I don't know what you're doing, but I don't have to take it." He turned and left.

We watched Abdul as he walked inside the building. Paoli turned to me, his usually easygoing expression now clouded.

"Nice work, Julie. I was easing up to the big questions, then you jump in and hit him over the head with a sledgehammer," he said.

"I guess I was too direct."

"Like a bulldozer."

I silently chastised myself for my big mouth, for acting so stupidly with Abdul. I felt some responsibility for Bernie's murder and as a result I was behaving impulsively, talking without thinking.

It was only moments before I felt the familiar burning in my stomach. I pulled my Maalox from my purse, and as I took a gulp I saw Paoli's disapproving gaze. He prefers that I avoid stress rather than douse its effects with antacids. But I always reply with How can you avoid stress and make a living?, after which he always suggests that we move to the Bahamas and become bartenders.

We went back to the office and put together the project information Jennifer had asked for that morning. Paoli offered to take the report to her, but I declined and dropped it off myself. By that time it was almost five and I checked our messages at our Data9000 office. Joshua had called and said he would be dropping by around six, so we packed our briefcases and headed back to Data9000.

It felt good to be at my own desk, in my own leatherette swivel chair. I got the phone book and looked for Gloria's number. I wanted to talk to her and thought she might loosen up away from the office, but there was no Gloria Reynolds listed. There were several listings with the first initial G, so I called them all, but didn't locate Gloria.

When I finished, Paoli got on the phone with the printing company doing our brochures and I turned on the computer to log in the hours we had spent that day on Bernie's case. I noticed a message telling me I had new E-mail. I hit a button and saw I had a reply from Alone on Pluto.

I stole a look at Paoli. He was completely absorbed in brochure talk, so I pressed a key and the message came up on my screen:

Dear Venus—I too am frightened by my loneliness. It's a black, hollow part of me. I think I'll go crazy with it sometimes. My need can't be satiated by shallow companionship or pleasant chatter. My need probes deeper. I lust for a spiritual, mental and physical connection. Do you feel the same?

ALONE ON PLUTO

I stared at the note. Did I feel the same way he did? As far as the depth of his loneliness, the answer was no, but I related to what he said about needing a connection that was spiritual, mental and physical. I just wondered if it was possible.

"Hey, Josh!"

I jumped, startled, when I heard Paoli's greeting, and saw Joshua in the doorway. Quickly I pressed a key to save Alone's message, then deleted it off the screen.

Joshua had worked for me at ICI. He was your basic stress puppy, a nervous overreactive type who on his bad days threw hysterical fits over water cooler malfunctions, but on his good days was an efficient worker and a nice friend to have around. Joshua was currently working as an independent programmer. Good programmers can make more money on their own than working for a company, and I had heard that Joshua was doing well. I felt a little embarrassed seeing him again, since the last time we met was a month earlier at Paoli's house when he and Paoli caught me sneaking around Paoli's shrubbery trying to look in the windows. I had mistakenly suspected Paoli of entertaining a woman in his house. It had not been my finest moment when they found me in the bushes, and I don't think they believed my raccoon story.

After a few minutes of catching up on our respective businesses, I described the basic design of the patient program for Josh. Afterwards Paoli couldn't resist filling him in on how we ended up with the programming job, including Bernie being stalked on the Net. When Paoli mentioned ErotikNet I noticed Joshua's face turn pink. When Paoli used the name Whip Boy, Joshua's mouth fell open.

"Whip Boy was murdered?" Joshua asked, his eyes wide.

"You know Whip Boy?" I asked.

Joshua squirmed in his seat. "Well, sort of. I mean, I saw his messages a few times. After you've been logging on a while you get to know the regulars."

Was everyone in Silicon Valley plugged into cyberkink? Were they all going home at night and putting on their black leather and iron studs, with me the only person left sleeping in T-shirts? On the other hand, I decided not to be so judgmental since I was currently exchanging messages on ErotikNet under the name Virtual Venus.

"Did you ever see any messages from somebody called Night Dancer?" Paoli asked.

Joshua shook his head. "Not that I remember."

We spent another half-hour with Joshua, then left for home, leaving Joshua at the office to work on the program. He promised to leave whatever he finished on our desk so we could take it into Biotech the next morning and pretend we had done it ourselves.

After picking up a couple of takeout burritos, Paoli and I went to my house. Going to Paoli's place is seldom an option since he has no furniture except a futon that serves as couch, bed, dining table and dirty clothes hamper. Stretched out side by side on the couch, we watched CNN while we ate, then Paoli clicked off the television and leaned back into the couch.

"I learned something interesting about the Net today," Paoli said.

My heart fluttered, worried that somehow he had found out about my message from Alone.

"What is that?" I asked innocently.

"That Night Dancer wasn't a regular user. Joshua recognized Whip Boy, but had never heard of Night Dancer. When you went to the ladies' room I asked Joshua if he logged on to ErotikNet enough to be really familiar with the regular users. He said he did, and that he had never heard of Night Dancer."

I breathed easier. "Which just confirms my theory that Night Dancer was targeting Whip Boy from the beginning. And that means that someone from Biotech is the most probable suspect. A computer literate person is much more likely to choose the Internet as a framework for murder."

Paoli stood up and began collecting the dirty plates and foil wrappers off the coffee table.

"But Julie, lots of people are computer literate these days, and lots of people use the Internet."

"But we have to look at the odds. I can't give you numbers, but I'm sure the majority of Net users are people who work in the computer industry or at least use a computer in their work or at school. And don't forget that Bernie's social life was wrapped up in Biotech as well. His girlfriend worked there."

Cradling plates, glasses and burrito debris in his arms, Paoli paused, looking uneasy. "I guess I'm at the point where I don't want to admit anymore that it's a probability," he said.

"Why?"

"Because I keep thinking about what Dalton said. That if someone at Biotech killed Bernie and if that person knew the real reason we're there, that we could potentially be targets."

"I've been thinking the same thing. It worries me a little, but I don't see how anyone could know about us. I'm not going to let it scare me off the case."

Paoli still looked troubled as he carried the dishes to the kitchen. Later that night I woke up around three and found myself lying in bed thinking about Bernie, about the blood on him that night we found him. In spite of dating Gloria,

Bernie had still felt lonely. Alone on Pluto's words came back to me: "It's a black, hollow part of me."

I unwrapped myself from Paoli's arm, careful not to wake him, and slipped out of bed and went into the living room.

There's a chair by the window that my mother gave me. The chair had been in our house when I was growing up, and when I found out my mother was going to sell it in a garage sale I saved it and had it reupholstered. I remembered my father sitting in that chair, watching television on our old black and white TV.

I sat in the chair in the darkness, looking out the window and thought about all the loneliness there was in the world. Bernie, Abdul, Gloria—they all suffered from it. And even me, sometimes. We all had black, hollow places inside us that needed to be filled. It crossed my mind that a need like that could drive someone to murder.

9

It looked ominous. Sure, it was just a yellow Post-it note, but it was stuck on the door of our office, and that was a bad sign. There's a hierarchy of intimidation in the placement of Post-it notes. A note on a document is innocuous. A note stuck on your desk is a step up in seriousness, a note placed on your computer screen another step up from that. But a note stuck to the door of your office: that means trouble.

The next morning Paoli and I saw it from a distance as we cruised down the hallway. We reached our door and inspected it. It was from Jennifer and it said Benjamin Morse wanted to see us as soon as we got in.

"You think we're in trouble?" I asked Paoli and he laughed.

"What are they going to do? Take our television away for a week?" He had a point. Paoli had this way of reducing things to the lowest common denominator.

We took the elevator up to the second floor and made our way to Morse's office. Gloria was sitting at her desk, her back to us. It surprised me to see her in the office since she had seemed so ill the day before. I thought she'd probably be at home.

"We're here to see Morse," I said. She turned around and the sight of her gave me a jolt. She looked worse than the day before. Much worse. Her face was ashen and her eyes dull.

"Gloria, are you okay?" I said to her, but she stared

down at her desk, busying herself with some papers.

"Mr. Morse wanted to see you as soon as you got in. Let me tell him you're here," she said without looking at us, her voice flat. She rose quickly from her chair and walked around the desk, but as she reached for the knob of Morse's door I saw her falter and, thinking she was going to fall, I caught her arm. She went stiff, pulled away from me and opened the door.

"Ms. Blake and Mr. Paoli are here," she said. I heard Morse mumble something from inside his office. "I was going to fill your pen today, Mr. Morse, but I couldn't find it on your desk. If you'll give it to me I'll take care of it before I leave."

There was a pause, then I heard him say, "I lost it."

"I'll order another one for you," she told him, then gestured for us to go inside. The girl was a slave to him, having to fill his damn pens with ink. It was fashionable for executives to use hundred-dollar Mont Blanc fountain pens, even though a good old Bic worked just as well. I wondered if he made her wash out his silk underwear during her coffee breaks.

"We're going to talk when I'm done here," I whispered to Gloria as Paoli and I went in.

Morse's office was cloyingly modern. His desk was comprised of a thick glass top laid over two rough blocks of gray granite, and the walls were covered with art that to me looked like someone had puked paint. I noticed a picture of him on the wall shaking hands with the governor, another one of Morse playing golf.

"Have a seat," Morse told us. He was parked behind his desk, looking grim. There were no polite offers of coffee, no chitchat about the weather. My Post-it theory was holding up nicely. Paoli and I sat down.

"Gloria looks ill. I think she needs a doctor," was the first thing out of my mouth. Morse tightened his lips, then opened them to speak.

"I'm sure if she's sick she'll take care of herself. I didn't ask you here to talk about my secretary's health. I've had a complaint about you," Morse said. He sat stiffly in his chair, trying to maintain a cool, corporate facade but I could tell by his clenched hands that he was angry.

"I didn't think we had been here long enough to offend anybody," Paoli said good-humoredly.

"You must work faster than you realize." Morse's voice was thick with tension. I recrossed my legs and got comfortable. This was getting interesting.

"Could you tell us what the complaint is about?" I asked politely. I wondered what trespass would merit the attention of the company president.

"Harassment," Morse replied quickly and I sat up in my chair. Morse's statement surprised me, and the first thing that came to my mind was sexual harassment. I shot Paoli a questioning look and he responded with a "beats me" shrug. The only woman Paoli ever sexually harassed was me, and I liked it.

"What are you talking about? Who harassed who?" Paoli asked, his good humor gone.

Now that he had us on the defensive, Morse leaned forward into a more confident posture.

"Abdul Jarrod complained that you've been badgering him with questions about Bernie Kowolsky. He says you've been pressing him regarding Bernie's death. Pressing him in an accusatory way. I'd like for you to explain yourselves."

"Abdul is overreacting, which is understandable, I suppose. He's upset about Bernie's death," I said. "We just asked him a few questions, that's all."

"What right do you have to ask questions?"

"It's called the First Amendment," Paoli chimed in. "We've really got a lot of work to do. We're leaving."

Morse's face turned hard as he pressed his hands against the desk top. He was all quiet anger, the way a mean dog looks when he's considering biting your leg off.

"Listen to me, both of you. You're temporary employees here. If I find out you're bothering anyone I'll have you taken off the premises immediately. Do you understand what I'm saying?"

I understood the words but I didn't understand why he was taking such an interest in Paoli and me asking a few simple questions, and I doubted that Morse gave a damn whether or not Abdul was upset. I doubted he'd even known who Abdul was before this incident. It would be natural for a company president to be concerned about gossip when an employee had been murdered, but I sensed something in Morse that went far beyond that.

I wanted to question him, but if I did I risked getting us kicked out of the building, and I didn't want that. Probably the only reason Morse didn't fire us straight out was because Jennifer was so desperate to get the patient program finished. I decided to get my answers by less direct methods. I smiled politely and assured Morse that Paoli and I would keep our questions to ourselves. We then left.

"What the hell was that all about?" Paoli whispered as we exited Morse's office.

"Abdul must have gone running to Jennifer after we talked to him yesterday, and somehow Morse found out about it. It's strange that Morse rather than Jennifer would dress us down. He's scared about something. I don't know what."

I looked around for Gloria, but she wasn't at her desk. We went out into the hallway and I saw her at the end of it carrying a cardboard box.

"I want to talk to Gloria. Leave me alone with her, okay?" I said to Paoli. "I think she's more likely to open up to me if it's just the two of us."

He nodded and took off in the opposite direction while I stood by Gloria's desk, waiting for her. When she saw me she stopped, her expression a mixture of worry and fatigue.

I thought she might actually turn around to avoid me, so I quickly headed her off.

"Gloria, we need to talk," I said.

"Can't. I'm packing." She tried to push by me but I blocked her path.

"Packing? Why?"

"I . . . I quit this morning."

The box fell to the floor, her hands hovering in the air as if the box were still between them, and I realized that it was weakness that caused her to drop it. Her knees began to buckle and I grabbed her. I'm not that large a person and we both almost fell over, but I steadied myself against her desk and managed to keep us upright.

"You're sick. You need to sit down." I moved her toward a chair by her desk, but she pulled back.

"No, not there."

I gave her a quizzical look. "Okay, how about outside?" She nodded. With me holding on to her, we slowly walked outside to the patio area where the smokers hung out. Luckily nobody was there and I sat her down on the steps.

"Take a few breaths," I said, and she did. "You should see a doctor. I can drive you right now."

She shook her head. "Can't. I have to pack. I have to get out of here."

"Why are you in such a hurry?" She didn't answer me, and I searched her eyes for a reason for her strange behavior. I soon found it. It seemed like half the people at Biotech were frightened. "What are you afraid of?"

She looked at me when I said the last sentence and, too weak to lie anymore, her barriers fell. I felt the light touch of her fingers on my arm. Her skin felt hot.

"Bernie knew something about the company. Something horrible. I think that's why he was killed."

"And he told you what it was?"

"I knew. That's why I have to get out of here. They could kill me too."

"Who would want to kill you?"

She shook her head. "I don't know. There's no way to know."

"Then, Gloria, please tell me what it is that you and Bernie knew. I might be able to help you."

She stood up shakily, and I rose with her to keep her from falling over. "You can't help me. Nobody can help me."

"You don't know that. Gloria, you have information that the police need. Tell me what it is. I'll tell the police, but I won't tell them where I got it."

She closed her eyes a moment, took in some air, then let it out. Then she opened her eyes and clutched my arm. The strength of her grip surprised me.

"It had something to do with a file on someone's computer. Bernie saw it. I saw it."

"What kind of file. Whose was it?"

She took a breath and her body shuddered. "Kaufman's. It was Kaufman's file. He called it Rambo. Stupid name."

"What was in it?"

"I can't say anymore."

I had a dozen questions, but she looked so feeble I was afraid to press her any further.

"Okay, no problem. I'm taking you to a doctor." I pulled her gently in the direction of the parking lot, but she resisted.

"No, I can't. I have to pack. I have to—" I watched with horror as her eyes rolled back in her head. Then her body went rigid and hit the sidewalk.

Frantically I dropped down beside her and called her name but she couldn't hear.

"What have you done to her!"

I heard the yelling behind me. Turning, I saw Abdul.

"You! You caused this! You won't leave anyone alone!"

Abdul stood there shaking with fury, but something kept him from coming too close. I think he was too panicked to get close to her. Some people are like that in a crisis. Luckily, I'm not one of them.

"Go call an ambulance," I told him, but he just stood there, frozen. "Now!" I screamed. I put my head to Gloria's chest and didn't hear her breathing. I gave her mouth-to-mouth, and her breath came back, but she was still unconscious. In five minutes an ambulance pulled up, although it felt ten times longer. I'm no doctor, but to me she looked like she was dying. Holding her hand, I talked to her encouragingly, even though I didn't think she could hear me. The paramedics pushed me aside and took her vital signs, gave her oxygen, put her on a stretcher and placed her inside the ambulance. I asked if I could ride along with her and they said okay.

As we rode to the hospital I kept holding her hand, not knowing what else to do. I wanted to comfort her, so I spoke to her, told her everything was going to be okay, even though I had no idea if it would. After a few minutes her eyes opened. She opened her mouth to speak.

"Don't say anything. You're going to be all right, Gloria. It's all going to be okay." As I said the words I remembered that I had said the same to Bernie, and things hadn't been okay. Not by a long shot.

When we arrived at the hospital nurses whisked Gloria away. I called Paoli and told him what had happened and he said he would pick me up as fast as he could get there. I felt stupid that I didn't even know the name of the hospital. I had to ask someone.

While I was waiting for Paoli a nurse came out and asked me if I was the one who had come with Gloria. I said I was and she told me to wait. She left and a few seconds later a doctor came out.

"I'm Dr. Backus," the woman said. She was a little smaller than me, about five foot one with curly auburn hair and freckles. She didn't look old enough to be a doctor, but I didn't say so. People are always telling me I don't look old enough to be out of college. I know it's supposed to be flattering, but I never like it and I had a feeling she wouldn't either.

"Were you with Gloria when she collapsed?" she asked. I said I was. "Can you tell me what happened? Did she simply faint or was it more like a seizure?"

"It was more like a seizure, I think. She didn't just collapse to the ground. She went stiff first. Her eyes were open."

"Had she been ill recently? Has she any history of seizures?"

I shook my head, feeling useless. "I'm sorry, but I don't know. I haven't known her that long. Do you have any idea what's wrong with her?"

"It's too soon to know. We need to contact her family immediately."

"Yes, of course," I said, stammering a little. "I'll call someone in Personnel. They should have a family contact in her file."

Dr. Backus left. I immediately called Biotech and got in touch with someone in Personnel but Abdul had beaten me to it. The girl on the phone told me that Gloria's sister had been notified.

I tried sitting in the lobby for a few minutes but I felt queasy, so I went outside and sat on the edge of a stone planter. When I saw the Porsche pull up I was so happy I decided never to say another derogatory thing about it. I got inside the car, and soon as I faced Paoli I started to unravel. He put his arms around me and held me. It didn't matter that I hardly knew Gloria. Seeing her collapse the way she did had been wrenching.

"I'm going to take you home," Paoli told me after we pulled out of the hospital parking lot. "You can just plop down on the couch and let me take care of you. I'll cook your lunch."

"You don't cook, Paoli. You've never cooked in your life."

"So how tough can it be to apply heat to raw foodstuffs? My mother did it every day. You have a stove, right?"

I smiled at him. I wanted nothing more than to go home and get away from Biotech, but I couldn't.

"As much as I appreciate the offer, we have something else to do this afternoon."

He shifted the car into first as we pulled away from a red light. "Oh, believe me, we'll do that afterward. It'll take your mind off things."

"I meant work, Paoli. We have to go back to Biotech so we can get the Rambo file out of Kaufman's PC."

"I've missed something here. What are you talking about?"

I told him what Gloria had confided about the Rambo file supposedly on Kaufman's computer. For some reason Paoli didn't share my hands-on attitude about the situation.

"Julie, I think we should just tell the police and let them get a search warrant."

"Are you joking? If they did that Kaufman would just destroy the file before they could get to it. It only takes seconds to erase something."

"He may have already destroyed it anyway. Besides, we have no idea what it is or if it even exists. Gloria doesn't seem too stable to me. What if she's making this all up? She's still a prime murder suspect as far as I'm concerned."

"I don't think she was lying. Lying takes too much energy. She was so weak she could barely walk."

"Okay, then let's assume for the moment that she was telling the truth. How do you suppose we go about getting Kaufman's file? I'm sure he locks his office at night."

"I've already thought about that and I have a plan."

Paoli slapped his forehead as he pulled on to the freeway. "Why didn't I guess that? Of course you have a plan. You always have a plan. And your plans usually involve breaking and entering."

I ignored his last remark. "Just drive to a software store. I'll explain on the way."

I took a swig of Maalox from the bottle, put the cap back on and returned the bottle to my purse. I was on my way to see Kaufman, but passing by Bernie's office, I was drawn inside. The police had already gone through everything, but I wanted to check it out on my own. I told myself that perhaps the police had missed something, that maybe because I knew Bernie I could find a clue they hadn't.

That was part of it, but there was more. I still felt connected to him. I had only known him a couple of days, but he had been one of our few clients and I had been moved by his predicament, grateful for his trust. I had tried to help him and I had failed, and the failure gnawed at me.

His office looked pretty much the same as it had on Friday, the day he died. I glanced around at his computer and his papers, then told myself I should leave, but I didn't. Instead I pulled open his top desk drawer and saw his Biotech card key lying there. Its presence bothered me. Why had he left it? Normally someone would take their badge home with them so they could use it the next day to enter the building. I wondered if that day Bernie, like Gloria, had decided to leave Biotech and never come back.

I picked the badge up and slipped it into my purse. I would need it later if I wanted access to the lab. It was then I noticed a document on Bernie's desk I recognized as Bernie's overview of the patient program. I picked it up, perused it and discovered that it was much more detailed than the information Paoli and I had scraped together. The police had already gone through the drawer so I didn't think it would hurt to take it, and it could be helpful to

Joshua. I closed the drawer and left Bernie's office.

Flipping through the document as I walked, my breath caught in my throat when I saw a blue paper stuck to one of the pages. The paper was small and lined, a type of note paper Biotech must have kept in stock, because I had seen it in my own desk drawer.

Words were scrawled in large print across it. I'LL KILL YOU, it said. The note paper had a sticky strip across the top and must have gotten stuck between the pages so the police missed it. I had suspected it before, but now I knew for sure—someone at Biotech had wanted Bernie dead.

I took a fortifying breath and knocked on Kaufman's door. Using Bernie's card key I had entered the lab easily, and since I had been in the lab area only a few days before, none of the technicians seemed to question my presence. Moira wasn't at her desk, so I went directly to Kaufman's office and tapped on his door. A gruff voice yelled, "Come in."

I tried to open the door, but it was locked. Through the glass wall I could see Kaufman sitting at his desk, the desk top piled high with papers and books. The whole office was a mess. With annoyance he got up and opened the door, looking at me like I was a tax auditor.

"What do you want?"

"Sorry to interrupt, but last week Bernie asked me to install some antivirus software on your computer." I held up the shiny box of software that I had just bought an hour earlier. I figured Kaufman wouldn't turn down a request from someone so recently and tragically deceased. I was wrong.

"I already have antivirus software." He looked at me cautiously.

"I know, but some files around the company have been infected. Bernie thought we should install better protection. This software is the best on the market." I held up the box as if I was Vanna White, but he just looked at me.

Time for a new approach. "Have you noticed anything funny about your files?" I asked. "Any lost data, any numbers transposed?"

"Numbers transposed?" he said with fresh concern in his voice. I figured any scientist would get extremely nervous about numbers being screwed up.

"That's what's been happening to other people. It's hard to detect. It'll only take me half an hour to get it installed. I could do it while you're at lunch."

"It's two-thirty. Too late for lunch. I don't eat lunch." I watched his face go through its paces as he considered the options. The man obviously didn't want me touching his computer, but on the other hand he couldn't risk numbers being fouled up, especially around budget time. "Is this authorized by Jennifer?"

"Of course. It was her idea. You can call her if you want," I said, knowing that only a few minutes earlier I had seen her get in her car and drive off.

"All right. I'm doing the budget and can work off my printout. Sit here."

He pointed to an uncomfortable-looking metal chair on the other side of his desk next to his own chair. It was stacked with old newspapers and tattered copies of *Scientific American*. I walked over to it, Kaufman right behind me.

"I'll just move these papers," I said. He grunted and sat down.

This wasn't what I had expected. With him sitting next to me it would be tough to go through his files without him noticing. I sat down next to him and spent the next five minutes taking the plastic shrink wrap off the software box and taking out the diskettes. I wasn't sure I would have time to sort through his files and actually load the software too. Chances were he would never notice whether the antivirus software was loaded or not, since that kind of software worked behind the scenes. It depended on how much he knew about computers. I decided to give him a little test.

"Is your IO bus dual modulated or single coded?"

He gave me a blank look, then answered "Dual modulated." Bingo. It was a nonsensical question, the type techno-dweebs like to use to make fools out of people, and Kaufman had answered, proving he was a neophyte. He would never know whether or not the software was loaded.

Just for show, I took out the diskette already in the hard drive and put in the antivirus diskette, then I scrolled through his files. Although he was buried in his paperwork, every once in a while Kaufman glanced in my direction, and that made me nervous since he could see the computer screen from where he was sitting.

"Darn. There's a glare from this angle," I muttered, then turned the screen toward me so it was now obscured from his view. He didn't seem to notice.

Kaufman had hundreds of files on his PC. They were grouped under subheadings and I searched them all, examining every file name, but there was nothing called Rambo. The process was taking much longer than I expected, and after an hour Kaufman started giving me funny glances. After an hour and a half he articulated his concerns.

"You said it would only take thirty minutes."

"Yes, well, I'm having a little problem. I'll have things worked out in just a minute."

I turned back to my screen to show him how furiously I was working, but out of the corner of my eye I noticed him watching me. Soon I felt a heavy hand on my thigh.

"You're a lovely woman," he said, his voice husky. "I would like to know you better." His hand squeezed my flesh. I considered sawing my leg off.

I opened my mouth to tell him that he would be singing soprano in the Vienna Boys Choir if he didn't remove his hand, but decided against it. I hadn't found the file yet and I might need to stay in his good graces if I was going to get another shot at it. If I was lucky maybe I would get the chance to nail him for murder.

"I'm dating someone," I said.

"Does that matter?" he replied, giving my leg a fresh squeeze for punctuation.

"To me it does."

I pushed his hand off my thigh, then faked a smile. It was then, over his shoulder, that I noticed the laptop computer sitting on a pile of books, and I realized that's where the file probably was. If the Rambo file were secret, naturally he would keep it on his own computer, one he could carry with him.

"Would you like for me to take a look at your laptop and see what antivirus software you have loaded?" I asked him.

"No," he answered quickly. "Leave that one alone. It's mine, not the company's."

His response only heightened my desire to get at that laptop. I continued working for another few minutes, long enough to go into his budget spreadsheet and change a few formulas so the next day when he printed out a fresh copy most of his figures would be wrong. He should be more careful about whose thigh he squeezed.

"All done now. Sorry if I interrupted anything," I said cheerily, then left. Once outside his door I shivered with disgust. Could I clean my leg with Clorox and a steel brush, I wondered? When I got back to the office, Paoli was there.

"How did it go?"

I showed him the blue note I found in Bernie's desk, leaving it stuck to the report just as I had found it.

"Don't touch it. There may be fingerprints," I said.

He looked at the writing, then back at me. "We'll have to give this to the police."

"Of course. You know what this means? It just confirms the theory that Bernie's killer is someone at Biotech."

"I thought we knew that already."

"We suspected it. Now we have more proof."

"So how did things go with Kaufman?"

"Lousy. I didn't find the file on his office computer. It's got to be on his laptop. We have to figure out a way to get to it."

"Can't we just go into his office tonight after he's left?"

"He's probably going to be working late tonight because his budget's due tomorrow." I failed to mention that Kaufman would be working especially late once he caught the recently introduced errors in his spreadsheet. "You call Dalton and tell him about the note. I'm going to call the hospital and see how Gloria's doing."

I called, but the ward nurse wouldn't tell me much over the phone, so I decided to go there myself. I made a quick photocopy of the note I had found in Bernie's desk, slipped the original in an envelope, then put both into my briefcase. Paoli drove and we swung by the police department first and dropped off the original note. When we arrived at the hospital Paoli waited for me in the lobby.

The receptionist scanned her computer and told me that Gloria was in the intensive care unit and that only family members were allowed in her room. After I assured her I just wanted to talk to her doctors, she told me where I could find the ICU area. I went up the elevator, turned left then found the door to Intensive Care. It was locked and had a buzzer by the double metal doors. Before I could push the button I saw Abdul and George in the hallway. Abdul was pale, his face like stone, and George's usually smug countenance had been replaced by a stunned gape. I went over to them.

"What's happening? How is she?"

George didn't say anything.

"She's dead," Abdul blurted out. "She died an hour ago."

I stared at him in disbelief. "What happened? What did she die from?"

"They're not sure," George said.

"The nurse told us it could have been bacteria. And Gloria was in the lab a few weeks ago. She was helping catalog the vials. She got infected and now she's dead! We could all get it!"

Abdul was hysterical and George put his hands on his shoulders to quiet him. When he felt George's touch, Abdul began to cry.

"I loved her," he mumbled through his tears.

"I better get him out of here," George said. Still holding on to Abdul, he turned his friend around and walked with him to the elevator.

Abdul's words about the bacteria spun in my head. Gloria had told me that she was afraid for her life because of what she knew, because of what Bernie had told her. Was it possible that someone at Biotech had purposely infected Gloria with toxic bacteria?

Nausea swept over me and I leaned against the wall and tried to breathe deeply, but my breath caught inside my chest. Clasping my hands together so they would stop shaking, I went back to the door to the intensive care unit and pressed the buzzer. A nurse opened the door.

"I need to find out about Gloria Reynolds. I have some questions I'd like to ask the doctor."

"Are you a family member?" she asked.

I hesitated, then spoke. "I'm a friend."

"Oh, I was hoping you were a relative. She died very suddenly. Her mother and sister are on their way but there are things that need to be taken care of—"

"I have to talk to the doctor right away."

The nurse looked disappointed that I wouldn't be making funeral arrangements, but she scurried off. A few moments later a bearded man in his thirties walked up to me.

"You're a relative of Gloria's?"

"I'm a friend of hers from work. A close friend. Tell me what happened."

He paused at first, not certain if he wanted to spill the details. "She died of cardiac arrest around an hour ago," he said after a moment.

"She had a heart attack?"

"Her heart stopped functioning, but Gloria had some virus or bacterium that we haven't been able to identify. It could even have been some sort of toxin. We're not sure."

"You're saying she could have been poisoned?"

"We're not sure of anything yet. There was no irritation in her stomach or lungs we could find that would indicate poisoning." His beeper went off. He stopped, took a look at it, then continued. "We need to do an autopsy to find out what went on with her."

Nice way to put it, I thought. "To find out what went on with her" sounds a lot nicer than "to find out what killed her."

"Gloria's mother will be here soon. I'm sure she'll want you to do whatever you can to find out what she died from."

I handed him my business card, introduced myself and asked if I could call him after the autopsy for more details about Gloria.

"Sure. I'm Dr. Horst. My office number's listed," he said. "I've got to go now. I'm very sorry about your friend."

I watched him as he walked back down the hallway, then I got a drink of water from the fountain and leaned against the wall, trying to stop my blood from racing. I had a suspicion and I didn't like it. If Gloria had died from something mysterious, then perhaps Abdul was right. It was possible she could have contracted it at Biotech. I just wondered if it was an accident. It was too much of a coincidence that both she and Bernie had known about the Rambo file, and now within a few days both she and Bernie were dead.

10

It took a jumbo shot of tequila to calm my nerves. As soon as Paoli pulled the Porsche away from the hospital curb I directed him to the Rainbow Lounge, a raunchy bar for Silicon Valley down-and-outers to which I had been introduced a month earlier by a woman friend. Only a year before I wouldn't have been caught dead in a place like the Rainbow. But then, a year before lots of things were different, including me.

Before we sat down I used the pay phone, keeping the greasy mouthpiece as far from my lips as possible, and called Lieutenant Dalton. I told him what had happened with Gloria, gave him Dr. Horst's name and suggested he look into the autopsy results. Dalton asked me a few questions about the threatening note we had dropped off earlier. I answered them, then joined Paoli at the bar.

He ordered a beer for himself and a white wine for me. When our drinks came I raised my glass to my lips, peered down into it, then held it up for a closer inspection. The wine looked like a urine sample, so I sent it back and got a shot of tequila, a drink I felt I could trust. Paoli looked at me with astonishment as I poured salt on my hand, licked it off, tossed the tequila down my throat, then sucked on a wedge of lime.

"Did you pick that up in the MBA program at Stanford?" Paoli asked as he watched my face pucker. It was hard to answer with my teeth clenched around the lime. Tequila is a rough drink and the lime tasted like it hadn't seen a refrigerator in a week, but after a few seconds I could feel a warm glow in my chest. I took the lime out of my mouth and put it down on a napkin on the bar.

"There were a lot of things they forgot to teach me at Stanford," I told him, my voice choked from the liquor. "They taught me about financial analysis and computers," I said, counting the subjects off on my fingers. "They taught me about the stock market and statistics and operating margins. But they didn't teach me a damn thing about humans. Kiss me."

I'm not a good drinker. About the only time I drink more than a glass of wine is when I'm working on a case, which had been infrequently, and I could already feel my head buzzing.

I don't know why I needed to be kissed at that moment, but I did. Paoli stood up, lifted me out of my chair, leaned me back into his arms and kissed me like we both had thirty seconds to live. I heard some faint applause from the bar patrons. Paoli kissed me for what seemed a long time, a luscious kiss, deep and aggressive, and we could have stayed like that all night for all I cared, but he pulled away.

"You're a cheap drunk, Julie Blake. I like that in a woman. Want another one?"

"Another kiss or another drink?"

"Your choice."

"What I want is for you to take me home, take all my clothes off and make me forget my job."

And he obliged. I awoke the next morning feeling restored and optimistic that maybe things at Biotech weren't as sinister as I had imagined. Maybe Gloria's death was from natural causes. Maybe Bernie's murder was a freak occurrence, the random act of a crazed killer but not a heinous plot by a trusted co-worker. Maybe Paoli and I would wrap up the Kowolsky case that morning and move on to a big corporate project. Maybe Prince Charles and Di would kiss and make up.

That morning a cold fog filled the valley, so we took my Toyota since the Porsche doesn't have a working heater. It took some convincing but Paoli finally gave in. First we stopped off at the office and picked up the envelope sitting in front of the door, Joshua's first installment on the patient software. Next stop, the Hard Drive.

Lydia looked at us suspiciously when we walked in, her arms filled with a tray of blueberry muffins. Her long brown hair was pulled with fat yellow yarn into a straggly ponytail that sat askew on top of her head, and she had forced her Rubenesque figure into a pair of turquoise stretch pants. It made me think she must have a new boyfriend. Her apron, the one she always wore, said KISS THE COOK.

"You weren't here yesterday," she said.

"Working on a case," Paoli answered. He winked, made a clicking sound with his tongue and pointed at her. "Got to make some money, honey, so one day I can whisk you off to Rio. You belong in a bikini, not an apron." Lydia scolded him but twittered happily as she made our cappuccinos.

Driving the Toyota, I felt warm and cozy, glad not to be riding in the Porsche. I like my cars the same way I like my men—efficient, dependable and with all their parts in functioning order. Paoli was a little short in the efficient category, but he topped the charts on everything else.

"We need to plan our day," I told him as I pulled onto the freeway.

His face turned overly serious and he raised his hands in the air. "Okay, here's the plan. We get to Biotech, solve the case by ten, be at the horse track by eleven, have at least five beers apiece by two-thirty—"

"Paoli, this is not a joking matter."

"Everything in life's a joking matter. It's the only way to survive."

"On the contrary, the only way to survive is through

brains and imagination. I have to get to Kaufman's laptop and I'm not sure how."

Paoli mulled it over a moment while I negotiated the commuter traffic. "Do you know if he locks his door when he's not there?" he asked.

"Yes, he does. I know because it was locked yesterday, even though he was at his desk. The door must lock automatically when it's pulled shut."

"I can take care of that," Paoli said, a little too easily, I thought.

"How?"

He grinned. "I'll show you when we get there."

But plans change, and when we arrived at Biotech fifteen minutes later we saw a sign in the lobby announcing a company-wide meeting that was being held that day in the lunchroom at eight-thirty. All employees, temporary as well as permanent, were required to attend.

We dropped off our briefcase and followed a small group to the lunchroom. When we got there all the seats were already taken, with people standing in the back. The room bustled with conversation, none of it too cheerful. I spotted Justin standing near the window and pulled Paoli in that direction.

"What's this about?" I asked Justin. He was wearing a green Nehru jacket, loose pants and high-top sneakers.

"Gossip is that Gloria Reynolds died from a disease she got from one of the bacteria samples. Everybody's hysterical."

"Can't blame them," I said. Just then the room became quiet. I stood on my tiptoes and saw Benjamin Morse walk to the front of the room with Kaufman in tow. They both looked glum. Placing himself behind a wooden podium, curling his fingers around its edges, Morse scanned the sea of faces with the somber deportment of a funeral director. The way things were going I guessed that was about right.

"First let me express my deep sorrow over the death of

Gloria Reynolds," he said. "She was a valued employee to all of us as well as a cherished friend. The company has started a memorial fund to be donated to our local SPCA in her name. The SPCA was a favorite charity of Gloria's. The company has already made a substantial donation, and if any of you would like to contribute please contact the Human Resources Department."

Morse cleared his throat and an underling scurried up with a glass of water. He took a sip, handed the cup back, then continued.

"It has come to my attention that rumors are circulating through the company that Gloria may have died from a bacterium that was being researched here at Biotech. Let me assure you that we have no information whatsoever that would lead us to that conclusion. Biotech has the highest standards of security and control, and it is only the remotest possibility that anything of that nature could have happened. But to make sure everyone here feels secure in their working environment, we will be glad to pay for any medical testing that any employee wishes in order to give him or her peace of mind. But let me assure you again, we have no information that would lead us to believe that Gloria died from contact with anything here at the company."

A few hands waved in the air.

"If you have any questions," Morse added quickly, "please feel free to take them to Human Resources. Thank you." Morse abruptly left the podium, exiting the room with Kaufman right behind. I guessed he didn't want to answer any irksome questions about how an employee ended up in the company incinerator.

"That was short and sweet," Paoli said sourly. "Naturally they don't have any information that implicates Biotech because Gloria's autopsy hasn't been completed."

"Or if it has, Biotech hasn't received the results yet," I added. "Did you see Kaufman's face? He looked like he was about to hurt someone."

"You know he killed a man."

I heard the words and wheeled around to find their source was Justin.

"What?" I said.

"Kaufman killed some guy back in Germany. That's why he came to the States."

"How do you know?"

"It's a rumor, but I heard it from someone in the lab who heard it from someone at Burlex Lab who came from Frankfurt. Kaufman threw some guy against a wall and cracked his skull open."

"But why?"

Justin shrugged. "I heard they got in some kind of argument. Who knows? But have you noticed that if you look in his eyes, really look into them, there's nothing there? Gotta go."

He wiggled his fingers at us, turned and moved through the crowd toward the exit.

"Do you believe that?" Paoli asked me.

I shook my head. "I don't know. It's an unsubstantiated rumor, yet there's something about Kaufman that makes me think he's capable of anything."

As the crowd dispersed I could hear discontented rumblings and I couldn't blame any of them for being worried. I was starting to feel very uneasy myself. If someone at Biotech found out that Paoli and I were investigating Bernie's murder, would we be the next persons taking a one-way trip to the hospital?

I shook off the thought. I had no proof that Gloria's death was from anything but natural causes, only there was this twinge in my gut telling me it wasn't—a twinge that several swallows of Maalox couldn't eradicate.

Back in our office, Paoli and I called Dalton and set up a time when we could update each other on the case. We agreed to meet at a nearby coffee shop that afternoon at two. I hung up the phone and faced Paoli. Although I was filled with anxiety up to my eyeballs, I did my best to sound self-assured.

"Okay, you were going to show me how to get past Kaufman's locked door."

Paoli swung his feet off his desk. "You said the door locks automatically when it closes, right?" I nodded. "No problem. I prefer to use beeswax for this, but chewing gum will do."

"What are you talking about?"

"I'm talking about sticking some gum inside the part of the doorjamb where the door locks. You stick the gum inside as far as you can. When someone shuts the door it'll close, but it won't lock." He scowled. "Where did you go to school, a convent? I thought everybody knew this."

"I studied books when I was in school."

"That's what you get for living in a good neighborhood. Your education gets limited. There's a vending machine in the cafeteria. Go get some gum."

Doubtful of Paoli's approach, but without any good alternative of my own, I got some change out of my purse, went to the cafeteria and came back with a package of Juicyfruit. Paoli was absorbed in an issue of *ComputerWorld* so I stuck it under his nose.

"Now what?"

"Chew a couple of pieces real well to get some of the sugar out. It sticks better that way. Then you go to Kaufman's office, stick the gum in the lock when he's not looking, then wait for him to leave. Child's play. I'm amazed at the things I have to explain to you." Paoli went back to his magazine.

"How do I get the gum in the lock without someone seeing?"

He kept his face buried in his reading material. "If I told you how to do everything you'd never learn on your own. What happened to all the brains and imagination you were talking about this morning?"

I chose not to grace the comment with a reply. Instead I marched over to the lab and used Bernie's card key to get inside, madly masticating my Juicyfruit as I came up with an inane plan to get the gum in the door.

When I reached Kaufman's office I stopped. Through the glass wall I could see him bent over his laptop and I stared at him a moment thinking about what Justin had told me. The thought of what I was about to do made my skin crawl, but I reminded myself that I was working on a case and had to push personal preferences aside.

I spit the gum into my hand and knocked on the door. When he saw me he looked irritated, but then Kaufman always looked irritated. He got up and opened the door.

"What?" he said gruffly as he sat back down, his eyes immediately glued back to his computer screen.

I leaned my hip and shoulder against the door in a manner I assumed was sexy since I had seen Lauren Bacall do it in *Key Largo*. I've spent too much of my life in front of computers to have built up much of a repertoire of sensual gestures. The only one I really knew was just to take my clothes off, and although it always worked with Paoli, I wasn't about to try it with Kaufman.

"I just wanted to see how your new software was working," I told him, my voice softened to a kittenish purr I was immediately ashamed of. The girls at the Association would have been so disgusted.

"Works fine. I'm busy."

His attitude threw me. I had expected a warmer reception from someone who had so recently fondled my thigh, but that's men for you. Kaufman had diverged radically from the script I had created in my head. Not sure of my next step, I winged it.

"Yes, well, I just was wondering if maybe you wanted to go for a drink," I said out loud. Slut, I said silently, the finer part of my conscience writhing with the indignity. "Tuesday maybe," I added, hoping like hell I would be out of Biotech by then. If not I could always throw myself under a train. Kaufman looked at me with new interest.

"Tuesday?" he asked with a leering half smile. "Yes, I would like that."

"Call me Monday, and we'll set it up. Oh, one more thing. I think I dropped an earring yesterday when I was installing the software. It's probably beneath your desk."

"Feel free to look," he said.

"Well, I was wondering if you could. I've got, uh, a knee injury from tennis."

Stupid, Julie. You get arm injuries from tennis, although since I'd never played tennis you could have gotten ear injuries for all I knew. But apparently not a tennis player himself, Kaufman bought my story and slid off his chair and onto the floor to look for the phantom earring.

"What does it look like?"

"It's gold and round," I said as I speedily pushed the chewing gum into the door lock. I couldn't see Kaufman because the desk blocked my view, but I could hear him rummaging around on the floor. I heard the words "I don't see it" come from underneath the desk.

"Try over near the wall," I said, stalling for more time while I pushed the gum in farther so it couldn't be easily seen. Paoli had provided very limited information about the actual gum placement process. It was a more complex operation than I had originally assumed, especially since the gum kept sticking to my fingernail.

"It's not here," Kaufman said. I heard a thump followed quickly by an *ouch*. I disentangled my fingernail from the Juicyfruit just as he emerged.

"No earring," he said grumpily.

"No problem. I have plenty more. See you later." I turned to leave.

"Wait."

I stopped, praying he didn't want to move up our date.

"Meet you at the Spatz bar on Tuesday? Around eight?"

he asked, his eyebrows rising lasciviously.

"Sure, eight. Sounds good." Like a root canal.

"Until then."

"Right. See you." I walked down the hallway feeling cheap and ashamed of myself.

"Well?" Paoli asked when I walked in. He was busy shooting rubber bands against the wall and he had been at it a while because there was a small pile on the floor near the window. I shut the door behind me.

"The operation was successful except that I feel like a ten-buck hooker. Only a ten-buck hooker is better than me because at least a hooker is upfront about what she does."

Paoli immediately swung his feet off the desk and sat up. "For chrissakes, Julie, what did you do?"

I dropped down into a chair. "In order to distract him I had to agree to have drinks with him next Tuesday."

"You're going on a date with the commandant? Shouldn't you have discussed this with me?"

"I was only using my brains and imagination," I said sarcastically, then slumped into my chair and crossed my arms. "We won't be here next Tuesday, because we're going to have this case wrapped up by then. I stuck the gum in the lock, so all I have to do now is wait for him to leave his office and sneak in."

"What is this 'I' pronoun?"

"I have to do it alone. The people around the lab are used to seeing me now. If we're both in his office looking at his computer it'll seem suspicious."

Paoli didn't appear convinced. The phone rang. He picked it up, said "sure" a few times, then hung up.

"That was Jennifer. She wants to meet with us at four-thirty to take a look at what we've done on the program. She said there's a budget meeting for the department heads from five until eight, so she only has half an hour for us."

"That's great!"

"Are you nuts? A half-hour could be an eternity. Since

we're not writing the program ourselves it's going to be a little hard for us to discuss it."

"No, I mean if there's a meeting for the department heads, Kaufman will have to be there. I can get into his office between five and eight."

"Julie, I don't want you to do it."

"Don't worry. Nothing will happen."

Famous last words.

"I got a call about Gloria Reynolds's autopsy about an hour ago. The hospital put a rush on it," Dalton told us. We were sitting at a small table at a coffee shop two miles from Biotech where our fellow employees would be unlikely to catch us cavorting with the cops. I was sipping coffee while Paoli and Dalton wolfed down apple pie, a gluttonous act I resented since I was still trying to lose five pounds.

"What were the results?" I asked.

"She died from a toxin. It's called—" He stumbled for the word, finally reached into his shirt pocket and pulled out a folded laundry ticket. "Grayanotoxin," he read.

"A poison?" Paoli asked.

"Sort of. The doctor says it's a weird thing to come across. The only way they figured it out so fast was because they rushed tissue and blood samples to UCSF."

"But Gloria had been sick for a few days. Does that mean someone at Biotech was slipping poison in her food for a while?" I asked him.

He shrugged as he put a forkful of sugary apple and flaky crust in his mouth. The pie looked homemade.

"That's the crazy thing about it. They don't know how she got it. She didn't ingest the stuff orally."

"How do they know that?"

"Because if she had, the autopsy would have shown irritation in her stomach lining or somewhere and they didn't find any needle marks either, so they can't figure out how she got the stuff inside her. It could have been an accident because she had been helping another secretary in the lab do some cataloging of test vials, and grayanotoxin was one of them. It's possible she could have picked up the toxin that way, I suppose, but Biotech management doesn't agree. They say you couldn't get it in your bloodstream if you bathed in it."

"She must have been helping Moira, Kaufman's assistant," Paoli said. "And Moira's fine. I saw her at the meeting this morning and she looked healthy."

"The other odd thing is that grayanotoxin isn't normally fatal," Dalton said. "It causes seizures, even comas, but you recover."

Nobody said anything for a few minutes. I grabbed Paoli's fork and took a bite of pie. A girl's got to keep up her strength.

"Did you get a chance to go over the personnel files and see if anyone had a heavy UNIX background?" I asked after I swallowed.

"We've gone through the records of everyone in the computer department and couldn't find anything like that," he answered.

For a few moments there was silence at the table.

"So what do you think?" Dalton asked, directing the question at both of us. "You've both been at Biotech for a few days now. Do you think someone there could have killed her?"

"Yes," I said, and filled Dalton in on what Gloria had said to me about being afraid for her life because of something both she and Bernie knew. After I had told my story, Dalton gave us his home phone number and told us to call him that night if we found out anything else, then we headed back to Biotech with Paoli driving.

"You didn't tell Dalton about the Rambo file. Isn't that a salient piece of information?" Paoli asked.

"I just want one more chance at getting it myself. Fifteen minutes with Kaufman's laptop and I'll have it, I'm sure. We'll take a look at the file then turn it right over to Dalton. If for some reason I don't get it tonight, I'll tell Dalton about the file first thing tomorrow. But trust me, he'll just get a search warrant, Kaufman will erase the file before the police get to it, and we'll end up knowing nothing."

Paoli considered what I had said as he turned a corner. "Okay, we should go after the file tonight, but I'm the one to do it, not you. Kaufman's a murder suspect, especially now that we know what killed Gloria. And after what Justin said about Kaufman's background in Germany I don't want him catching you in his office."

I waved the idea away. "He won't catch me because he'll be in a meeting for a good three hours. I have to be the one to do it because I'm already familiar with Kaufman's files. I'm sure he uses the laptop for backup, and I won't waste time looking at files that were on his company computer."

Paoli stopped the car in the middle of the street. I heard honking behind us, but Paoli ignored it.

"The only way I'll let you do this is if you check in with me every ten minutes while you're in Kaufman's office. I'll wait at my desk. If you miss a phone call I'll come looking for you."

"That's stupid. Someone could hear me making the calls." I twisted my neck to see the angry drivers behind us. "Could you move the car? We're blocking traffic."

"Make the calls or you're not going."

"You don't decide what I do or don't do, Paoli."

"When it comes to your safety, I do."

"You do not."

"I do."

It was obvious where the conversation was going. Luckily for us and the people behind us we both shut up and Paoli drove on. When we got back to Biotech it was almost time for our meeting with Jennifer. We took a few minutes to go over Joshua's program so we wouldn't look ignorant, then went to her office.

She was at her desk talking on the phone and she looked worn out. It was that time of day. All her makeup had worn off and her eyes looked small and glassy. She hung up the phone and asked us to sit down.

"I never asked you about your meeting with the police lieutenant. Did you give him everything he needed?" she asked first thing.

"I think so," I answered.

"Well, please cooperate with him as much as possible. Anything we can do to find out what happened to Bernie."

Her mouth tightened, her eyes began to redden and she quickly changed the subject to the patient program. She looked at what we had done, made a few suggestions and that was it. Her suddenly cursory attitude toward the program surprised me. Maybe she was too overwhelmed with the two deaths at Biotech to get deeply into detail on anything else.

Paoli and I got back to the office a little after five and putzed around until six bickering over whether or not I was going to Kaufman's office, which of course I was. I did agree to call him every half-hour and that seemed to mollify him. At ten after six I was on my way.

I didn't think there was much risk involved in what I was about to do. Kaufman's meeting was supposed to go until eight, and meetings like that usually went over their allotted schedule. I had fixed the door earlier so I could get in easily. Still, I felt an excitement pulsing through me as I walked to the lab. If I had known how, I would have whistled.

All my life I'd been a Girl Scout, always being responsible, always following the rules, doing what was expected of me. That was the old Julie Blake. Since I had started Data9000 with Paoli, for the first time in my life I was taking a few risks. I mean, talk about risk. Even halfway living with a man like Paoli was jumping off a cliff as far as I was concerned. And sneaking into someone's office, well, it was kind of thrilling. I felt like a spy, and the thought of it made me laugh.

I used Bernie's card to get in the door. There was only one technician still left in the lab and he looked like he was finishing up. He looked at me when I walked by but didn't seem overly interested.

Confident that I would be able to waltz right into Kaufman's office, I twisted the doorknob. Nothing happened. I tried it again, shaking it this time, but it still wouldn't budge. So much for Paoli's adeptness at schoolboy pranks.

I left the office and peeked out into the lab area, finding it empty, the lab assistant gone. Time for Plan B. I knew from my corporate days that there was always someone in any department who had a master key to all the doors and offices. People constantly forgot their keys. And if someone was at home sick, whoever filled in for them had to have access to their desk and files. I looked around the lab area. There was a master key in that room and I was going to find it.

The logical place would be Moira's desk. I tugged on her top desk drawer but it was disappointingly locked. The key could be on top. I looked around the photos of Moira's two kids and the usual clutter of knickknacks, including a framed "Cathy" cartoon, a few birthday cards, a couple of coffee mugs filled with pens. Near Moira's computer was a photo of her hugging an elderly woman I assumed was her mother or grandmother. Moira looked bubbly. Poor woman, I thought, having to work for a lech like Kaufman.

I checked underneath the mugs, the paperweight, ran my hand underneath the desk to see if the key was taped on, then zeroed in on the mugs again. Any secretary with kids had to miss some work. Kids got sick, didn't they? All the secretaries at ICI were always running out of the office in the middle of the day because their kids were sick or bruised on the playground or something. My own experience with children is very limited, and in my mind's eye I pictured all young children as bruised and scraped all over with their noses constantly running. The point was that a mother had to have her master key accessible to others in the department. Ergo, the mugs.

I stuck my hand in the first one and felt around, found nothing, but with the next one I hit pay dirt. I pulled out a small ring with three keys on it and one had a dab of red nail polish on it.

I tried that key on Kaufman's door and the lock clicked open. Kaufman's office light was off and the room was half dark, being windowless and only partially lighted from the hall. His laptop computer was sitting on his desk. I closed the door behind me and sat in front of the computer, then picked up the phone and dialed Paoli's extension.

"I'm in."

"What took you so long? I was getting ready to come look for you."

"Yeah, well, sorry to discredit the Eagle Scouts, but the gum-in-the-lock trick failed miserably."

"You must have done something wrong. Did you chew the sugar out of it first?"

"I masticated it flawlessly. There's no time to discuss it now. I had to scrounge around for a master key, so I'm getting a late start. I should be back in the office in half an hour. If I'm going to be late, I'll call you."

I hung up, turned on Kaufman's laptop and scanned through his files, but didn't see anything named Rambo. I went through the same laborious process I had gone through with his other computer, opening every subgroup of files and scanning the contents. It seemed like it was taking forever. Finally, when I had opened the second-to-last group, I found it. A group of files named Rambo sat innocently among the rest. A shiver of excitement ran through me. Life was good. I pressed a key to open the first one, but was met with disappointment.

The files were encrypted, a scrambled compilation of numbers and letters. Encryption is a protection device formerly used by the government to protect files from unauthorized eyes, and now encryption increasingly was used in everyday business. In order to read the file you had to first process it with decryption software to put it back into readable English. But if Kaufman had encrypted the file then he had to have the decryption software as well. I made a copy of the files on a diskette I had brought with me, then called Paoli to check in. I quickly told him what had happened, then turned back to the computer.

I pressed a few keys to get back to the master list of files, but didn't see anything that looked like encryption software. It had to be there, so I kept looking.

I don't know how much time had passed when I first heard the noise. I had been concentrating so hard that the time had flown by without my noticing. But I heard a door down the hallway open and close. My hands froze over the keyboard. There were footsteps that sounded like they were coming from the lab. Quickly I shut down the computer so the glow from the screen couldn't be seen in the hallway. My stomach twisted into a knot as the footsteps came closer, then closer, reminding me of ghost stories I had heard as a child. And I was just as frightened.

I ducked down underneath the desk and rolled the chair in close to me so no one would look into the office and see anything out of place. I heard the doorknob turn.

11

My mind raced with the options but there were basically only two—reveal myself or stay hidden. Small and with only one door, the office allowed no opportunity for escape, and whoever had come in was bound to find me crouched beneath the desk. I heard a rattling noise. Apparently the gum in the lock had caused the door to stick, because I heard the doorknob being jiggled, giving me a few extra moments to come up with a plan.

Unfortunately for me, all scenarios looked bleak. If it was Kaufman who found me, he would probably call the police, and the idea of jail didn't appeal to me at all. I doubted if Paoli had enough cash in his checking account for bail, and I was the shy type who didn't like showering with other women. But then I looked at the bright side. Maybe it was a security guard at the door, one with a gun and an itchy trigger finger.

When I was taking my MBA courses at Stanford the professors had neglected to cover this type of business scenario in their lecture material. Why had I let myself get into this ridiculous position in the first place? Paoli had tried to talk me out of coming to Kaufman's office, but would I listen? Of course not. I never listened to anybody. That was my trouble.

I decided to do the reasonable thing—stand up with dignity, then lie like crazy. I could always use the lost earring excuse one more time. But as I prepared to straighten my knees the sound of the door opening followed by footsteps into the office forced my mind into a panic and my body into a fetal position.

The door closed and I silently chastised myself for my reactions. I, Julie Blake, president of her high school graduating class, graduate of MIT and Stanford, would not be discovered cowering like a frightened rabbit beneath a desk. I would stand up and take my medicine, and I was getting ready to do so when I heard a thump against the desk. The thump surprised me, but not as much as what I heard next.

"Take your blouse off. I want to see your breasts."

My mouth dropped open and I clutched the collar of my blouse in chaste resistance before I realized the command was not directed at me. There was more than one person in the room. I recognized the unmistakable voice of Kaufman, but the lech had apparently lured someone into his lair. Someone with breasts. But who was this poor, cursed creature?

"No, I can't," a female voice replied.

Good for you, sister. Keep your skivvies on and make a break for it while you still can. But my mental telepathy wasn't working, because I next heard the sound of hungry kissing, heavy breathing and of papers being hastily pushed off the desk. As papers fluttered down, a stapler hit my foot and I mouthed an *ouch*. I hoped they would be cognizant enough not to hurt the computer.

"What if someone walks by?" was the next thing she said. Too late to worry about that now, honey, I thought, as her blouse dropped to the floor beside me. Slowly, with a single finger I pushed it safely away from me, figuring correctly that they were busy and wouldn't notice. It struck me that the woman's voice was familiar, but I couldn't identify it. An aroma of perfume laced with a sweet cinnamon fragrance reached my nostrils. I sniffed the air. I had smelled it before.

"No one will walk by. Forget about it. I know you want me."

Good old Franz, be he ever so humble. There was more kissing.

"I was getting so hot sitting next to you, Franz."

It was at that moment I recognized the voice of Jennifer Bailey. At first I couldn't believe it. Surely she could do better than Franz, although I supposed some women found foreign accents sexy. I gave her the benefit of the doubt and decided she had cracked under all the job pressure, then I made a mental note to try and find her a decent date. Maybe Paoli had a friend.

At this point, there was a lot of bumping against the desk. I tried to get comfortable since the point had long passed where I could jump up and say "howdy," but if I was lucky they would make love, then leave without either of them pulling the chair away from the desk. I doubted that Franz would have hot sex with Jennifer, then sit down at his desk and do paperwork. At least that was what I was hoping.

As things got hotter and heavier above the furniture, I remained curled beneath it feeling stupid and embarrassed and longing for the safety of my old job at ICI. Sure it got boring sometimes, but I had a salary, health insurance, paid vacations and no compelling reasons for breaking and entering. On the other hand I knew that some people paid big money for noises like this, and I was certain what I was hearing was much better than any 900 number.

Just then I heard something that made me shiver.

"Punish me with your mouth," Jennifer muttered.

I had heard those words before. They had been in the note that Night Dancer had written Bernie. I heard Jennifer laugh softly, then the two of them went at it like bunnies. Could Jennifer be Night Dancer? I wrapped my arms more tightly around my knees and shuddered.

After three minutes and forty-five seconds Kaufman exhausted his passion. I'm certain about the time because I was repeatedly checking my watch, wanting to keep track of when I was supposed to call Paoli. As a lover, Kaufman was definitely more of a sprinter than a long-distance man. Afterward there wasn't a lot of cooing and kissing. In fact Jennifer put her clothes back on while they discussed the budget. What kind of love affair was this? I had a feeling Jennifer would not be receiving flowers the next morning.

With relief I heard Kaufman tell Jennifer that he would walk her to her car. As soon as I heard their footsteps down the hall I tiptoed out of the office and around the corner. I called Paoli, but got no answer. I waited a little longer and when I saw Kaufman go back in his office, I slipped out of the lab.

Paoli was waiting for me in the paved area that separated the lab from the main building. His arms were crossed, his hands tucked in his armpits while his foot tapped the ground nervously.

"Where have you been?" he said testily with the same tone my mother had used on me when I was six. "When I saw Kaufman and Jennifer come out I decided to come get you but the damn lab door was locked and my badge didn't work. I was about ready to beat the door down. Why didn't you call me?"

"Because I was hiding underneath the desk while Kaufman and Jennifer—" I stopped short. I found the idea of sex with Kaufman, like certain voodoo curses, something that shouldn't be uttered out loud.

"While they what?" Paoli asked impatiently.

I had no choice but to spit it out. "While they had sex."

I started walking briskly, Paoli quickly at my side.

"You were in the office while they had sex?" I looked at him and nodded, and Paoli's eyes widened to golf ball size. For a moment he was speechless. "Were you watching?" he finally asked.

"What do you take me for? I was under the desk. They were on top of it. But forget that."

"It's hard to."

"Try. Here's the point. I heard Jennifer say to Kaufman, 'Punish me with your mouth.' "

Paoli just looked at me. "So, she's a talker."

"It's like the phrase that was in one of Night Dancer's notes to Bernie. Night Dancer said, 'I want to punish you with my mouth.' I think Jennifer could be Night Dancer."

Paoli looked incredulous.

"I don't know, Julie. I don't think you can nail the woman because of one phrase. Lots of people say things like that while they're having sex. It could just be a coincidence."

"Well, I'm going to tell Dalton about it."

"Oh, yeah? And just how are you going to tell him you got the information?"

"I'll tell the truth, naturally."

"And you know what Dalton's going to think? He's going to think you were listening to them on purpose. That you're kinky."

I let out a derogatory *hah*. "Impossible."

"I'm not so sure, Julie. The hiding-under-the-desk story sounds shaky."

"You believe me, don't you?"

"Of course, but I know you. You would never do anything kinky."

I squinted my eyes, but decided to let the comment pass.

"Did you at least find the Rambo file?" Paoli asked.

I patted my purse. "I've got a copy of it, but it's encrypted and I didn't have time to find his encryption software."

"No problem. I'll give it to Jeff. He can probably make it readable."

Jeff was one of Paoli's buddies at the NSA where Paoli had been working when we met. We continued on to the parking lot, then I broke the silence, stopping Paoli from walking.

"What did you mean by that?"

"By what?"

"That I would never do anything kinky."

"Just that. You never would."

"How do you know that I haven't done something already?"

Paoli chortled and put his arm around my shoulders as we walked to the door. "Julie, my love, you are wonderful and brilliant and incredibly sexy, but kinky you're not."

The words stung. Not kinky? I opened my mouth to tell him I was exchanging notes with Alone on Pluto, but wisely decided against it. It reminded me, though, that I hadn't responded to Alone's last message.

On the way home we stopped off at the Data9000 office while Paoli called Jeff about the Rambo file. Thrilled with the challenge, Jeff said he would start work on it as soon as we could get the file to him. We loaded the file onto my PC and transferred it to Jeff over the Net.

I called Dalton at home and told him what I had heard in Kaufman's office. I also told him how I had heard it. After he stopped laughing he suggested that I avoid such activities in the future, since breaking into someone's office is generally frowned upon by law enforcement agencies. He also said that Jennifer didn't have a decent alibi for the night Bernie was murdered. She said she had been alone, reading.

When Dalton asked me what I was doing in Kaufman's office in the first place I told him I was just searching for any files that might be incriminating. I had been more than ready to tell him about the Rambo file, but decided it would be best not to mention that I had actually stolen something from Kaufman's computer. At least not yet.

After I hung up I turned on the computer and brought the Kowolsky case file up to date, logging in our additional hours. We had already used up Bernie's two-thousand-dollar retainer, not that it meant we would slow down on our work, but I logged in all our hours anyway just in case I could use it as a tax deduction. When I was finished I looked over at Paoli and saw that he was wrapped up in his mail. He said he wouldn't be able to leave for a few minutes, so I took the opportunity to bring up Alone on Pluto's last message. Keeping one eye on Paoli, I began typing in my reply:

Dear Alone, We all need connections to other people, physical, mental and spiritual. You seem like an intelligent and sensitive person and I'm sure you would be a delightful companion in all those areas. A few years ago I took a night course and met lots of interesting new people. Have you considered something of that nature?

VIRTUAL VENUS

I logged off and we headed home. I had sex on the brain that night, but not in the usual way. It had gone from physical to conceptual. You would think that hearing two people make love only inches from me would be a turn-on and that as soon as I got Paoli alone I would jump on him like a fat lady on a milkshake, but the experience had the opposite effect on me. Sex seemed to be the central theme of this case, but it was a greedy, self-serving, loveless sex. Kaufman and Jennifer did the deed, then coldly buttoned up their clothes and discussed the budget. Bernie and Night Dancer developed a sexual relationship via machine that had turned fatal. It all left me feeling a little wary of sex as a hobby. Maybe Paoli and I could play gin rummy together instead.

Paoli was already lying on my bed in his tightie-whitie underwear reading *Byte* magazine when I stepped out of the bathroom in a long plaid flannel nightgown my mother had given me for Christmas a few years before. It had a high neck with ruffles around the throat. Paoli eyed me over the top of his magazine.

"Does this mean the honeymoon's over?"

I crawled into bed facing away from him and pulled the covers up to my chin. "I just feel like flannel tonight."

I heard Paoli put down the magazine and felt him lean over me.

"Julie, is there something wrong?"

"Why would you think something's wrong?"

"Because you're wearing a nightgown that reminds me of my Grandma Lily. It looks better on you. That I'm not denying, but what if this is a trend and tomorrow night you traipse in wearing a hairnet and terry-cloth house slippers? It doesn't make any difference to me now, of course, because I'm young and virile, but as a man gets older sometimes he needs a little—"

"Oh, shut up." I clenched my eyes shut in a vain attempt to force sleep.

"Okay, no joking, Julie, I'm worried about you," he said, his tone now different. "You're edgy, out of sorts. If this case is starting to get to you then you should back out of it. I can finish it up on my own."

I pulled the covers up a little higher. "I'm not backing out of anything."

I was prepared to hear an argument and instead felt Paoli's lips on my ear. Admittedly the feeling was delectable, but it wasn't enough to change my black mood.

"I'm tired," I said. I couldn't see Paoli's face but I could imagine the surprise on it. Since Paoli and I first began our romance I had never turned down lovemaking with him. He didn't say anything, but turned off the lights and got under the covers next to me, our bodies touching.

I couldn't sleep. I kept thinking about Jennifer and if she could have been Night Dancer. Maybe since she was having an affair with Kaufman she also knew the contents of the

Rambo file. Did that mean she could be a killer or that she could be the next victim?

When I finally fell asleep I dreamed about Kaufman. I was in his office. He grabbed me and violently kissed me, his mouth hungry like an animal's, like he was trying to devour me. *I want to punish you with my mouth*, he said. I struggled to get away from him, but I couldn't move. Then, humiliated, I realized we were both naked. I looked down and screamed. Where Kaufman's penis should have been there was a large hypodermic needle.

12

The next morning the mood between Paoli and me was cautious as we stopped by the Data9000 office and picked up Joshua's latest installment on the patient program. Not that we were bickering. Quite the opposite. Like two matrons at a church tea we were excruciatingly polite to each other, evidenced by the fact that Paoli didn't emit one argumentative peep when I suggested that I drive. We made the usual pilgrimage to the Hard Drive in diplomatic silence.

"You don't look good," Lydia said as soon as she laid eyes on me. Personally I felt she was in no position to talk about appearances since she was wearing pink leggings, red cowboy boots and an oversized purple T-shirt covered with multicolored rhinestones. Although they were obscured by her apron, I was pretty sure the rhinestones formed the outline of a poodle. To augment the French effect she had fastened a red beret to her hair with bobby pins, but it was hanging precariously on the side of her head, threatening to slide off into the sticky buns. Although her fashion sense was questionable, her demeanor was upbeat. I couldn't say the same for myself.

"I didn't get much sleep last night."

She winked and wagged a finger at Paoli. "That's your fault, you bad boy."

He had the good taste not to say anything. We got our usual coffees and a couple of muffins and headed for Biotech.

I kept my eyes on the road while I negotiated the morning traffic, but in my peripheral vision I could see Paoli watching me from his side of the car, the flannel nightie having a residual effect on him.

As I pulled into the Biotech parking lot he bolted up in his seat.

"Julie, turn the car around. I think we should take today off," he said. I gave him my best "you're crazy" look.

"Don't be ridiculous. We have work to do."

"A day off wouldn't hurt. We could go to the city, prowl through the museums, take a stroll through the park, maybe catch a movie."

"And what would Jennifer think if we didn't show up today?"

"Jennifer is probably still basking in her orgasmic glow from last night. She won't notice."

Any orgasmic glow on Jennifer's part would have to come from a couple of D batteries since Kaufman had pulled off a world speed record the night before. But I didn't mention this to Paoli since men get their backs up about these things.

The chance to take the day off appealed to me more than I wanted to admit. My body was tired and my mind muddled. More than that a part of me just wanted to escape for a while. But when I saw the Biotech building looming in front of me with its black glass and sharp edges, I felt it was posing both a threat and a challenge directly to me and I wasn't going to back down.

I pulled the Toyota into an empty space and turned off the engine.

"Listen, Paoli, Data9000 Investigations is never going to be successful if we let ourselves get scared off a case so easily."

His eyebrows rose. "Easily? Two people have died, both in ways I don't like to think about. Besides, Julie, this is all having a bad effect on you and you know it. And I'm not talking about flannel nighties. It's the look in your eyes.

You're stressed and you're exhausted."

"I'm just not sleeping well, but I feel fine, really. I was a little down last night, but I'm not anymore. I feel ready to tackle anything," I said, tapping on my chest with my fist. "And we have a very important task on today's agenda."

"Like what?"

"Like figure out how Gloria got the toxin."

Paoli looked disgruntled as we got out of the car and walked to the front entrance.

"Dalton said it could have been an accident," he said.

"He's wrong. My intuition tells me it wasn't."

"Your intuition also told you to invest your IRA money in the Mexican stock market."

"But this time I'm right."

"Let me guess. You have a plan and it has a couple of prongs."

"As a matter of fact, yes."

We both halted, him first, me second. He took my hand in his.

"Listen, Julie, I didn't like this case from the beginning when all we were doing was finding Whip Boy's wank master, and that's before people started dropping dead. If you're insistent that we find Night Dancer, then fine, I'll take care of it. I'll handle the case on my own from here, but it's too dangerous for you to be involved anymore." He pointed at the Toyota. "I want you to get in the car and go home. Pick me up at six."

I jerked my hand out of his. "Okay, fine, you investigate the murders and I'll go home and bake some cookies." I brushed past him toward the doorway. "Fat chance, Paoli," I said, throwing my hands into the air. "Why even start this argument?"

I could hear him muttering as he caught up with me, and we walked into the building in stony silence. After dropping our briefcases in our office, I marched up to the second floor to Gloria's desk, or what used to be her desk, with Paoli right beside me. We found someone sitting there—a lanky redhead with too much lipstick and a cocky look on her face like she only worked as a hobby. When I saw her I pulled Paoli back around the corner and into a doorway, out of view.

"You wait here," I told him.

"I'm not the waiting type."

"Well, then don't say anything to her," I whispered to him. "Let me do all the talking."

Paoli's already annoyed expression intensified. "You know, it really pisses me off sometimes when you use that schoolteacher tone."

He was very sexy when his eyes got that burning look in them, but at the moment I had to stay focused.

"I have a good reason for this. Just don't say anything. We're saving your golden voice for later. Trust me."

The girl at the desk looked up at us as we walked in. I noticed the young trollop give Paoli an appreciative glance and I knew how hard it was for him to keep his mouth shut in such a situation, but he did. I looked over the desk and found it the same as I remembered it.

"Hi," I said. "Are you Gloria's replacement?"

"I'm a temp," she replied in a tone that meant, So don't expect anything. Good. That meant she wouldn't have taken the trouble to rearrange things on Gloria's desk.

"Is Morse in?"

"No, he's in San Francisco all morning but he's calling in for messages."

"No problem. We'll talk to him tomorrow."

We walked away. As soon as we got out of earshot Paoli spoke to me, his voice low.

"What was that all about? Why couldn't I talk? She liked me, I could tell. I could have gotten information out of her."

We stopped and I playfully pressed him against the wall. "Believe me, I'm well aware that the girl would have told you all her childhood stories, her lingerie sizes and any state secrets she happened to know, but we don't need anything from her. Now we wait a few minutes, then you call Gloria's extension and tell the temp that you're from Human Resources and that you need to talk to her about her paycheck.''

"And what does this accomplish?"

"It gets her away from Gloria's desk so we can search it. Here's my theory. If I worked at Biotech and I wanted to murder Gloria by getting a toxin into her bloodstream, I'd do it in a way that would target only her. I couldn't put it in the water cooler or anything like that because I would risk killing the wrong people. One good way to target only her would be to use her desk somehow. That's the only thing in the company I can think of that Gloria used that wasn't accessed every day by multiple people."

Paoli turned over his palms. "But secretaries' desks get rummaged through by everybody. You were going through Moira's desk just last night."

I held up a finger. "Correct, except that executive secretaries are different. The secretary to a CEO and president has more status; she's part of the executive inner sanctum. Her desk is off limits."

"If you say so."

I checked my watch. "It's time. Let's make the call."

Paoli and I found a pay phone in the lobby, called the Biotech main number and asked for Morse, which put us through to the temp. We didn't want to use the in-house phone system since the caller's extension might show up on the digital readout on the temp's phone. Paoli told her he was from Human Resources and needed to see her immediately. He also directed her to one of the lab buildings so it would take her longer.

We walked back toward Morse's office, saw the temp scurrying in the other direction and made a beeline for Gloria's desk.

"Okay, now what do we look for?" I said.

Paoli rolled his eyes. "What do you mean, 'now what do we look for?' I thought you knew what you were doing."

"In a strategic sense, I do. I just need help with the tactical part of the plan."

Paoli shook his head but started scanning the top of Gloria's desk. "Whatever it is, it won't be obvious. It could be something she inhaled, maybe, like on her Kleenex."

I got down on my knees to view things from a different angle. "Or the killer could have placed a needle with the toxin somewhere on or under her desk," I said, still kneeling. "Thinking it would hit her in a place that would be difficult to spot, like between her fingers or her knees or something."

Paoli got down on the floor with me, checked under the desk, then opened her bottom file drawer. I prayed that no one would walk by, but it was a risk we had to take. I could always use the dropped earring excuse again. That gave me an idea. I snapped my fingers.

"What about putting the toxin on a pierced earring?" I asked.

Paoli nodded. "That sounds good. Women take off their earrings to use the phone, don't they? Someone could easily swipe her earrings and dip the little post part in the toxin."

After considering it longer it didn't sound so good. "The problem is that when you pierce your ears, after a while they heal completely," I told him. "I don't think the toxin would have a good chance of getting in her bloodstream. Our killer needed more of a sure thing."

I thought of all the orifices in the human body that could contract disease, and none of them seemed likely for this particular murder, but I kept looking. I searched the contents of her top desk drawer, then back under the desk to see if anything could have scraped her leg. I checked out everything on top of the desk one more time, but came up with zero.

I was getting frustrated. Maybe my theory was wrong. Maybe Gloria got hold of the toxin accidentally when she was in the lab, or maybe she got it in a restaurant or somewhere else completely accidental and nonsinister. My mother had spent years trying to convince me you could pick up horrible diseases from a toilet seat.

I saw Paoli running his hand underneath Gloria's chair, and at the moment my hands felt dry. Dry skin runs in my family and I always keep a tube of hand cream on my desk at our regular office, but I had forgotten to put an extra tube in my purse. I saw a ceramic pump bottle of lotion on Gloria's desk. I reached for it and pressed a small amount into my hand. I was just about to massage it into my skin when a terrible idea struck me. I looked up and saw Paoli watching me, his expression puzzled.

"Julie, what is it? You were looking at your hand like you saw the face of Jesus etched on it."

I held my palm out to him. "The cream. The hand cream," I said, my voice a horrified whisper.

He shrugged. "Yeah, right, hand cream. Am I missing something?"

"This is how Gloria could have gotten the toxin in her bloodstream. Dealing with paper all day is hard on your hands. Secretaries get paper cuts. Or Gloria could have had a torn cuticle."

The realization of what I was saying crept over Paoli's face. "You know, I remember her rubbing cream on her hands that first day we met her," he said. "It makes sense. It's something that normally only she would use, and it would be fairly simple to get the toxin in the pump bottle."

We both looked down at my hand, then at each other before Paoli grabbed a Kleenex and frantically rubbed off the cream. I used another Kleenex to pick up the bottle, then we hustled out into the hallway. I rushed into the ladies' room and washed my hands more times than Lady Macbeth, stopping just short of taking the skin off, then we started in the direction of our office. All of a sudden Paoli grabbed my arm and I almost dropped the bottle.

"Wait, shouldn't we get this bottle out of the building?" he asked.

"I think we should call Dalton first."

"We can use a pay phone somewhere, but let's get the hell out of here. I don't want to risk someone seeing us with it. You can't put it in your purse because it might smudge fingerprints."

"You think someone who is clever enough to put poison in hand cream is really going to forget to wipe their fingerprints?"

"We might as well play it safe." He had a point.

So we made our escape, hurrying through the halls, staying close together to obscure the bottle I held between us, and I was relieved when we finally made it to the Toyota. We stopped at the closest phone and called Dalton. He was on another line, so we decided to drive straight to the police station and hand him the bottle in person.

"Why do you think the toxin was put in this?" was the first thing Dalton asked. The pink ceramic bottle did look innocuous. I mean, it had a picture of two teddy bears on it.

"We looked all over her desk and couldn't find anything else that seemed like a possibility. Besides, if I were the murderer, this is how I'd do it," I said.

Dalton looked at me funny, then Paoli and I listed for him all the reasons the hand cream was the logical choice, which included the fact that it was a personal item Gloria used every day and it would be easy to tamper with. When we were done he agreed with us at least partially and made a call to a lab in San Jose. They said they could have the tests run that afternoon if they got the cream that morning.

Dalton said he would have an officer drive it over.

"Have you found anything out about Kaufman?" I asked him.

Dalton was at his desk. He leaned back in his chair and crossed his legs and I noticed he wore those thin executive-length socks. "We interviewed him again late yesterday and asked him about any toxins he was experimenting with. He claims he was working with a grayanotoxin derivative, but he says all of it is carefully tracked and none of it is missing. We found a lab assistant, though, who says he noticed some vials mislabeled. We're checking into it."

"That's it," I said, jabbing my finger into the top of Dalton's desk, which I quickly stopped because it hurt. "Kaufman admits he was working with grayanotoxin. That has to move him up to the top of the suspect list."

Dalton held up one hand. "You're right, but it still isn't proof. Other people had access to it, and Kaufman says that grayanotoxins are sometimes found in foods. Anything with honey in it, he said. She could have gotten it by accident."

"Except you told me she didn't get it orally."

"And I reminded him of that." He paused for a minute. "But don't they put honey in cosmetics and lotions? Like hand cream?"

"If there was honey in a hand cream it would only be a trace," I said, but I thought a moment. I remembered girlfriends who used honey as a facial mask. I didn't remember what it was supposed to do, cleanse your pores or something, but I told Dalton about it.

"We'll check everything out completely," he said, then paused and took a breath. "There's something else I should tell you. One of our officers let it slip that you're the ones who gave us information about Kaufman."

I grimaced. That wasn't the best of news. If Kaufman killed Gloria and he knew we were giving information to the police, how safe were we from him? The man had access to all kinds of lethal stuff. I told Dalton I wasn't worried, but I was.

When we got back to the Data9000 office Paoli called Jeff at the NSA. Jeff said he was still experimenting with decryption software and thought he would have the code broken by that afternoon.

Sitting at my desk I attempted to concentrate on a copy of the Biotech organizational chart, trying to figure out who had access to the laboratory, but I was too jumpy to focus on anything. The fact that Kaufman knew we were giving information to the police had me feeling edgy and it only worsened an already disturbing feeling I had about Gloria's death. Bernie's death was a horrible thing, but his murder was a physical attack. It came from the outside, and that simple fact made it seem more manageable to me. Gloria's death was even more insidious because the murderer killed her from the inside. She never had a chance to fight.

And if Gloria had been murdered in such a vicious way, then were Paoli and I safe? A wave of nausea swept over me as I remembered Leonard showing us the vial of the flesh-eating virus. You feel like you can protect yourself from an external attack; you can carry a gun, stay in well-lighted, populated places. But how do you protect yourself from an attack on the blood in your veins? I felt exposed and vulnerable and I didn't like it.

I inspected everything on my desk, eyeing with suspicion the most harmless-looking, ordinary articles, wondering if they could transmit a disease or toxin. Then I had an unsettling thought about my purse. I picked it up and looked inside. It would have been so easy for someone to put something in my purse while I was in the ladies' room or down the hall for coffee. A poison could be in my lipstick or a toxin on the travel toothbrush I carried with me.

I put down my purse and massaged my throbbing forehead. I could make myself crazy this way, and I had no sound reason for thinking someone would want to harm me. So Kaufman knew we had given information to the police. He wouldn't kill us for that. At least it's what I told myself.

Jennifer stopped by and asked us about progress on the patient program. She was wearing a black suit that had a serious slit up the skirt and I immediately identified it as the slut suit George had mentioned that first day we met him, the suit she wore when she had a hot date after work. She said that Morse wanted a demonstration of the interface screens and that he had cleared some time on his calendar for the following day. It was hard for me to make eye contact with her after what had happened the previous night. It didn't matter that she didn't know that I had been there. I was embarrassed to even talk to her, and Paoli's smug grin didn't help.

"The project should come to a climax in a couple of days," Paoli said to Jennifer, emphasizing the word "climax." I shot him a look, which he ignored. When she tried to set a specific time for the meeting with Morse, Paoli kept talking about when Jennifer could "come" and how he knew she was "in and out" all day. I was annoyed with him for being so childish, yet at the same time trying hard not to laugh.

At two o'clock we grabbed takeout sandwiches at the deli and were at our desks eating when Kaufman burst in.

"What do you think you're doing," he said, his whole body bristling. He shut the door behind him. Paoli and I swiveled our chairs in his direction.

"What?" I garbled through a bite of turkey on whole wheat.

"Don't play innocent. The police. They keep questioning me. I asked them 'Why do you pester me?' and one of them tells me that you have made an accusation that Gloria was murdered." He pointed a finger at me the way I imagined they had at the Salem witch trials. "You suggested her death could be connected to me. To my lab. I will sue you. I will make you pay. No one defiles the name of Franz Kaufman!"

Lobbing the words at us like stink bombs, Kaufman vibrated with Teutonic fury, and I was afraid of him. Paoli stood up and placed a hand on Kaufman's shoulder.

"Now, now, Franz, let's not get excited," Paoli said, his voice low. Kaufman shoved off the hand and shook his fist in Paoli's face.

"Touch me again and I will beat you until . . ." Kaufman said, letting the sentence hang so we could use our imaginations to fill in the blanks. It crossed my mind that this man was more than capable of killing us right then and there.

Paoli stepped menacingly toward him and Kaufman retreated a few inches. Paoli's basically a lover not a fighter, but when pressed he'll step up to any physical challenge, and a guy who pumps iron three times a week can use his biceps when biceps are called for. I would have enjoyed seeing Paoli give Kaufman a good uppercut to the jaw, but there was always the possibility that Kaufman might hit back and mar Paoli's adorable baby face, so I decided to play referee. I inserted all five foot three inches of me between them.

"Calm down, Mr. Kaufman. There's no need for a fight. There's a possibility that Gloria was murdered, and if she was, her murder could be connected to the work being done here. *Your* work. The police didn't need my help to figure that out."

"The policeman said you're a friend of the lieutenant's and that you implied I had something to do with Gloria's death."

"I didn't imply anything." No, because I stated it quite directly.

"I barely knew the girl," Kaufman said.

"If you're innocent, then you have no problem, do you?"

That stopped him for a few seconds though his anger didn't subside. He turned away from me, then spun back again.

"Why are you meddling in this? The two of you are stinking programmers. Why do you persecute me?"

"No one's persecuting you. I was with Gloria when she became ill and I'm interested in what happened to her. The autopsy report showed that she died from grayanotoxin. You work with it in your lab. It doesn't take a rocket scientist to make the connection."

He threw his hands up into the air. "Yes! Yes! I have samples of it in the lab! That doesn't mean I killed the woman. I know little about grayanotoxin. Several people have access to it. I already told the police that none of it was missing.

"One of your assistants says some of the vials were mislabeled," Paoli said.

Kaufman showed his teeth but he wasn't smiling. "Yes, but that's a technician or clerical issue. It has nothing to do with me."

"So who had access to grayanotoxin?" I asked.

"The lab assistants. Morse. Why am I telling you this? I should tell you nothing."

"Morse had access to grayanotoxin?"

Kaufman's irate expression relaxed a little. Sensing that he had successfully cast suspicion on someone else, he decided to maximize it.

"Of course. He is the president and chairman. He has keys to everything, including the lab storage."

"And who has access to his keys?" Paoli asked.

He looked at us haughtily. "I can't answer that accurately. You'll have to ask him." He checked his watch. "I'm very busy. I have to go. I'd like to leave you with one thing."

"Which is?" Paoli asked.

"Benjamin Morse has had a troubled past."

"What does that mean?"

"I can say nothing more." Kaufman opened the door and exited.

"What was that all about?" Paoli said after Kaufman was gone.

"I think old Franzie is trying to point the finger at Morse," I said.

"But why tell us? Shouldn't he be telling this to the police?"

"Maybe he already has, but more likely he's giving the information to us to protect himself. He has to work with Morse. The last thing he wants is for Morse to find out he's giving incriminating tips to the cops. Better to give the info to us and let us pursue it. That way he's insulated." I picked up the phone and dialed.

"Who are you calling?" Paoli asked.

Max picked up before I had time to answer him. I wanted to get the gossip on Benjamin Morse, and nobody was plugged into the Silicon Valley grapevine like Max. Her fiancé, Wayne Hansen, knew everybody associated with the high-tech world.

"Hi, Max. I need a favor."

I heard a sigh. "You're not the only one, sweetheart. Since you're my singular bridesmaid, would you like your data goggles to match your dress? I found a place that will spray-paint them purple."

The wedding. I had been so wrapped up in the case I had forgotten all about it, and it was only two days away. I hadn't even picked up my dress yet. I quickly scribbled down a note to call the dressmaker.

"It's up to you. No one's going to see the goggles much anyway. Aren't all the guests going into the Saturn experience as soon as they enter the ballroom?"

The wedding was being held in a hotel since the local churches didn't have enough electrical power to handle the cabling.

She sighed dramatically. "I suppose. This whole thing's making me crazy."

"It'll be over in two days and then you'll have Hansen making you crazy. Just kidding. Is there anything I can do to help?"

"Help me take my mind off of it before I run down the street shrieking."

"Okay, how about assisting me with a case?"

"The kinky one?" She sounded interested.

"The same. I want you to check out a guy named Benjamin Morse. He's the president and CEO of Biotech. I want to know the gossip on him."

"So you think the president of Biotech is engaging in sex chat on the Net?"

"Who knows? What I need from you is background info on him."

"Are you talking personal or corporate?"

"Both. Anything you can get."

We exchanged goodbyes and when I hung up the phone I noticed that I had gotten the phone cord caught on the metal spiral spine of a notebook. As I leaned across the desk to untangle it I felt a prick on the underside of my arm. My blood froze.

"My God," I said softly.

Paoli heard me. "What is it?"

I didn't answer him. I looked at my arm, saw a drop of blood oozing from my skin and the image of the vial of the flesh-eating virus flashed in my head. Desperately I searched the desk for whatever had pricked me, shoving papers and pens onto the floor as I looked.

"Jeezus, what is it?" Paoli leaped up and came over to me. Finally I found it. A pushpin was lying on my desk, the kind you use on a bulletin board. I held it in my hand, my fingers trembling as I examined the tip.

"This pricked me," I said, my voice quivering.

Paoli looked at me, his expression troubled. "It's just a

little pin prick. I don't think you're going to die or anything."

That was the wrong thing to say.

"What . . . what if someone put something on the pin? Someone could have put poison or bacteria on it."

Paoli kneeled down so he could look me in the eye. He took my hands into his.

"Julie, I opened a new box of pushpins just a few minutes ago. See up there?" He pointed to a cork bulletin board. "I pinned up a Bizarro cartoon. They were new pushpins. The box was sealed. No one had a chance to put any poison on them. Julie, you're starting to get paranoid."

But the word implied that I was afraid of something that wasn't really there, and there was something out there to be afraid of. We may not have been able to see it, but I sensed its presence.

13

Was there poison in my lip gloss? Toxin in my toothpaste? I've never been the skittish type, but now I was making myself nutty with worry and suspicion. While I sat at my desk I questioned every innocent object around me, wondering if it was a murder weapon. I stared into my cup of coffee instead of drinking it, thinking maybe someone had added a little something extra. I picked up the telephone, then slammed it back down again because something deadly could be on the mouthpiece. To say I was a little nervous was an understatement. I warned myself that I was going to end up as one of those weirdo women who wander the streets, living out of a grocery cart and wearing a surgical mask, if I didn't get ahold of myself. But fear had its grip on me and I couldn't seem to shake it.

Problem was, I just wasn't busy enough to keep my mind occupied. As far as the case was concerned, we were temporarily at a standstill, and that gave my imagination plenty of free time for ill-used creativity.

Reason and intuition told me that the murders of Bernie and Gloria were connected, but I was a little short in the evidence department and had no proof positive that poor Gloria was murdered at all. All I really had in front of me to connect the two murders was the fact that both Bernie and Gloria knew about the Rambo file. Until I discovered exactly what data the file contained, I was stuck. And that meant I was forced to cool my heels in the Biotech office with too much time on my hands, time that I could spend wondering if the envelope flap I licked was laced with cyanide.

But at least part of my problem was soon corrected for me. The phone call that afternoon from Jennifer Bailey was polite but brief, as if she had learned how to ax employees from Miss Manners.

"I'm sorry, but we won't be needing you after today. You can pick up your paychecks Monday morning," she said.

I was flabbergasted. "Are you unhappy with our work?"

"No, it's not that. Your work is fine. The truth is, it wasn't my decision, but I'd be glad to be a reference for you . . ."

She continued on about how tight money was and how terribly sorry she was, blah, blah, blah. I had fired a few people in my time. When you're a manager sometimes you have to. But I was always honest with people and told them exactly what was going on, and I had this feeling that Jennifer was being less than candid. Since Kaufman was a director at Biotech, he was probably on the management committee, and I suspected he had told Jennifer to give us the push. I would have called it pillow talk, but I doubted the two of them ever did it anywhere near a pillow.

I thanked Jennifer for the reference offer, hung up the phone and gave Paoli the news. To my amazement he started whistling cheerfully and immediately began packing up his things. It was the most contented I had seen him in days.

"To tell you the truth I've been thinking it was about time to blow this stink hole," he said, sliding his notebook in his briefcase. "First thing we'll do is jump on the Pacific Bank job, then when that's finished I'll get on the phone, make some cold calls and churn up a new client. I'll be dialing for dollars by eight-thirty. Yes sir, we'll have a new case in no time."

I sat in my chair, not moving a muscle to pack. "We don't need a new case."

He stopped what he was doing. His countenance was crusty for a moment but it soon relaxed into the type of quasi-smile I've seen adults use with naughty children.

"Listen, Jules, sweetheart, I can appreciate the fact that our client dying wasn't enough for you to quit the case. Sure, working for a corpse would stop some people, but you're a tenacious girl and I like that about you. But there comes a point when we all have to face reality. Our client is dead, and now we've been tossed out of this company. We're out the door, no longer on the premises, de-installed. We're gonzo."

I didn't say anything and he sat down across from me and gently patted my cheek. "Julie, are you hearing me? My mouth is moving and I can feel air over my lips and tongue, but I must not be talking because I can tell by your face that the words aren't getting through. Let me put it this way. The great Computer God, that big mainframe in the sky, is sending data to us. He's saying the party's over, pack up and go home."

I stood up and, in a huff, began shoving my things in my briefcase.

"I may pack up and go home, but I'm not quitting. We were paid to find Night Dancer and we're going to find Night Dancer," I said as I stuffed a fistful of papers in a side pocket.

Paoli held up his hands in frustration. "Fine. Wonderful. It's no use arguing with you, but at least we can do our investigating outside of this hellhole. It's like the twilight zone around here. I keep waiting for Rod Sterling to walk in any minute, not to mention that people around this company have a nasty habit of dying."

He ranted on for so long it was after six when we finally left the office. I was rattled over Jennifer's call, but the good news was that at least being fired took my mind off being poisoned. To calm my frayed nerves we decided to take a joint bubble bath when we got home, complete with candlelight and wine. I was looking forward to it, but, alas, it was not to be. As we started out the door, the phone rang. It was Dalton.

"The lab in San Jose looked at the hand cream," he said.

"And?" I held my breath.

"It's just hand cream. Nothing more." Dalton said the words slowly, carefully enunciating each syllable. He didn't sound happy. "They're making jokes about me now. The Jergens Jerk studying lotion potions. Thanks, Julie."

"I'm sorry if you're embarrassed, but if the toxin wasn't in the hand cream it has to be in something else. Kaufman admitted that some of the vials were mislabeled," I said in a rush of words. "Someone took the toxin and somehow he or she got it into Gloria. We've got to find out how. When we do, it will lead us to who."

Through the phone line I heard Dalton take a long breath to compose himself.

"I have a problem with what you're saying."

"Like what?"

"Like the word 'we.' I'm sorry, Julie, but it's not going to be 'we' anymore. Our guys are working hard on the case and they have it handled. I appreciate the help you've given us, but we're taking over from here."

Paoli waved his arms in front of me and mouthed "Who's on the phone?" but I was too absorbed with rebutting Dalton to stop and tell him.

"So, you're going to let one minor embarrassment veer you off course?" I said, my voice raised. "One little lab weenie calls you a couple of names and you run off with your tail between your legs? I thought you had more backbone than that, Dalton."

There was a pause on the other end of the phone. "I have quite a bit of backbone, thank you," Dalton said. "But I'm up for a promotion and having guys call me the leader of the Cream Team doesn't move me up the ladder. It was outside of protocol for me to get you involved in the first place. I should have remembered more clearly what you were like during the ICI case. You're trouble. I let you stick one toe into something and before you know it you're in up to your eyebrows. If you want to stay at Biotech I can't stop you, but as of this moment our unofficial relationship is officially over."

At this juncture I suppose I could have told him that we had just been fired, but somehow I didn't feel like it.

"You're forgetting that you're the one who asked us for help, Dalton."

"Well, I don't require it any longer. I've got some reports to do. Goodbye."

He hung up. I slammed the phone back onto the cradle. So that was that. Me, Julie Blake, being tossed aside like an empty beer bottle. Slam bam, thank you, ma'am.

"We'll see who needs who," I said.

"What? Who was that on the phone?" Paoli asked.

"A VUP," I said.

Paoli crossed his arms. "Translation, please."

"A very unassertive person."

"Dalton?"

I told him what Dalton had said, and Paoli pressed his palms together and looked up toward the ceiling.

"I'm listening, oh mighty Computer God. You're sending us another signal." He came over and jauntily slung one arm over my shoulder. "Maybe we should stop off at the store on the way home and get a good bottle of wine, the kind with a cork in it. It'll ease the pain."

I pretended I didn't hear him. "Two rejections in one day. First Biotech doesn't want us, then Dalton doesn't want us," I said. "And they were both over the phone. I prefer my rejections face to face."

"To be honest, Julie, I thought the hand cream angle was a long shot."

"*Et tu, Brute?* Gloria didn't get that toxin accidentally. At least I don't think so. Dalton said his men were working on it, but I don't have confidence in them."

"Julie, they're professionals. Maybe Dalton's right. Maybe we should leave it to them." I shot him a look and he raised his hands. "Okay, okay, maybe not, but we can worry about it tomorrow. Tonight we have plans. Bubbles. Wine. Me kissing your toes." He nuzzled my neck.

"Sounds great, but we have things to do first."

Paoli groaned. "Like what?"

"Like call your friend Jeff and see what progress he's making. He's had the document a whole day."

"Julie, call me crazy, but tonight I would rather watch you naked in a bathtub than have an decryption conversation with Jeff. We'll call him first thing in the morning."

"Let's go to the office just for an hour so we can talk in private. Please?"

He acquiesced and we went straight to the Data9000 office and called Jeff on the speaker phone. Not only had Jeff finished the decryption on Kaufman's document, he was ready to fax it over to us.

"The letter was bizarre, but the encryption was straightforward. It was basically a simple version of PGP," Jeff said.

"We're in a hurry," I said, interrupting. A guy like Jeff could wax on about algorithms like some guys wax on about football, and I was anxious to see the document. We gave him our fax number and within a few minutes I heard the machine begin to churn.

Paoli and I stared at the fax and both leaped for the papers when the machine began spitting them out. Paoli got to them first but we read them together. There were several pages of what looked like test results, but the most understandable and damning item was a letter to a member of the Saudi government.

According to the letter Kaufman was in the final stages of animal testing on a drug referred to only as R32. The tests confirmed that the drug was fully capable of altering DNA and was designed to be used against military troops. The method for delivering the drug wasn't yet confirmed, but would probably be in a liquid form that could be used to taint a water supply. At the end of the letter Kaufman reminded his reader politely that his next payment was due.

Kaufman was researching biological warfare. I could feel a lump rising in my throat.

"Kaufman is human sewage," I said. Paoli dropped into his chair and I could tell he felt the same way I did.

"Do you understand the implications of altering DNA?" he asked me. "It means that you infect soldiers with this liquid or gas or whatever and it not only messes with their genes. It messes with the genes of their future children. The letter doesn't give any information about what sort of damage this drug could do, but the possibilities are pretty awful."

"You mean it could cause the soldiers' children to have birth defects?" I asked.

"That's what happens when you start cooking someone's genes. And if it could be added to a water supply the potential uses go far beyond just the military. It could be used for terrorism. Someone could dump it into a city's water supply. I can't believe Kaufman would be cold enough to work on anything like this."

We were quiet a moment as we absorbed the terrible information.

"So at last we have our motive," Paoli said quietly. "Kaufman could have killed Bernie and Gloria because they knew about the Rambo documents. If the information became public his reputation would be ruined."

"That's plenty of motive for murder right there, but also I don't think the government would look kindly on what he's doing," I said. "Kaufman could wind up in prison."

"Do you think Morse is in it with him?"

I pondered it a moment. "It's possible but seems unlikely. Morse is sure to make millions when Biotech goes public. If what Kaufman is doing got out, it would bring an avalanche of bad publicity on Biotech and would kill off the company's chances of a stock sale. Who wants to buy the stock of a company engaged in biological warfare? It would be all over the press, plus the fact that the government would be investigating them."

"So that gives Morse plenty of motive for murdering Bernie and Gloria. Maybe he didn't know what Kaufman was doing with the Saudis at first, but suppose he found out? He would be desperate to keep it quiet," Paoli said, and I had to agree.

I was silent a few seconds as I considered this new data when a thought struck me.

"Paoli, remember that last day we saw Gloria outside Morse's office? Didn't she ask Morse about his pen?"

He cocked his head to one side. "Yeah, I think she said she was looking for it, but he said he lost it or broke it or something."

"Maybe he attacked Bernie with a knife, and the pen was in his pocket. He was probably so used to carrying it he didn't think of removing it, but he and Bernie struggled, and the pen broke. After Bernie was dead Morse noticed ink had gotten onto Bernie's clothes."

"So you're saying Morse removed Bernie's body because the ink would tie him to the murder?"

I nodded.

"Do you remember seeing any ink on Bernie that night? I don't," Paoli said.

"I just remember a dark stain, but there could have been ink."

"But we'll never know, will we? Bernie's clothes were incinerated along with the rest of him."

I sighed and sat back in my chair. "Okay, so here's where we stand. Kaufman has a motive and Morse has a motive. They both had computers and could access the Net, so they're possibilities for being Night Dancer. They both had access to grayanotoxin. But let's not forget that there's someone else with plenty of motive for murder. Abdul wanted Bernie out of the way."

Paoli put his feet on his desk and his hands behind his head. "But why would he kill Gloria? He loved her."

"Because after going to all the trouble of eliminating Bernie, Abdul gets rejected again by her. I saw Gloria tell him to leave her alone. She was quite emphatic about it and Abdul looked devastated. So he takes his revenge and kills her. But did he have access to the grayanotoxin?"

"Maybe he got it somewhere else," Paoli said. "He knows that the lab has grayanotoxin. He gets his own from an outside source and uses it to murder Gloria, knowing it implicates someone in the lab. But here's something else to consider. Gloria had to be getting the poison for a couple of days before she died. That means Abdul had to have started poisoning her about the same time he killed Bernie. Why would he do that?"

I gave my desktop a karate chop. "I just thought of something. Didn't Dalton tell us that grayanotoxin wasn't supposed to be fatal? Maybe Abdul just wanted to make Gloria sick so he could come to her rescue and get back in her good graces. He could have started slipping the stuff to her days, even weeks before. Only Gloria's system overreacted to the toxin and she died."

Paoli looked at me with an incredulous squint. "Sounds like a tough way to get a date. First you poison the girl, then you nurse her back to health so she'll go out with you. Wouldn't it just be easier to try the personal columns?"

He was right, of course, but then a lot of things about

this case didn't make sense. My watch said seven-thirty. We were both starved, but the local library only stayed open until eight-thirty, so we raced over to look up everything we could about grayanotoxin on the theory that if we knew more about our murder weapon it could help lead us to our killer. While we sat there, our stomachs rumbling, Paoli focused on poison books and medical guides and I checked references on the library's on-line information system.

"Here it is," he said, tapping on a page. "Grayanotoxin is found in the nectar of rhododendrons."

I looked up from my issue of *Scientific American*. "That means anybody could get ahold of it if they knew what to look for. Does that book show a picture of the plant?"

"You mean so Abdul could take this book and go tramping through the forest looking for it? Sorry, no pictures. The problem is that the toxin is only found in a certain species of rhododendron, a species only found in Oregon and Washington, at least in the States. Do you really think Abdul had time to make a short trip to Portland and hike around the woods extracting nectar? And why would he go to the trouble if grayanotoxin was right there in the lab?"

"To frame Kaufman, only I'm beginning to think Kaufman didn't need framing. Here, look at this. Grayanotoxin was the original experiment in biological warfare. It was used in 67 B.C. by a Greek king to beat Pompey in battle. Pompey's soldiers ate honey laced with grayanotoxin, and while they were convulsing they were massacred by the Greek army. Do you know what this means?" I asked.

"Stay away from baklava?"

"It means Kaufman was lying when he said he knew hardly anything about grayanotoxin. If I could find this historical data so easily, it must be fairly well known. I'm sure Kaufman's done plenty of research on biological warfare, enough to be familiar with grayanotoxin."

Paoli took the magazine from me and perused the article a few minutes. "It also says here that there are plenty of cases of people getting it accidentally."

"If you read further it says that in those cases people got it through food. That's not what happened to Gloria. Remember, the autopsy showed that she didn't ingest the poison orally."

We made photographs of the articles and went back to the office. Normally Paoli would have complained about going back to the office so late, but this time he said he was willing to work all night if necessary. He wanted to nail Kaufman for the murders. Besides, he was going to be performing his favorite activity next to sex—he was going to break into someone's computer.

Paoli had learned his computer infiltration skills during his time at the NSA when he was chasing hackers, but even though he had the knowledge, he rarely used it. It's illegal, after all, but catching a killer was a worthy cause for breaking some rules.

Although we had already determined that Kaufman, Morse and Abdul were murder suspects, we wanted to know if anyone else at Biotech was a possibility. To do that we needed to see a Biotech stock listing to find out who at the company owned enough stock to provide a motive to murder Bernie and Gloria.

On the way to the office we stopped at Taco Bell for takeout and ate burritos in the car. I couldn't remember the last time I had a meal that wasn't cooked by a stranger wearing a white paper hat.

We already had Bernie's ID and password for the Biotech system, so we easily gained access to the outside shell of their computer, but getting to the actual stock listing was tougher. It was eleven-fifteen by the time Paoli isolated the Biotech stock program, and it took another two hours for Paoli to break into it by using some password-busting software he had developed at the NSA. We sat in front of the computer screen feeling tired but determined, and the information proved worth the wait.

The listing in front of us showed all the Biotech employees who currently owned stock. As I went over it, my finger sliding down the screen, I found something interesting.

"Bernie owned about twenty times as many shares as anyone on this list, other than Biotech directors." I did some quick calculations in my head. "Almost three hundred thousand dollars worth by my estimates. Look at this. All the other employees, including Gloria, owned small amounts. You can tell by the dates that everyone got the stock as year-end bonuses except for Bernie. He received large chunks several times in the past few months. The last transfer date was only five weeks ago."

"You think Morse gave Bernie stock to bribe him not to say anything about the Rambo file?"

"It's sure possible."

Paoli smiled. "There's only one way to find out."

By eight-thirty the next morning we were parked on chairs outside of Morse's office. The temp, whose name turned out to be Lori spelled with an *i*, was sitting primly at her desk wearing a bright magenta sweater and what must have been a whole tube of matching lipstick. She informed us that Morse was expected in just a few minutes, a fact she knew for certain since Morse just called her on his car phone, but Lori assured us that Morse would not see us without an appointment. When I suggested that he might make an exception in our case, she shook her head emphatically, suggesting an inflexibility I felt certain would preclude her from any future career in diplomatic service.

So we sat. Paoli had the foresight to bring along some doughnuts. I had wanted him to leave them in the car, but after the first ten minutes of waiting I was glad to have them. A girl's got to eat. Every couple of minutes Lori would look up from her computer and give us a nasty look.

I offered her a doughnut, but she said she was watching her figure, which only lowered my opinion of her.

It was close to nine when Morse waltzed in, wearing an expensive dark suit I had to admit looked good on him. He laid eyes on us and immediately gave Lori an accusatory look. She pressed one hand to her buxom breast.

"I told them you wouldn't see them," she said, defending herself. He shook his head with indignation. Paoli and I stood up, just to let him know we were serious.

"I thought you two were gone," he said, regarding us with distaste.

"Not quite. We want to talk to you," Paoli told him.

Morse chuckled without smiling. "Like I have time for that. I'm busy."

I had Kaufman's letter ready in my hand and I shoved it in front of him. While he scanned it I realized I had sugar crumbs on my lip and quickly brushed them off. As Morse read the letter his gruffness wilted.

"Come in," he said without looking at us. Lori gazed with astonishment as we followed Morse into his office. "Close the door behind you."

Paoli shut the door and we stood by the two visitor chairs. Morse went behind his desk but he stayed on his feet. He laid the letter on his desktop.

"Who gave this to you?"

"I can't tell you that. What's important is that we have it. That we know what Kaufman is doing with the Saudis," I said, not wanting to tell Morse that I had stolen it. Morse's face was turning the color of Lori's sweater, and I could see the tension in his neck and jaw. For a moment he was too dazed to speak.

"Is it money you want?" he finally asked, leaning forward on his desk, his voice a low growl. "Are you extortionists?"

"No, but I think Bernie Kowolsky might have been," I said, and Morse's eyes reacted immediately. "We know that Bernie owned a lot of stock for a midlevel manager."

"How do you know that?"

I dug in my purse and handed him one of our business cards.

"We were hired by Bernie Kowolsky to investigate some threats that were being made against him." I was hoping that giving him the real reason we were at Biotech would distract him so I wouldn't have to answer his question, and I could avoid telling him we had hacked into the Biotech computer.

"We're trying to find out who murdered him," Paoli said.

Morse's eyes narrowed. "And why are you bringing this to me?"

I stepped close to his desk, leaned one hand on it and leveled my eyes at him. "Both Bernie and Gloria knew about this letter, a letter so secret it was encrypted. Now both Bernie and Gloria are dead. If Kaufman's activities had been made public you could have lost a lot of money, not to mention your reputation."

Morse went all stiff and quiet, and when he sat down his eyes were on me. He considered what I had told him, then lowered his head in his hands. When he tilted up his chin again he looked sick.

"I didn't know what Franz was doing until four months ago. Believe me, I would never condone activities like that. The whole idea of it disgusts me."

"How did you find out?" Paoli asked.

"Kowolsky. He told me. He came in here and said he was fixing something on Franz's computer and found a letter. He showed it to me. It wasn't this one," he said, pointing to the document we had brought to him. "It was an earlier letter, but just as incriminating. Kowolsky asked me for money to keep quiet."

"And you gave it to him?" I asked.

"Of course not," he said, his indignation sounding phony.

"Then how did he end up with all that stock?"

Morse frowned. "All right, all right, I gave him the stock. Kowolsky was a quiet person, but I found out he could be very aggressive where money was involved. He said if I didn't give him the stock he would make the whole thing public, tell everyone I had authorized the research. The idea of being associated with it sickened me. Plus the fact that it would screw up the public offering."

"Naturally you wouldn't want a little thing like biological warfare to cut into your bank account," Paoli said.

Morse's eyes flashed. "Think what you like, but there are plenty of people in this company who stand to make money off their stock options. People with families, people who were counting on the money."

Paoli didn't let up. "I'm sure you were only thinking of the charitable aspects of the situation."

"Listen, my hands were tied." Morse hit his desk with his fist. "I had no choice but to pay him. Kaufman promised he would cut off the Saudi deal and that would be the end of it. Only it wasn't. The bastard kept working on the project behind my back. Then Kowolsky came in here about six weeks ago and told me he'd found another letter."

"So Kaufman was still letting Bernie play around with his computer? That seems unlikely," I said.

"Kaufman is anything but stupid. The first time was an accident. Bernie was fixing something on Franz's hard drive and he found the information. Once Franz knew what had happened he transferred all the files to his personal laptop and encrypted them."

"So how did Bernie get the second letter?" Paoli asked.

"A fluke. Franz wanted more memory on his company computer. Bernie ordered an upgrade for him, but he couldn't wait and he was yelling about it, so I told him to switch computers with Gloria. She had a top-of-the-line system, but she only used it for word processing and keeping my calendar. After Gloria got Franz's computer she lost a file or something, and when she was looking for it, somehow she came across Franz's stuff."

"You mean Kaufman was dumb enough to leave the files on his company hard disk?" I asked.

"He thought he had erased them, but they were still there. I don't know how it happened. Gloria must have told Bernie what she found. They were dating, you know. They had been for a year."

Paoli nodded. "Some people don't realize that when you erase a file on your computer, it doesn't actually go away. Erasing it only means that the disk space the file was written on becomes available for something else. The file stays there until something is written over it."

"Is that what happened?" Morse asked, his eyes wide. I would bet a week's wages that as soon as we left he would be frantically checking his computer for all the incriminating information he thought he had erased.

"Look, Morse, you can't keep this Saudi thing secret anymore. Two people who knew about that letter are dead. The police have to know about it," I said.

"Their deaths had nothing to do with Franz's research! Kowolsky was murdered by a crazy person. Gloria's death was accidental. We still don't know what happened to her. You think I don't care?"

Paoli moved toward the door and put his hand on the knob. "Let's get out of here," he said to me.

"What are you going to do?" Morse asked, his voice fearful.

"Talk to the police," Paoli said.

"Not yet. Please. Give it a week, I'm begging you. I'll pay you," he blurted.

Paoli looked at him like he was something a dog left on

the sidewalk. "We don't want your money, Morse. People are being murdered, and Kaufman isn't the only one with a motive."

"What do you mean?"

"I mean you had plenty to gain by killing Bernie and Gloria and the cops will be delighted to hear about it. And what happens to Bernie's stock, now that he's dead? Since the company is private, does the stock revert back to Biotech?"

"No, it doesn't. We have a bylaw that you can't sell the stock to an outsider. If you want to sell it while the company is privately owned, only the company can buy it back, and at the original price. But if you die you can leave it to someone. It will probably go to Kowolsky's relatives."

"We'll be sure to confirm that," I said. We started out the door.

"Let me tell you something before you go. Kowolsky asked for more money. I told him I wouldn't give him anything more."

"We know he got the stock five weeks ago," I said.

"I gave it to him, thinking the company would be going public in the next ninety days and I'd be off the hook. But Franz threatened him. I heard it. We were all in this office and Franz said to Kowolsky's face that if he didn't keep quiet he'd kill him."

I remembered the note I had found in Bernie's desk.

"Did you tell the police about the threat after Bernie turned up dead?" Paoli asked.

"No. I . . . I didn't think there was any way Franz could have done it. Franz made a big point of telling Kowolsky that he could kill him and no one would ever know. The implication was that he would use something in his lab, a drug or something. Why would he go to all the trouble of stabbing him?"

"Maybe so it would look like someone else did it," I said and gave Morse one last look before we exited. His mouth was twisted and his eyes looked feverish. I thought he looked nice that way.

Lori was gone when we passed her desk, but I saw a stack of stapled documents that looked like the department budgets. I casually pointed this out to Paoli, then he stopped and began flipping through them.

"What are you doing?" I whispered, trying to see if we were still in Morse's view.

"Looking for Kaufman's budget. There might be a note attached to it." He pulled out one of the budgets and looked at the note paperclipped to it. "Here it is and here's a little note to Morse saying that something went wrong with his spreadsheet program and that some of the numbers might be wrong."

I smiled. Paoli slipped the note into his pocket.

"Souvenir?" I asked.

"Hardly. I just want to compare the writing to the note you found in Bernie's drawer."

We hurried outside, and once in the car we got out the photocopy of the threatening note. Paoli held it next to Kaufman's budget note. The writing was the same.

14

*T*erminated. It wasn't the kind of word I wanted associated with the name of Julie Blake, especially at Biotech where lately it had a particularly literal meaning, so I didn't tell George that Jennifer had fired us. I just said that Paoli and I had been let go. It sounded so much nicer, like you caught a fish and tossed it back in the water.

After the meeting with Morse, Paoli and I went back to our office—our real office, the one with the DATA9000 sign on the door. I gave the sign an affectionate pat as I walked inside. Maybe our office was a little dingy, maybe the furniture was rented, but it was home.

I called George first thing to ask him the whereabouts of Bernie's parents, saying I wanted to send a sympathy card, which was true, except that I wanted much more than that. I wanted information.

"I think he only has a mother and she's in Nevada some-where," George said, sounding preoccupied. I could hear the keys of his computer clicking and knew he was working as we talked.

"Could you go to Personnel and get her phone number for me? I'm sure there's a next-of-kin name in his file." The clicking of the keys stopped.

"I thought you wanted to send a card. Why do you need a phone number?"

"Well, a call is nice. More personal."

George was quiet a second but then said okay. We hung up and he called back ten minutes later with Mrs.

Kowolsky's phone numbers, both home and office. Since it was the middle of the day I called the office number first and got a recording that told me I had reached Sierra Power and Electric. A computerized voice sounding like a robot on Valium asked me to enter the name I wanted using the keys on the phone keypad, which I did. After some Muzak I reached the billing department and asked for Mrs. Kowolsky. In a few seconds I heard a click on the line.

"Brenda Kowolsky." The voice sounded husky and thick, a smoker's voice.

"Mrs. Kowolsky, my name is Julie Blake. I'm an investigator. Your son hired me a few days before he died."

She didn't respond and I felt uncomfortable. She probably didn't feel like talking to strangers.

"I'm very sorry about your loss. He was a fine person," I said.

"Not really. He treated me like shit. What were you investigating?"

Her words gave me a start, but in spite of her harshness there was a lethargy and sadness in Mrs. Kowolsky's speech. I couldn't see the woman on the other end of the phone line, but her voice alone told a story. I pictured her in her early sixties with permed hair dyed a flat brown, her skin darkened and thickened from years of smoking. Her eyes I imagined as dull and lightless since the death of her son.

"Someone on the Internet computer network was making threats against Bernie, and he hired me and my partner to look into it. Now we're working with the police to find out if the threats are connected to his death."

"You mean someone threatened him with a computer?"

"Kind of."

She exhaled slowly. "He was always a weirdo. Treated me like crap but I loved him. Hadn't seen him in five years."

"That's a long time," I said.

"Well, he didn't like me much. He was holding a grudge against me for things that happened when he was a kid. Silly things, looking back on them, but he was bitter. Now my boy's dead." There was a silence. "What do you want from me? I'm on my break."

"Bernie owned a lot of stock from his company. Did he leave a will?"

"That's kind of private, don't you think?" She sounded angry at first, but then I heard her sigh. "What the hell, it doesn't affect me anyway. Yeah, he left a will, but nothing to me. He sent me a copy of it about a month ago. I guess he wanted to throw it in my face that he finally owned something and didn't want me to have it. Not that I ever expected to outlive him." Her voice cracked and she sounded like she was starting to weep. "Like I said, we didn't get along too good."

"Who did he leave his things to?"

"Ah, some guy I never heard of."

"Do you remember his name?"

"I wrote it down and brought it to the office with me. I was gonna call him and give him a piece of my mind, but then I thought, hell, it's not his fault. Hang on. I think it's in my purse." She put me on hold and I listened to Muzak. "Here it is. Ricky Larson. That's who got the money. Listen, I've gotta get back to work. My supervisor's coming through."

"Thanks for your help. I'm so sorry about Bernie."

"Find out who killed my boy. He didn't deserve to die like that. I loved him."

After I hung up I felt that Brenda's sadness had crept into me. She sounded so hopeless. It was hard to believe that Bernie had left stock worth so much money to a friend when he had a mother slaving away at a power company. I supposed it made some sense if he and his mother weren't close, but still, it bothered me. She said he was holding a grudge against her for something, so maybe that was it. I guess we all hold some sort of grudge against our parents, but with luck we get over it. For a long time I held a grudge against my dad for dying. Stupid.

I called George back, and after I dialed I heard a clicking noise on my phone. It was the sound the phone makes when you have the call-waiting feature, only I didn't have it. George picked up.

"Is this by an chance an SSG?" he asked after he knew who he was talking to.

I really wasn't in the mood, but I played along. "Excuse me?"

"A subversive sexual gesture. If you want to go out with me just say so. You don't have to keep making up excuses to call."

"You're very attractive, George, but that's not why I'm calling."

"Yeah, right."

Was there something in the water at that company?

"Do you remember Bernie ever mentioning a guy named Ricky Larson?"

"Sure. Larson worked here. He was fired a year ago."

"How come?"

"The company made everybody do a drug test and Ricky flunked. Amphetamines. It didn't take a test to figure it out, either. Everyone knew. He was barely making it into work. We all covered for him."

"Was he a programmer?"

"Sure, he started out as a programmer, but then he transferred over to the lab. He said it was more interesting. Yeah, sure. The guy was a drug freak and wanted to be close to the chemicals."

"Were he and Bernie good friends?"

"I don't know. They hung out together some, I guess." He paused a beat. "Why are you asking about him?"

"His name came up, that's all. Do you know where he is?"

George hesitated, then continued. "I haven't talked to him in a year, but he used to live in Redwood City on Travers Street. He had a Super Bowl party there a few years ago. The Niners won. I don't know the address, but I remember the house was sort of a crummy pink and had a mailbox painted with idiotic little birds on it. A real dump. Are you sure you don't want to go out sometime?"

I assured him politely that I didn't. When I hung up I swiveled my chair in Paoli's direction. He was sitting straight up looking as eager as a terrier.

"What happened?" I asked.

He smiled. "I have something to show you," he said and gestured me over. I walked up and he pointed to his computer screen. I took one look and thought I recognized what I saw.

"You logged onto ErotikNet."

"Wrong. I've spent the morning hacking into Jennifer Bailey's computer. I didn't want to tell you what I was doing because if I didn't make it in you might think me less of a man, but naturally I did get in. What you're looking at is Jennifer's files. She was quite a regular ErotikNet user and she had a lot of different aliases, including Looking for Love and Testy Tina."

I raised my eyebrows. "Testy Tina?"

"That was only one of her personas. She had several. I doubt anyone realized that all of them were the same person. You have to see all the notes together like I did to get how similiar they are."

I perused the note he had on the screen. It was your basic ErotikNet fodder.

"Are any of the notes signed Night Dancer?"

"No, but what's interesting is that some of the language is like the Night Dancer notes. For instance, she uses the 'punish me with your mouth' line a couple of times."

"So if Jennifer was Night Dancer she had to send the notes to Bernie using a separate Net ID, right? In order to be routed through the Wisconsin computer."

"Right, but I'm not so sure she's Night Dancer." Paoli settled into his chair and looked at the computer screen. "After reading her notes, Jennifer just doesn't sound like Night Dancer to me. She comes off as too lonely, too passive," he said. "Who were you just talking to?"

I gave Paoli a brief rundown of the information I had gathered, including the fact that Ricky Larson had plenty of motive to murder Bernie. Larson also had knowledge of the Net and of Biotech's lab, since he had worked in the lab as well as in the programming department. We looked in the phone book but didn't find a Richard Larson, so we decided to take a drive over to Redwood City and look for the house on Travers Street that George had described.

Travers was narrow and lined with small, badly kept houses, the kind of street the city forgets to maintain properly. After a few blocks we came to a house matching George's description. It was pink, it was a dump and it had a mailbox with birds painted on it, only the birds looked like they had landed beak first in some toxic waste. Whoever Larson was, I hoped he would use his largesse from Bernie to fix up his house.

We walked up a cracked cement walkway to the front door and rang the bell. I didn't hear a ring so I knocked, lightly at first, then harder. No answer. I put my ear to the door and heard a television.

We went around the side of the house and I was peeking into a window when suddenly the blind shot up with a snap. Surprised, I jumped backward, falling into Paoli, who barely managed to stay on his feet. We regained our footing while the window opened and the barrel of a gun emerged, pointed directly at us. Paoli gallantly pushed me behind him.

"Get outta here or I'll blast your knees off. I got nothin' worth stealing."

The voice was crackly, and looking over Paoli's shoulder

I saw that the hands holding the gun were covered with ridges of blue veins and age spots. Soon the deeply lined face of a woman in her eighties appeared in the window, her silver hair trapped underneath a faded red bandana. I could only see her from the chest up, but I could tell that her aged cotton blouse was so thin from washing you could see through it.

"We're not trying to steal anything," Paoli said. "We're looking for Ricky Larson."

The woman poked her head closer to the window and squinted at us.

"Huh? You looking for Ricky? Well, he ain't here. If he owes you money it's nothing to do with me. Lord help me, I know how to shoot this thing, so you best be off. I ain't foolin'."

There's something incredibly disconcerting about the barrel of a gun when it's pointed at you, but I felt fresh courage building inside me, probably because Paoli was standing between me and the bullets.

"Please, we only want to talk to him. We work at Biotech. We just want to ask him some questions," I said. "We're friends of Bernie Kowolsky's."

The names Biotech and Kowolsky seemed to have a pacifying effect on her, because the gun barrel moved downward and she stuck her head farther out the window.

"I thought you was drug dealers."

"We're not," I said. She looked us over. I stepped out from behind Paoli so she could get a good look at my Ann Taylor suit and sensible shoes. She put her gun down on the window ledge.

"You looking for Ricky?" We both nodded. "My name's Mamie and Ricky's my grandson, but he ain't here. He left a few days ago and I ain't seen him since."

"What day did he take off?" I asked her.

"Friday. Not that him taking off is unusual. He goes off on a binge and it takes him days, sometimes a week to make it home. So you two kids work for Biotech?"

We were actually ex-employees, but I didn't think it was time to cloud the issue with confusing details, especially when her hand still rested on the barrel of the gun, so I said yes.

"Good company. That was the last job poor Ricky had. I don't suppose there's any chance of him going back there."

"I can't really answer that, but I'll check into it," I said. Mamie's hand finally left the gun. Recovered from the possibility of taking a bullet for me, Paoli decided it was time to jump into the conversation.

"Is Ricky friends with Bernie Kowolsky?" he asked.

Mamie nodded. "Sure. Bernie's one of the best friends Ricky ever had. He tried to get him off drugs, even got him tested. You know, for AIDS." She whispered the last part and shook her head. "Ricky uses needles. I don't try to hide it anymore. Best to be open. That's what they said at the meeting I went to."

Without a gun in her hand she was sort of sweet, and I didn't have the heart to tell her that Ricky was about to inherit the big bucks and had perhaps left his little old granny high and dry.

"Mamie, when Ricky left, did he take any clothes with him?" Paoli asked her. She gazed off at a tree for a moment, concentrating.

"Yup, you know, he sure did. Took his backpack and some jeans and things. He had a couple of paperback books by his bed and I noticed those gone too." She looked back at us. "You think he took a trip or something? He didn't have no money. Only money he gets is his unemployment check, and he spends that the day he gets it."

"Does he have a computer?" I asked.

"Sure. In his bedroom. Sometimes he stares at it so hard I think his eyes are gonna bug out. Works with it all the time. Really keeping his hand in, so if you know of any computer jobs anywhere I sure wish you'd give him a call."

Reaching in my purse, I tore off the edge of an envelope and wrote down our phone number, handed it to her and asked her to call us if Ricky showed up. She said she would.

Paoli and I left Travers Street and stopped by the Biotech Personnel Department to pick up our paycheck. We deserved it since we had produced at least part of a patient program, and the money would go directly to Joshua. Afterward we headed back to the Data9000 office.

We got on the speaker phone first thing and called Dalton. He sounded less than pleased to hear from us, but when we told him about the Kaufman letter he perked up. I told him about our conversation with Morse as well as the ErotikNet notes from Jennifer. Then we dropped the news about Ricky Larson.

"You've been busy," he said dryly, but thanked us for the information, sounding a little sheepish. He said he would put someone on the task of finding Larson.

Paoli called Pacific Bank about the job we were supposed to be starting for them. The applications manager said he wanted to meet with at least one of us to help him write a description of the project for his quarterly budget. I guess it was just that time of year. We flipped a coin, Paoli lost and he took off for Pacific. We agreed to meet at my place later.

It was early afternoon when I got the call from Gloria's mother.

"Someone at Biotech told me that you helped Gloria when she had the seizure. A man named George. He said you even rode with her to the hospital. Both my husband Stan and I wanted to thank you for your kindness," Mrs. Reynolds said.

I stammered around a few minutes, then told her how sorry I was about what had happened to her daughter. At a moment like that everything you say seems trite and phony, no matter how sincerely you mean it, but Mrs.

Reynolds accepted my condolences with gratitude.

"The police said that maybe it wasn't an accident." She said it calmly, but I could hear the pressure in her voice. I knew she wanted to talk about it.

"That's a possibility," I told her. I had to be honest.

"If it wasn't an accident," she continued, her voice beginning to shake, "then whoever did it should burn in hell."

"I promise you, I'll do whatever I can to help find out what happened," I told her, blurting the words awkwardly.

"But what can you do? What can any of us do?" She couldn't hold back the tears any longer and I couldn't blame her. A male voice in the background spoke soothingly. When she apologized to me I told her it wasn't necessary, then she thanked me again and said that Gloria's body was being shipped home to McCall, Idaho, for burial.

When I hung up, all the good vibrations I'd felt earlier had vibrated away. After hearing the grief in the voices of Brenda Kowolsky and Mrs. Reynolds I wondered what it really felt like to lose a child. It was hard to imagine the pain. Sometimes when I'm honest with myself I think the reason I haven't committed to marriage and children is because I'm afraid of the risk. Having my father die when I was so young left me with the realization of how hard it is to love people, then lose them.

I scrounged in my purse for my Maalox, unscrewed the cap and found it was empty. Muttering a curse I shook it, then put the cap back on and balanced the bottle upside down on my desk in hopes the dregs would slide down and pool into a mouthful. Mrs. Reynolds had said there was nothing I could do to help her, but she was wrong. I could find out who killed her daughter.

I looked at my desk and tried to imagine that I was an executive secretary like Gloria. What motions would I go through each day? It shouldn't be tough to figure out since I had observed my own secretaries for several years.

Opening my desk drawer, I considered which of the objects inside provided an opportunity to expose me to something lethal. I focused on it for five minutes before slamming the drawer shut in frustration. I had gone through this exercise already and had only come up with some innocuous hand cream.

I grabbed my shoulder bag and dumped its contents on the desk, fanning out the items. Women kept purses in their desks. I did, every woman did because at an office there was nowhere else to keep it. I looked at the stuff in front of me—a wallet, loose change, wads of receipts, a calculator, a small flashlight, keys, a lipstick, compact and a frayed coupon for Lean Cuisine that I would never remember to use. Then my eyes zeroed in on something. In the pile sat a small plastic container for tampons. Opening it, I pulled out a tampon and stared at it. A cold shiver ran through me as I realized I was looking at the perfect murder weapon.

15

I had to reach Gloria's mother but she hadn't left a phone number. I closed my eyes, my hands drumming the desk as I struggled to remember the town where she lived. Finally I got it. It was in Idaho. McCall, Idaho, and her husband's name was Stan.

I called the operator to get the area code for Idaho, then dialed information for Stan Reynolds's number. It was Mrs. Reynolds who answered. I told her who I was.

"Mrs. Reynolds, did you receive Gloria's personal property, like her handbag?"

"Why, yes. Why do you ask?"

"I need to know if she had tampons in her purse. I know it sounds like a strange request, but—"

"You think maybe she had toxic shock?"

"Something like that. Could you check her handbag for me? Please, it's important. And if you do see tampons, please don't touch them."

I heard the thump of her setting down the phone, then footsteps across a hard floor. I said a silent prayer. A few minutes later she came back.

"Yes, there were several in her purse."

"Can you send them to me Federal Express? I'll give you a billing number. I know this sounds unusual, but please pick them up with a Kleenex, put them in an envelope, then seal it. I think those tampons might help the doctors figure out what happened to your daughter."

She agreed to send them to me with overnight delivery,

refusing to use my billing number, insisting she pay for it herself. As soon as I hung up I called Dalton, but he wasn't in. I left a message for him to call me at home.

It was after five when I checked my Daytimer and remembered with a jolt that Max's wedding was the following evening. With everything that had been going on I had completely forgotten about it. Amazing. I made a frantic phone call to the dressmaker and she agreed to stay open for another half-hour, so I jumped in my car and fought the rush hour traffic. I just barely made it in time.

The dress was a deep purple with velvet on top and some frothy material in the skirt. Trying it on, I faced myself in the dressmaker's mirror and decided I looked like an eggplant. The dress was lovely, but I'm not the frothy type. I feel more comfortable in business suits.

I stopped by Max's place to check in and see if the wedding was still scheduled. She and Hansen had a very turbulent relationship and it was always best to confirm whether the relationship was off or on. Max said it was definitely on.

Dressed in an old chenille bathrobe, her hair atypically mussed, poor Max looked distraught. She was carrying a champagne bottle in one hand and I could tell by the lipstick marks around the bottle's neck that she was drinking from it directly. She shoved the bottle at me, wiggling it in my face. I politely declined the offer.

"I'm going to ask you one more time, are you sure you don't want some kind of bachelorette party tonight?" I said, following her into her living room. "It's not too late to call a few friends and go to a bar or a restaurant."

I had repeatedly offered to throw a party for her, but she had always refused. Even though I had plenty on my mind and wasn't in the mood to hang out in a smoky bar, I felt like Max would only get married a few times in her life and that she deserved a party if she wanted one.

Max shook her head then blew a strand of hair away

from her face. "A bachelorette party? The last ten years of my life have been a bachelorette party. No, tonight I just want to be alone. I want to meditate on the grave step I'm about to undertake. It's a momentous thing, you know, marriage is."

Starting to slur her words a little, she plopped down into a chair and threw her bare feet over the side. I had never seen Max so distracted and disheveled. Is this what getting married did to you?

"Are you okay, Max? Do you want me to stay with you tonight?" She belted down some champagne.

"I'm fine. Just dandy." She kicked off her house slippers and waved me toward the door. "Go. Don't worry about me. I'm getting married tomorrow and I couldn't be happier."

Personally I thought she looked like her dog had died, but I was in no position to give premarital counseling. After she rejected several more offers of my companionship I decided she meant what she said and headed for home.

It was a day for surprises and when I walked into my house I smelled aromas I had never encountered in my own home before. It took only a second for me to recognize the smells of cooking. I threw my things on the couch and hurried into the kitchen where I found Paoli wearing only blue-jeans and a long chef's apron over his bare chest. He was stirring something.

"What are you doing?" I asked. He grinned.

"Cooking dinner."

Disturbing images of boiled wieners and frozen Tater Tots filled my head as I walked over and inspected the pan in which a morass of unidentified food items simmered.

"Seems radical, Paoli. If God had intended for us to cook she wouldn't have invented takeout."

He tossed salt into the pot then stared at it as if something was supposed to happen. It didn't. He kissed me.

"The goal is to create an atmosphere in which you can relax. You've been doing a fair imitation of a banshee lately."

"Thanks for the compliment. You've been a little high-strung yourself. What are you making?"

He put his face closer to the pot and inhaled. "I have no idea. I just went to the store and bought the kinds of things my mother always bought and threw them in. We'll see what happens."

I put my arms around him from behind and kissed his shoulder. "I've never had a man cook for me before."

"Take a Polaroid, sweetheart, this may never happen again. It's more complex than I expected, but fortunately I took chemistry in college. Tell me this, is the garlic supposed to be chopped up?"

"Beats me. Seems like you're supposed to crush it or something."

"That's what I thought, but when I tried it on the countertop the garlic kept slipping around. Finally I just put it on the floor and stepped on it."

I grimaced. "Is that sanitary?"

"Don't worry, the heat kills the germs."

Here I was worried about being poisoned at Biotech when the real danger was in my own home. I was about to suggest we eat out when the doorbell rang and I jumped, startled. Hardly anyone ever rang my doorbell. Paoli and I exchanged a quizzical look then I went into the living room and opened the door, finding Dalton on my doorstep.

"Hi," he said with a shy smile. "I have some information for you and I thought I might as well drop by and give it to you in person."

"How did you know where I live?"

"Your address is in the file from the ICI case. I was in the area and wanted to apologize for the way I acted before on the phone. This case has been crazy and I've got a dozen other cases on my plate. Anyway, I'm sorry if I acted like a jerk."

I accepted his apology and invited him in, thinking maybe he had stopped by in an attempt at a subversive sexual gesture. Surely he knew I was involved with Paoli. But I had overestimated my charms, because when Dalton saw Paoli in the kitchen he smiled broadly and I knew it was general companionship the man was after. I gave him a glass of white wine and sat him down at the kitchen table before I told him and Paoli about my tampon theory. Both of their faces twisted into frowns.

"A tampon?" Dalton asked. Paoli looked at me with a repulsed expression. It amazes me that men can act so weird over a little thing like a tampon. Do women turn red and start choking at the mention of a condom, which is just as personal an item? Of course not.

"Listen, Dalton, you said yourself that Gloria didn't take the poison orally and that it wasn't injected into her. So how did it get into her bloodstream? A tampon is the perfect method. Someone could easily sneak into her purse and use a syringe to inject a small amount of liquid into the cotton right through the paper wrapper. A tampon is something only the victim would use, and then, after she has gotten the poison in her bloodstream, she flushes the murder weapon down the toilet. It's the perfect crime. Almost."

"Why almost?" Paoli asked.

I jabbed my finger in the air. "Because whoever is responsible isn't going to get away with it. Mrs. Reynolds found tampons in Gloria's purse and she's overnighting them to me. You'll have them tomorrow," I said, directing the last part to Dalton. "I'll bet you both a dinner in San Francisco they're loaded with grayanotoxin."

Dalton leaned on his elbows, his fingers pressed to his temples. "After all the jokes they made about the hand cream I can only imagine what's going to happen with this," he said unhappily.

"You'll sleep better if you don't think about it," Paoli told him, giving him a friendly slap on the shoulder. I went to the fridge to find something for us to munch on.

Dalton gulped his wine. "I have some bad news for you. Kaufman has an alibi for the night Kowolsky was murdered. We checked it out and we think it's good."

Not finding anything edible, I shut the refrigerator door. "It can't be," I said. "Where does he say he was?"

"With a woman. We called her and she backed him up."

"Jennifer Bailey?"

"No, it wasn't anyone he works with. She was some young thing he met in a bar a couple of months ago."

Kaufman had to have something going for him that I wasn't aware of. How did he do so well with women?

"She could be lying for him," Paoli said.

"I talked to her myself and my instincts say she's telling the truth. She was scared as a rabbit. We'll work on her some more, but here's what's interesting. Benjamin Morse has no alibi at all. He claims his wife was out with girl-friends and that he was home alone, but he didn't get any phone calls that would corroborate it. He had access to the drugs, he had a motive and as far as we know he had the opportunity."

"What about Jennifer?" I asked.

"Her alibi's looking more solid. Even though she says she was home alone, she got a phone call that corroborates it. It's Morse that I'm focusing on now. That's why I came over. I wanted to get your impressions of him."

I sat down at the table with Dalton. "I think he's a slime-ball and a liar. But a killer? I don't know if he has the guts for it. I still think Kaufman is our man," I told him. "Morse told us he heard Kaufman threaten Bernie. He threatened to kill him."

Paoli cocked a thumb in my direction. "She doesn't like either one of them. What about Ricky Larson? He had as good a motive as anybody to kill Bernie. Any leads on him?" he asked as he stirred his concoction.

"We haven't found him yet, but we've got a guy working on it. I just can't see a motive for him murdering Gloria Reynolds." I poured him more wine as he pondered it. "If she was murdered at all."

Paoli put a lid on the pan and picked up his wineglass but still held on to his wooden spoon. "Larson's grandmother said he has a computer. If we could log onto it we could probably find out if he was Night Dancer," he said.

"How?" I asked.

"Today I called that systems administrator in Wisconsin. She said she has a computer terminal at home where she can monitor the university mainframe. If we set it up with her in advance we can log onto Larson's computer, send a message over the Net and then she can tell if the message is routed the same as Night Dancer's." Paoli turned to Dalton. "She gave me her home phone number in case we needed her over the weekend. I saved it on our office voicemail. Could you get a search warrant?"

Dalton started to answer, but I interrupted. "If Larson's our man, he probably got rid of his Net connection along with anything else incriminating."

Paoli pointed his spoon at me. "But we know Bernie received a Night Dancer threat the day he was killed, which was last Friday. We know Larson left Mamie's on Friday night. Even if he canceled his Net connection before he left, we still might find a file or something that would give us some information," Paoli said, his excitement obvious.

"I'll get a search warrant tomorrow. Could you two take some time to look at his computer?" Dalton asked.

Paoli and I both let out an enthusiastic yes. In the midst of our conversation, Paoli hadn't been paying attention to his cooking, and the pan began to smoke ominously. I jumped up, ready to locate the fire extinguisher.

"What are you making?" Dalton asked.

"All I know is that it has something to do with his mother," I told him, once I was sure the stove wasn't going to burst into flames.

Dalton walked over to the stove and peered down at the smoking pan. It didn't take much convincing for Paoli to turn over the cooking operation to him, including the apron. Paoli put on a sweatshirt and the two of us sat at the kitchen table sipping wine while Dalton happily chopped more onions and garlic and ultimately made a very edible spaghetti sauce. We shared an excellent dinner, managing to discuss at least a few topics that extended outside the range of Biotech and murder, but ended the evening with my promise to get the tampons to Dalton as soon as I received them. I was starting to like Dalton. It even crossed my mind to fix him up with Jennifer Bailey once I was absolutely certain she wasn't a murderer.

Later that evening after Dalton had gone, Paoli and I were doing the dishes, with me rinsing and him loading the dishwasher, an unusually domestic scene for us.

"So I've been going over the Ricky Larson scenario in my mind," Paoli said as he put a plate in the wire rack.

"And?"

"And it would have to be like this. Bernie and Larson stayed friends after Larson got fired. Maybe Bernie felt sorry for him and tried to help him with his drug problem."

"Mamie said Bernie helped Larson get an AIDS test. You would have to be a pretty good friend for that," I said.

"Maybe Bernie was bisexual and he and Larson were lovers. That would be a good reason to test for AIDS."

"It's possible, but just the fact that Larson is an intravenous drug user is enough justification to test for HIV."

Paoli nodded. "True. Anyway, lovers or not, let's assume they were close. So close that Bernie left all his worldly possessions to Larson in his will." He handed a bowl back to me. "You didn't rinse this one enough."

At his place Paoli never used anything but paper plates, so I doubted he knew much about dishwashers, but I went ahead and rinsed the bowl again, just to keep him happy.

"But why would Bernie make a will?" I asked. "He was only in his early thirties at the oldest."

"Because he knew he had the stock, because he didn't get along with his mother and didn't like the idea of her getting her hands on his money."

I handed Paoli the rerinsed bowl. "You think maybe Bernie had AIDS and that's why he made out a will?"

"I don't know. It's possible. The important thing is that Larson could have found out about Bernie's will. Bernie probably told him about it, and Larson decided to get early payment. We know that Larson used to be a programmer, and Mamie told us he still has a computer. Maybe Bernie told Larson he was logging onto ErotikNet, so Larson gets an idea and starts responding to Bernie's notes as Night Dancer. He sets up the murder, kills Bernie, dumps him in the incinerator, then leaves town." He took the glass I handed him. "How many dishes did we use, anyway? Seems like I've already put in a hundred."

"This is why we don't cook. So tell me this. Why did Larson get rid of Bernie's body? He didn't need to go to all that trouble after setting up that elaborate Night Dancer scheme."

"Don't you remember what Dalton told us the night Bernie was killed? He said that the murderer may have been worried about leaving evidence. Maybe there was a struggle and Bernie scratched him. Larson didn't want his skin found under Bernie's fingernails." Paoli put the last glass in the dishwasher. "We're done. Finally. Let's go to bed."

I closed the dishwasher and turned it on. "Your theory about Larson sounds good, but like Dalton said, it leaves out Gloria."

"Let me sleep on it. I'll come up with something." He looked me up and down, then gave me a leering smile. "Julie, the rubber gloves. They're a turn-on. Can we go in the bedroom and you make them snap when you take them off?"

"Is this some sort of surgeon/nurse fantasy you got from ErotikNet?" I asked.

"I'm interested in playing doctor, if that's what you mean."

Then he picked me up, carried me into the bedroom and made passionate love to me right on top of the flannel nightgown I had left lying on the bed.

On Saturday morning I groggily opened my eyes to find Paoli deliciously wrapped around me, still sound asleep. I kissed him before I untangled myself. Today was Max's wedding day. The ceremony wasn't until seven that evening but I needed to get there early to help Max get dressed and to provide any last-minute pep talks. Paoli had been tagged by Hansen to get to the hotel early in case there were any glitches with the virtual reality equipment.

I woke him up and pulled him into the shower with me, Paoli yelling as the water hit him. While he was waking up under the massage showerhead I made a world speed record for showering and washing hair. Normally I like to take my time in the shower, but that morning I was in a rush to get to the office and get a few things done so I'd be ready when Dalton called with the search warrant for Larson's computer. With any luck, Dalton would call early enough so Paoli and I could go to Larson's house and still have plenty of time to help out with the wedding.

On the way to the office Paoli had to drop by the hotel where the wedding was being held to check out the wiring for the computer setup, so we agreed to take separate cars and meet later.

I dried my hair, threw on some jeans and a turtleneck

and put the bridesmaid dress, shoes and makeup in the car, deciding to dress at the office to make sure I was there when the package from Gloria's mother arrived. While I was driving I found myself distracted, jittery, honking madly at other cars for the most minor infractions. As soon as I reached the office I went straight to the Hard Drive for a cappuccino.

"Is that what you're wearing to the office these days?" Lydia asked me, eyeing my outfit with disapproval.

"Give me a break, it's Saturday. Besides, I have to change into my bridesmaid dress later. You remember, don't you? Max is getting married today. God, I have a million things to do. Give me the usual."

She looked me in the eye. "You don't need any caffeine."

"Lydia, I'm fine. I want my cappuccino."

"You're jittery."

"I'm a paying customer and I'd like my coffee."

Lydia leaned over the counter. "I'm like a bartender. I can cut you off if I think you could be a danger to yourself or others. You're nervous because you're going to a wedding and being near a wedding makes you think about marriage in general and thinking about marriage in general makes you think you and Paoli, and thinking about you and Paoli—"

"Okay, how about a decaf?" I could get real stuff at the 7-Eleven and not have to bear the litany. Thinking she had won, she smiled and poured me a decaf.

The phone was ringing when I got back to the office. It was Dalton. He had gotten the search warrant for Larson's computer and wanted to officially hire us to examine its hard disk. I called the hotel, and after talking to at least six employees, finally got someone to locate Paoli. Paoli said he would call the woman in Wisconsin so she would be ready for us, then meet me in half an hour in Redwood City. When we got to Larson's house we met up with

Dalton and another policeman named Jack.

"I knew you was lyin'," Mamie yelled at us as we stood on her dilapidated front porch. "You don't work for Biotech."

She allowed the four of us into her house only after Dalton threatened to arrest her. Mamie wasn't much of a housekeeper and her home was small and dingy, the rooms piled with clothes and old newspapers, the walls in need of paint. Hovering angrily near us as we walked into the living room, she wore the same bandana and faded housedress, her ensemble accessorized by a pair of old wool socks. I noticed she walked with a stooped shuffle and I made a mental note to take my calcium.

I pulled her aside to try and explain. "We didn't lie, Mamie. We were hired to do some work at Biotech. Now the police have hired us. We're consultants," I told her.

"Consultants, schmultants," she said, shaking a bent finger at me. "Ricky ain't done nothin' wrong. He's got a few problems, so what?"

"Where's Ricky now?" Dalton asked her.

"I haven't seen him since late Friday."

"Do you know where he was around ten Friday night?"

"Sure, I know. He was sitting right here with me watching *The X-Files* like he does every Friday night. After that we watched the news. If you don't believe me ask Harry next door. He was here."

Dalton sent Jack next door to question Harry. When he turned back toward Mamie he noticed a pistol sitting on a coffee table on a stack of old *National Geographics*.

"You have a permit for that?"

"You bet I do, Buster. You wanna arrest an old lady? Here, take me, A-hole." She shuffled up to him and held out her wrists. "But touch something on me you shouldn't and I'll sue you for sex harassment. I know my rights."

Dalton stepped back from her while she laughed derisively, then turned her attention to Paoli and me. "Okay, so do your dirty work. The machine's over here."

Larson's computer was a kludge of different brands of equipment wired together. Paoli called the woman in Wisconsin, sat down and turned it on. While he worked Mamie kept muttering "fascists" under her breath and haranguing Dalton with her opinions on police brutality, the flagrant misuse of taxpayers' money and the fact that Travers Street needed a stop sign. I can't say I blamed her for being snippy, having strangers barge into her house, and all for nothing because Paoli couldn't find any evidence that Larson had a Net connection at all.

"Larson's computer didn't even have communications facilities so he couldn't have had a connection to the Net," I told Dalton. I twisted my neck in Mamie's direction. She stood there, hands on hips, glaring at us. "Mamie, did Ricky ever hook his computer up to your phone line?" I asked her, and she responded with a blank look, so I phrased it another way. "Did Ricky ever tell you not to use the phone while he was on the computer?"

Mamie looked at Paoli and threw up her hands. "What's she blabbing about?"

Just then Jack returned and told us that Harry next door had backed up Mamie's story.

"See, I told ya. Ricky was here till almost eleven. Then he went out," Mamie said.

"Does he usually go out that late?" I asked her.

With her fists back on her hips, she shook her head. "That Ricky, he's a night owl. Sleeps all day, plays all night. Don't leave much time for work, though. It's the drugs that does it."

I got up from the chair in front of the computer and walked over to her. "Mamie, did Ricky say anything about coming into some money?" She looked at me like I was crazy.

"Ricky never had any money and didn't expect to come into any. I know 'cause last week he said his unemployment was running out and he was thinking about getting a job down at the Pak N' Save. He applied and everything."

Having encountered another dead end, we left Mamie's feeling low. Ricky Larson couldn't have been Night Dancer, he had an alibi for the time Bernie was murdered, and I doubted he thought he would be receiving an inheritance if he was applying for a job at Pak N' Save. I expected Dalton to be upset, but he seemed to take the disappointment in stride. I think he was just glad to get away from Mamie.

I dropped Paoli at his car so he could go back to the hotel, and I went to the office. It was close to two and it took me an hour to get myself wedged into the dress and shoes and my face suitably covered with the required makeup. Max said it was fine to leave my hair down since the VR headgear would mess it up anyway.

It was after three when I heard the door open. I looked up, assuming it was the Federal Express person, but I was wrong. Kaufman stepped inside the office, slamming the door behind him.

"I always thought there was something strange about you," he said. "You didn't seem like a simple programmer. You're much too cunning."

I didn't like his face. He wore a slight smile but his eyes looked deadly and I wished Paoli was with me. But he wasn't and I was certain Kaufman was keenly aware of his absence.

"What are you doing here? How did you find our office?"

He walked up to my desk and looked me up and down. "Nice frock, but a little dressy for the office. Morse showed me your little business card."

In a single second his expression turned spiteful and his fist crashed down on top of my desk.

"What do you think you're trying to do to me?" he yelled. "You have brought the police on me! You have told them things you have no right to!"

"I have plenty of right," I said, trying to be brave in spite of the fact that my hands were trembling. I leaned back in my chair to get as far away as possible from him without actually running out of the room. "I'm trying to find out who murdered Bernie Kowolsky."

"And you think I did?" His volume was back down again and his eyes burned into mine.

"It's possible."

He grabbed my wrist, holding it so tight it hurt. I tried to wrench it away but he held fast.

"I will tell you this once and once only," he said, his voice low and menacing. "Stay out of my affairs. They are no business of yours."

His grip tightened until I thought my wrist might break. I could feel my face turning hot, the beginnings of tears in my eyes.

"Let go of me," I said, but he only squeezed tighter.

"If you don't do as I say, I will break you into pieces."

A knock at the door startled him. A UPS guy in his twenties stuck his head in the doorway.

"I have a package," he said in a breezy manner that contrasted sharply with the moment.

Kaufman threw my wrist down, smirking at me as I held it with my other hand, wincing with pain. I was frightened that maybe he knew what was inside the package, that he would take it and destroy the evidence, but he didn't even look at it.

"Don't forget what I said to you," he said, then exited, brushing past the delivery man and out the door.

I watched him as he left. Maybe Paoli was right that we should be looking at everybody as a murder suspect, but in my book Kaufman was numero uno in spite of his so-called alibi. He had the motive, the means and the temperament. He also had the eyes of a murderer.

16

An hour later, swathed practically to my eyeballs in purple chiffon and still shaken from my encounter with Kaufman, I swept into the Monte Cristo Room of the San Jose Westin Hotel and stared around me in disbelief. I've seen lots of computer equipment in my life, but my jaw dropped when I saw the virtual reality setup that Wayne Hansen had thrown together for his walk down the aisle.

The wedding was going to be small, only about forty-five people, but everyone was going to participate in the Saturn experience. To accommodate this size group Hansen had brought in forty-five VR treadmills and arranged them in five rows, the entire treadmill grouping surrounded on three sides by large screens.

Wearing VR headgear, the wedding guests would use the treadmills to simulate walking across the Saturn landscape projected on the screens at the front and sides of the room. The headgear would transmit 3-D visuals and sound. By Silicon Valley standards this was a fairly low tech VR configuration, but concessions had to be made to accommodate the number of participants. Max and Hansen would have a much more authentic VR experience by wearing full datasuits and sophisticated headsets.

I looked around the room trying to figure out how Hansen came up with that many VR treadmills when I noticed a dozen engineers huddled together looking sweaty. The room was so chilly I had goosebumps, so I assumed it was stress creating the perspiration on their brows.

As I got closer I saw two computers at the center of the group, each one about the size of a clothes washer. Paoli was sitting on the floor staring into the back of one of the machines. I eyed the equipment with keen interest.

"Having problems?" I asked, knowing very well they were. They all looked like someone had just run over their pet turtle, which meant the equipment wasn't running properly. Only Paoli maintained an optimistic smile, but that's Paoli, always the odd man out. When he looked up at me he let out a wolf whistle.

"You look great, sort of like Scarlett all gussied up for a big dance at Tara."

"Can the comments," I said with a smile, leaning over so I could see inside the equipment. "What's the glitch?"

"Problems with the communications. This one isn't talking to that one," he said, pointing to each of the computers. "Everyone else has taken a shot at fixing it and gotten nowhere and now it's my turn. Any suggestions?"

"I'm assuming that's a rhetorical question," I said as I bunched up my skirt and sat down on the floor. I realized at this point that it had been stupid of me to put my dress on so early. I had bluejeans and a sweater in my car, so I could have waited until just before the wedding to change into the dress and had less risk of ruining it. But I was a neophyte at this wedding business. Besides, the fabric was so frothy I figured I had more of a chance of it melting than wrinkling. As I sat cross-legged on the carpet the skirt floated up around me like a purple cloud. I swatted it down and stared into the guts of the computer.

I like to think of myself as self-confident but never to the point of arrogance, and it would have been sheer arrogance to think that I could fix a malfunctioning piece of high tech equipment when a whole gaggle of Wayne Hansen's best engineers had failed. Still, my days as a programmer had left me with an unabashed lust for hardware and software, and like an old lech's love of a bare thigh, I couldn't resist peeking at any computer with the cover off.

Hansen's techno-jockeys stood around sulking, gazing down their noses at me with the priggish reserve of old schoolteachers, certain my failure was imminent. Although I had an excellent reputation in Silicon Valley, Hansen's keyboard cowboys would never believe that I could succeed where they hadn't, plus the fact that I was just a girl. In spite of all the advances of feminism most of the high tech world was male, and there was an unspoken but prevalent belief that you needed a Y chromosome when it came to computers. Of course, the fact that I was wearing a prom dress didn't enhance my credibility. I could see the doubt on their faces and was determined to prove my worth.

"Have you checked the TCP/IP connection?" I asked Paoli. I could hear a few chuckles from the group, the boys amused at my naiveté. "I suppose you did."

Paoli crossed his arms and curled up his lips, enjoying the pressure I had put myself under. Tucking my legs tighter beneath me, I leaned forward from the waist and peered into the naked flesh of the machine, deep into the bowels of the boards and circuitry. If I were going to unravel this enigma I would have to attack it from a different angle than the engineers had. I knew from my days as a vice president at ICI that sometimes the most technical minds failed to solve a problem because they probed its complexities, when often the solution was simple and straightforward. Since I was certain they had covered the most complicated issues, I focused on the mundane, and that's how I fixed the computers.

I picked up a flashlight off the floor, shined it into the computer and after a few minutes thought I had uncovered the problem. I was able to detect it mainly because I was shorter than everyone else, my height allowing me to see in between some wires where no one else had been able. But I decided to let them think my discovery was due strictly to raw skill. I held out my hand with the solemnity of a neurosurgeon who had just drilled open a patient's skull.

"Screwdriver," I commanded, my eyes glued to the computer. Paoli put the screwdriver in my palm. Carefully I poked it inside and unscrewed a communications board, which I could see wasn't seated properly in its slot. Once loosened, I jiggled it into its correct place, then I leaned back and handed the screwdriver to Paoli with confidence.

"You can turn it on," I said, trying not to sound too smug although I doubt if I achieved it. The machine began to hum.

An engineer sauntered over to the computer screen and hit a few keys on the keyboard. He looked at the screen, narrowed his eyes to slits, then leaned closer to it. He then faced us, his eyebrows near his hairline.

"She fixed it," he said flatly. I smiled. It was one of those glorious times when you hit just that right combination of savvy and luck, and you emerge victorious, a hero for a moment.

"Good work, Julie!" Paoli shouted happily. "We've been trying to figure this out for an hour."

I was still on the floor, and they all stared down at me, their expressions as arid as the Sahara. In a group of humans from a normal gene pool there might have been a few "Atta girls" tossed in my direction or maybe some pats on the back, but the highly technical mind living in the Silicon Valley culture doesn't allow for such open displays of emotion. Silicon Valley has a frontier mentality, and its best engineers, like old cowboys, are a somber, jaundiced bunch.

"Cool," one engineer finally muttered, obviously overwhelmed with gratitude. The rest of them nodded in my direction and I felt properly lauded. Paoli held out his hand to me as if I was the queen of England, helping me to a standing position as I smoothed down my chiffon with pride. Having solved one crisis I felt confident enough to tackle one potentially more vexing. I told Paoli I was going and left to locate Max.

I was afraid of what condition I might find her in, but was determined to do my bridesmaidenly duty. I went to the hotel registration desk where she had left her room number for me, then took the elevator up and rapped on her door. After a few seconds Max answered, dressed only in white silk lingerie. A bellman pushing a luggage cart down the hall caught a glimpse of her and his mouth dropped open. Max turns heads when fully clothed, but the sight of her in her underwear left the poor man ruined for the rest of womankind.

"Thank God you're here," she said, pulling me into the room. "My mother's been hovering around making me nuts, pestering about the prenuptial agreement. I said, 'Mom, it's my damn business, all right?' I finally sent her off on some errand." Max looked me up and down. "You look great in that dress."

"Thanks. I feel like I'm going to the prom," I said as I walked farther into her room. She couldn't have been in the hotel more than a few hours but the room already looked like a typhoon had hit it, with clothes, towels and pantyhose thrown everywhere. "Which isn't too bad since I never made it to a prom. Not as a participant anyway." I made the remark flippantly but it had a sobering effect on Max.

"Why not?" she asked, her tone serious.

I laughed. "Because no one asked me." I saw Max's lovely forehead furrowed with compassion. "Oh, don't worry. It was a long time ago. Lisa Friedman and I checked coats in the lobby and had a good time. Really. While everyone else was feeling each other up on the dance floor we did our statistics homework. I aced the exam."

Max looked at me with pity, which was completely unnecessary since I really did have a good time with Lisa Friedman. She knew a lot of dirty jokes. But Max couldn't understand it since she would have been suicidal if she'd had to check coats at her prom.

Wanting to get my mind off my lackluster high school years, Max fluffed up my chiffon skirt and gave me a compliment.

"You look so beautiful, Julie, you really do. The dress is a little poofy, but I thought somebody should dress up since I can't." She smiled at me. "Besides, you're my only bridesmaid and I want you take up a lot of space."

I walked over to the window and checked her view. San Jose's a nice town but it doesn't have an inspiring skyline. "I don't see what difference it makes. Everyone's going to have on VR goggles anyway."

"They'll see you when you walk in, and I want you to fully participate in the ceremony. Practice, you know. You and Paoli are probably headed up the aisle soon." She winked at me.

I turned from the window and aimed my eyes at her. Normally that sort of comment would have ignited a minor skirmish between us, but I was so glad that Max had regained her composure, I just smiled complacently.

After seeing her the previous night I had no idea what I might find that day, and I was relieved she didn't require any woman-to-woman premarital counseling. Not that I minded being a sounding board for her, but I was more worried about what I would say to her if she asked for advice. If she still professed doubts minutes before the wedding, would I tell her it was merely prenuptial jitters or suggest she book a midnight flight to Rio?

Fortunately for both of us Max was calm and self-assured except for a few minutes when her mother knocked on the door demanding the name of Max's lawyer. Max blew up at first, then sent her mother down to the Monte Cristo Room to check the decorations. Of course there weren't any decorations in the Monte Cristo Room but Max told me it would take her mother a good hour to figure that out.

It was close to wedding time and I helped her step into

her bridal gown, which was a datasuit made of white stretchy fabric with wiring trailing behind it, the normally black cables spray-painted white. While she finished dressing I told her the latest about Bernie's case, including what had happened to Gloria and my theory about the tampons. Suddenly she jumped up off the bed, almost tripping on her cables.

"Jules, with the wedding and my mother and everything I almost forgot! I got some information on Benjamin Morse. He was fired from another firm two years ago."

"What for?"

"Fraudulent accounting practices is the way I heard it. He was president of a company called Ren Technology and got axed by the board. Does that help you?"

I wasn't sure. Any company about to go public would have its accounting records audited by the Securities and Exchange Commission, so I doubted Morse could cook Biotech's books and get away with it. And with that black mark on Morse's past, Biotech's records would most likely undergo special scrutiny. Did Kaufman hint at Morse's past to provide a real clue to the murders or merely to confuse us? I suspected it was the latter.

I thanked Max for her help. It amazed me that she didn't seem nervous at all about the wedding. On the contrary, she was eerily calm, like the eye of a hurricane. Just before seven, Max took a split of champagne from the minibar, popped the cork into the air and poured two glasses. We toasted our friendship and her marriage, in that order, then went arm in arm to the Monte Cristo Room with me holding on to her cables so they wouldn't drag. We stood outside the doorway and I gestured to one of the engineers to let him know that Max was ready to take the plunge.

There was never much of a chance of any Hansen project being ordinary, but with his wedding he achieved new levels of the bizarre. By the time Max and I got there the guests had all arrived and the room was dimmed with brightly colored lasers bouncing around the walls and ceiling. The traditional bridal march was replaced with New Age drum music blasted out of huge Bose speakers, it all seeming more like some primitive rite than a wedding.

Several engineers obviously uncomfortable in their tuxedos began hustling everyone onto their treadmills and helped them put on their VR goggles. Hansen was standing at the front of the room looking antsy and the minister next to him didn't appear much calmer as Hansen helped him with his goggles. I scanned the room and located Paoli in the third row of treadmills.

I walked solemnly down the aisle with Max right behind, our pace set not by the traditional bridal march but by African percussion music. After I got Max's cables plugged in, she took her place next to Hansen on a treadmill draped with white flowers and I stepped onto a treadmill in the first row.

We all donned our goggles. After I tightened mine around my head, I couldn't see much and all I could do was just stand there, half blind, and wait for the show to start.

Suddenly the screens surrounding us burst into color and I heard Rachmaninoff through my earphones. The best way I can describe the virtual reality experience is that it's like a very realistic video game, only you have to imagine you're inside the game surrounded by a make-believe landscape. You can see your make-believe world around you, walk through it, even feel it if you have the right equipment. It's a little frightening at first, but once you get used to it it's fascinating.

I looked around me and saw a rugged terrain of red sand and strange rocks that protruded from the Saturn land as if they were statues. It occurred to me that it was Mars and not Saturn that was supposed to be red, but I supposed Hansen wanted to use a vivid color. Regardless, the effect was inspiring.

I have to admit that I originally cast some disparagement

on the Saturn idea, but now I was impressed. Behind the music I could hear a harsh wind and over the red horizon was a remarkable pink sky filled with silver-ringed moons and streaking comets. Blue and yellow rings of light rose up across the horizon, glowing like neon, and the whole experience was bizarre and wonderful. I jumped when I heard the minister's voice coming through my headset.

"Welcome, my friends, to the planet Saturn and the mystical valley of Landar," he said uncertainly, apparently reading from a script. "Follow me as we approach the wedding altar high on a bluff across the Ayanmar cliff, where dwell strange creatures adapted to the severities of the Saturn environment."

I could see the minister in front of me waving for us to follow him. I walked forward on the treadmill, and with each step I took the Saturn landscape changed. I looked to the left and saw a huge crimson cliff towering over me. To the right I saw the bluff where a stone altar rose into the sky. As I moved forward the computer program veered me toward the altar, and from behind it crept a humpbacked three-legged creature with green warty skin, huge yellow eyes, no nose and a black hole for a mouth. The creature eyed me warily, hissed, then scampered away. Weird wedding.

As we reached the altar the computer program moved us up a steep flight of green stone steps chiseled roughly out of the side of the bluff. The altar looked more like a place for a human sacrifice than a wedding. Once at the top I could see Max and Wayne. In "real" reality they were standing on a platform in front of the screen, but in our make-believe world they were high on the bluff. As they held hands the minister went through a fairly typical ceremony, but the typical part didn't last too long.

As Max was about to say that she took Hansen in sickness and in health, a hail of meteors flew toward us and I heard several guests scream. I hoped the vows were extensive enough to cover Hansen's mental as well as physical health. Even though I knew the meteors weren't real, they sure looked real, and I ducked as a chunky one headed straight for me.

I wondered what Hansen had planned for his wedding night. Was it, too, going to be a virtual reality sexual experience? Max always joked that Hansen was so interested in computers she had to make noises like a disk drive to get him in bed with her.

Once we had survived the meteor shower the ceremony continued in a comparatively normal fashion, and although I tried to listen to the vows my mind kept veering toward the Kowolsky case.

I couldn't help it. I had all these pieces laid out in front of me—the Night Dancer threats, the murders of Bernie and Gloria, the Biotech stock and the too coincidental exit of Ricky Larson. I knew they all added up to some logical conclusion, but the conclusion escaped me. There were too many suspects, too many alibis and nothing tying the pieces together.

Behind my thoughts I heard Hansen repeating his wedding vows. Doing my best to direct my attention to the sacrament of marriage, I straightened my posture and looked at Max and Hansen while the minister spoke about commitment and eternal love, but I felt removed from the ceremony, as if I was looking at something through a window. Someone had committed murder. But who and why?

I fixed on Larson. Although I had never laid eyes on the man, he definitely had a motive for killing Bernie and he had a strong enough knowledge of Biotech to carry out the murders. But why would he kill Gloria? For that I had no answer, yet I felt certain the two murders were connected. They had to be.

Kaufman seemed the most likely suspect, but Dalton was convinced he had an alibi. And as far as I was concerned, Jennifer didn't have a motive and Morse didn't have the nerve. As for Abdul, the possibility of his killing Gloria just didn't sit right with me.

At that precise moment an idea began to take form in my head, a solution to the problem almost too obvious to be believable. It was like fixing the computers that day by looking for something simple rather than something complex. All of a sudden I thought I knew how to find Night Dancer.

When I looked back at the altar Max and Hansen were taking off their headsets, apparently having tied the nuptial knot without any more meteor showers. As the rest of us took off our goggles, the lights came on and we found ourselves back in the relatively mundane confines of the Monte Cristo Room. We all crowded around, congratulating the happy couple, and I did my compulsory share of it, even though my mind was still whirling around the theory forming in my head.

Paoli fell in by my side as we all moved to the large ballroom next door for the reception. Although the wedding itself was small, the reception included hundreds of guests, most of them already swilling champagne and eating the vegetarian hors d'oeuvres by the time we walked in. The Saturn theme was continued in the ballroom decorations, with planets affixed to the walls, laser lights bouncing on the ceilings and the members of the reggae band dressed in space outfits that contrasted sharply with their dreadlocks. Dozens of waiters dressed like extraterrestrials maneuvered through the room offering champagne and food.

"Cool wedding," Paoli said to me as we stood on the sidelines watching the people crowd around the tables, edging their way toward the pesto crudités.

"*Great* wedding. I think I still have meteor dust in my hair," I joked. Paoli kept his eyes on the crowd, but leaned closer to me.

"Julie, all this has me thinking. What do you say we move in together? I mean formally, same address and everything. Mingle our underwear, share the toothpaste. You can have the right side of the bed, I'll take the left."

I could feel a familiar tension filtering through my body and wished like hell I had some Maalox in the small evening handbag I had with me.

"This isn't the time to discuss it."

He turned up his palms as he looked around the room. "This is a wedding, right? The union of two souls and all that? Not that I'm ready to start picking out dinette sets or anything, but I'm definitely talking about a union between us. Definitely a union. Sort of."

I waved to a few people I knew as I talked. "Paoli, this isn't the time to start talking unions. You're supposed to stay focused on what's at hand. It's like discussing your upcoming appendectomy during someone's open heart surgery. It's in bad taste."

I looked at him and could tell he wasn't buying my hastily composed appendectomy theory, but I couldn't tell him that the topic of marriage made my stomach clench into an object you could bowl with. And at that particular moment I was too absorbed with my new Night Dancer idea to focus on such a serious and disconcerting topic as formal cohabitation. I decided to tell Paoli what was really on my mind.

"Listen, I have this idea," I said. He looked down at me, his expression surly and I knew I had blown it.

"I'm not interested in ideas tonight. I'm interested in drinking. And right now I need a drink."

Paoli turned and stomped off in the direction of the champagne fountain, which was a mechanical creation shaped like a spaceship with champagne spurting out its fuselage. As soon as he left I began kicking myself for what I had said to him. I started after him, but stopped to mull it over. Of course, he was behaving like a child. On the other hand, was I behaving like a neurotic bitch?

I quickly decided on the latter and again started off after him, but was grabbed by one of the engineers who had earlier been working on the VR equipment. I didn't know his name and he didn't introduce himself.

"I just want you to know that I liked what you did today. It was way cool, how you slapped that board in place with that dress on and everything," he said, slurring his words. He hadn't had time to have more than one or two drinks, but he probably wasn't much of a drinker and the champagne had gone right to his cerebellum. To be honest, I would have liked a little champagne myself, but I needed all my brain cells. I thanked the engineer for the compliment and continued my search, but couldn't find Paoli.

By this time, around eight, the party was going strong and the reception had turned into a big dance, bringing up for me with dismal vividness my own teenage dance experiences. Suddenly the more humiliating aspects of checking coats at the prom came back to me.

Admittedly I was sulking because of my tiff with Paoli. I stood around for the next hour making small talk with a few acquaintances and eating my weight in egg rolls and tiny spinach quiches. Finally, ready to throw myself at Paoli's feet and beg his forgiveness for my cold reaction to a proposal that would have made any woman proud, I circled the room once more and at last found him on the dance floor. Concealing myself behind a potted palm, I clamped my teeth as I eyed the young wench writhing to the music in front of my beloved. She was young, blond, and attractive in a tawdry Victoria's Secret sort of way I supposed some raw-beef-eating, overly hairy men would find appealing.

Paoli knew from our brief history together that the sight of him dancing with another woman would arouse juvenile feelings of jealousy in me, and I wasn't about to let him see me in that disgusting emotional condition. Besides, I had work to do. Maneuvering through the crowd, I found Max so I could say goodbye, but she hardly gave me the chance.

"Jules, my mother's making me crazy. Now she's following me around giving me advice about my wedding night, like Wayne and I haven't done it before."

"That's probably natural for a mother," I said.

"So finally I told her, 'Mom, we've had sex already. We've had sex wearing wet suits and flippers, okay? So I think I can handle a little postmarital coitus.' But would she drop the subject? This whole wedding thing just isn't what I expected." At this point Max grabbed both my hands and pulled me over to the bar where a guy wearing antennas on his head was pouring green-colored drinks. "Jules, listen, remember the ICI Christmas parties when we would grab a bottle and go have a drink in the parking lot by ourselves? Let's do it right now. I'll get a bottle of champagne and we can sneak outside, just for a few minutes."

"Max, I can't. I have to leave. Something has come up with this case I'm working on, and—"

She cut me off. "You and Vic had a fight, right?"

"How did you know?"

"Because the two of you haven't been together for the last hour, because you're both wearing expressions like the Grim Reaper, because he's slow-dancing with Wayne's niece, who has the cranial capacity of a single-celled organism. I know you, Jules. I can look at your face and know what you're thinking. Is there anything I can do to help? Slap him around a little? Lock Wayne's niece in my hotel room?"

"Thanks, but it's okay. Yes, we had a fight, but that's not why I'm leaving. I have work to do. I know it's bad of me to leave the reception like this, but I've got this idea in my head and I need to sort it out."

"What could you be doing this late?"

"I'm going to Biotech."

She gave me a suspicious look. "I thought they fired you."

"They did, but I think I can still get in the building. Anyway, I'm going to try. It should only take me an hour. When I'm done I'll come back."

Max took hold of my arm and pulled me close to her. "Let me go with you. I can help. You know I can. I've helped before," she whispered.

I looked at her with puzzlement. "You mean leave your wedding?"

"If it only takes an hour I'll never be missed. Wayne invited the president of every high tech company in the valley and he'll be schmoozing for hours. Right now he's over in the corner with Randall Schmidt deep in a discussion about three-dimensional data types. He'll never know I'm gone. Please let me come along. You're going to break into that building, I can tell by your voice, and I want to help."

"I don't know, Max. To leave your wedding. It's not normal."

"Jules, I'm fresh off the planet Saturn, dressed in a white stretch suit with cables attached to my butt. Don't talk to me about normal."

She had a point.

Max found Wayne and told him she was going upstairs for a minute. Before we slipped out of the reception we grabbed a plate of brie and stuffed mushrooms, then went to her room where she quickly changed into a pants suit. I had misgivings about taking her with me, especially since the last time Max helped me with a case she got knocked unconscious, an accident which catapulted Hansen into a form of dementia heretofore unseen by the hospital personnel. But how could I deny my best friend on her wedding day? Besides, I wanted the company.

While she changed clothes I called my office voicemail and checked the saved messages to get the home phone number of the systems administrator in Wisconsin. I called her and found out her name was Janet. I told Janet I needed her assistance and she agreed to help me. By the time I hung up, Max was dressed and we sneaked out of the hotel and got in my car.

I had left my regular handbag underneath the car seat,

having replaced it temporarily with a small black velvet clutch large enough to hold two quarters and a pocket calculator. I've never understood the concept of the tiny handbag. Scrambling through my purse I came up with the two things I was after—Bernie's Biotech badge and my Maalox bottle. Max saw me take the bottle out of my purse.

"I thought when you quit your job at ICI your bad stomach days were over," she said.

"That's what I thought, too, but I was wrong. They were just beginning." I took a gulp and put the car keys in the ignition.

"That's the funny thing about life," Max said. "It never turns out the way you think. Like me, for instance. I never thought I would marry a guy like Wayne. I thought I'd end up with a Cary Grant type—smooth, suave, you know, more tranquil. You couldn't call Wayne suave or tranquil."

Tranquil? I'd met toy poodles more tranquil than Wayne Hansen but I didn't say so. I used to make a lot of cracks about Hansen, but now that he was my best friend's husband I was determined to treat him with more respect.

I kept my mouth shut while Max discussed her plans for her wedding night. I was too busy thinking about Biotech to pay complete attention, but Star Trek suits were mentioned. Sometimes it's best not to ask for details.

17

Twenty minutes later we pulled the Toyota into the Bio-tech parking lot, gazing up uneasily at the black glass mono-lith in front of us.

"Who's the architect, Darth Vader?" Max asked. I laughed and told her my first impression had been the same. It was after nine o'clock and the parking area was empty except for a couple of cars. I let my seat back so I would have enough room to get out of the bridesmaid dress and into more comfortable clothes, but even with the seat reclining it was hard shimmying myself out of that dress. The skirt alone took up half the car. Finally Max had to help me.

"Be careful!" she said as my foot snagged the hem. "You're going to rip it."

I unwrapped the fabric from my toe. "Well, I'm sorry, but it's not like I'm going to wear it again."

"You can't be sure."

"Believe me, I'm sure. The dress is gorgeous, but wear-ing it I feel like I'm smothering in purple meringue."

Max shoved her fist into her waistline. "It's your brides-maid dress, Jules. You can be so unsentimental some-times."

I reminded her that she had just left her own wedding reception so she clammed up.

Once untangled from my chiffon, I squeezed into the jeans and the sweater I had left in the backseat. Then I rum-maged around the car for my loafers, couldn't find them and had to put on the purple high heels. Seems I remember high heels and jeans being fashionable sometime in the seventies, but I was never on the edge of fashion anyway.

Max and I went to a side door and with naive confidence I pushed Bernie's badge into the card reader. The light blinked an unrelenting red, the door refusing to open.

"Hah. So much for your plan," Max said, apparently still miffed that I wouldn't be wearing my purple chiffon on a regular basis to the grocery store. I tried the badge again with the same disappointing result.

"It worked fine the other day. I guess the administrative folks at Biotech are more on the ball than I thought. Someone canceled Bernie's badge."

Max made a face. "Of course. He's dead. He's not supposed to be using it. So now what?"

I looked at her and smiled. "We at Data9000 Investigations will not be stopped by such minor roadblocks."

If the theft of Bernie's badge had failed me, the next plausible option was deceit. We walked around to the front of the building while I explained to Max what we were about to do. Only months earlier I would have considered the deception I was planning beneath me, but that was when I was receiving a regular paycheck and full health benefits. Times change.

I paused in front of the glass doors leading to the Biotech lobby. A graveyard shift security guard sat at the front desk. I took a moment to get into character then I pushed on the door handle. It was locked. What was this, the Pentagon? I rapped on it loudly and twisted my features into an expression of stunned despair.

The guard looked up from his paperback. He was young. Good. He would be more malleable. I pointed to the door and gave him an imploring look that convinced him to leave his post, unlock the door and open it a whole six inches.

"The building's closed," he said.

I sighed with desperation and mimicked an expression of feminine helplessness I had seen once in an old Gloria Swanson movie. The security guard gave me a quizzical look that made me wonder if I was overdoing it. The dramatic arts were new to me and it was possible that my facial expression more resembled gastrointestinal distress than emotional desolation. I relaxed my face a little.

"Is something wrong?" he asked.

"Well, you see, I'm Bernie Kowolsky's sister. This is my cousin Maxine." He looked at us with a blank expression. "You know, Bernie Kowolsky, the employee who was murdered?"

His eyes grew large. "Oh yeah, sure. I heard about that. Hey, I'm really sorry. I saw him around here a couple of times. Nice guy. You know, you look like him."

"Uh, thanks," I said, trying to decide if I'd been insulted. "Listen, we were supposed to be here this afternoon to pick up some of his personal things, but the traffic was awful and then I got lost."

Max edged her way up where he could see her better. "Things are just so different here than in Arkansas," she told him. I gave her a sideways look and continued.

"So we were wondering if we could just run back to his desk real quick and get his things," I said.

The guard's shoulders stiffened.

"Aunt Edna wants them," Max chimed in again, really enjoying herself. "She's so destroyed by what happened."

Rubbing his chin with his hand, the security guard mulled it over. "Do you have any identification?"

Identification? I groped for a plausible answer. "Hmm, let's see. When I married Vic I changed my name on everything," I said, immediately wondering about the Freudian implications of the statement. I scrambled through my purse, stalling for time while Max looked on with amusement. "I have a credit card here." I took it out of my wallet and held it up for him. "See, it says Juliet K. Blake. The K's for Kowolsky." It was actually for Katherine, but it gave him enough justification to open the door a little wider.

"Look, I really should walk you back to his desk, but I'm not supposed to leave the lobby."

I could tell by his knitted brow that the strain of this seemingly unsolvable dilemma was causing him mental and emotional distress. He was slipping away from me, but then Max made her move.

Stepping forward and resting her fingers on his arm, her eyes locked onto his like lasers. "Why don't we just slip back there really quickly? No one will ever know," she said softly and I saw her fingers give his arm a gentle squeeze.

"Okay, but be fast." He opened the door so quick it almost hit me.

Max and I thanked him profusely, assured him of the brevity of our visit and hurried on our way.

"Men can be such weak specimens. One little press of the flesh and he crumbled like a homemade cookie. Makes you wonder about our armed forces," I said as we race-walked back to the Applications Department. Max gave me a punch on the arm.

"Are you kidding? I've been practicing that look since I was thirteen. Plenty of strong men have fallen for it. Executives, generals, heads of state." She noticed my incredulous look. "Well, Wayne falls for it and he's got fortitude."

I'd seen tapioca with more fortitude then Wayne Hansen, but I kept my mouth shut about it. When we reached the Applications Department we stopped and took a look around. The place appeared empty but earlier I had noticed a couple of cars in the parking lot, so I was still worried about being seen.

We made our way to Bernie's old office and tried the door. It swung open. Max and I entered, closing the door behind us. Quickly I sat in Bernie's chair and turned on his computer.

"After a while the security guard is going to come looking for us, so I have to work fast. You stay by the door and tell me if you see him coming," I said to Max.

I typed in commands, navigated my way to the Net menus, then I called Janet in Wisconsin and told her to stand by.

"What on earth are you doing?" Max asked from her sentry position at the door.

"Just trying something out." With Janet on the phone and ready at her computer, I created an E-mail message, sent it to my computer back at the Data9000 office and held my breath. To my great disappointment Janet told me that the message wasn't routed the same as the Night Dancer messages. I thanked her for her time and we hung up.

I spent the next few minutes looking through all of Bernie's computer files, in every nook and cranny I could think of, not sure what I was looking for, but I didn't come up with anything that helped. I was bent over the keyboard trying to decide my next move when I heard a noise. I froze.

"Max, is someone coming?" I asked, my voice lowered.

She peeked out the doorway. "I think I heard something, but I'm not sure."

"Get over here with me, quick."

I didn't have to tell her twice. Max sidled behind me, and I pushed her to a crouching position so my body was between her and the doorway. I didn't know what good this was supposed to do, but when Paoli had stepped in front of me that day we came nose to nose with Mamie Larson's gun it had seemed so gallant. I thought I owed the same to my best friend, especially on her wedding day. There wasn't much in Bernie's office that could be used as a weapon, so I grabbed a stapler.

Max looked at it discouragingly. "If someone jumps us you're going to staple his fingers together?"

"I'm going to bash him over the head with it," I answered with a lot more bravado than I felt.

I sunk farther down into my chair and hoped like hell I

wouldn't have to actually try it. As I sat there stiff with fear it occurred to me that Biotech was a very dangerous place. And there we were alone, vulnerable, our only protection a stapler and a twenty-year-old security guard sitting too far away from us to hear a scream.

I must have been crazy to take Max away from her wedding and into a potentially dangerous situation, and even though she had asked to come, I knew better than anyone that in certain areas Max had no sense at all. She had married Wayne Hansen, hadn't she?

Silence surrounded us, but I was certain that someone else was there. I slid up in my chair and hastily logged off Bernie's computer.

"Are we leaving?" Max whispered. I nodded and she looked disappointed. "But why? I don't think there's anybody out there. We just heard the air conditioning come on or something."

"Listen, Max, I like to think of myself as brave, but not to the point of stupidity. We're getting the hell out of here."

I made sure I left Bernie's desk and screen exactly as I had found it, then Max and I scurried out.

"So you found what you were looking for?" Max asked as we hurried down the hallway.

"No, I didn't."

She tugged on my sleeve. "Then let's go back, Jules. I can stall Kojak Junior and you can keep working."

I shook my head. "It won't help. What I tried didn't work. Besides, hearing that noise back there spooked me. Somebody around here has murdered two people. We should play it safe."

"Play it safe? That doesn't sound like you."

"Yeah, well, I'm getting older."

The truth was that I had plans for the evening that weren't safe at all, but I didn't want Max to know about them since she would probably insist on coming. I conjured up this laughable image of Hansen crawling into his marriage bed wearing his silk Star Trek jammies and finally noticing that his bride was missing. Besides, what I was about to do I wanted to do alone.

As we passed by the security guard I thanked him again and patted my shoulder bag as if it held a plethora of sentimental family treasures. He asked me to express his sympathies to Aunt Edna. I winced with guilt as I told him I would.

I dropped Max off at the hotel. She wanted me to come back to the reception, but I told her I was tired and was heading home.

"Should I tell Vic you went home?"

"Don't say anything. Let him wonder."

She twittered deviously. "Good plan. Don't worry, if Vic's still in there I'll monitor his every move and report back to you," she said, reading my mind. Before she got out of the car we hugged and I wished her a great wedding night, whatever that might entail.

As I drove away I pressed hard on the gas pedal, the engine accelerating along with my blood pressure. If what I was looking for wasn't in Bernie's office computer, it had to be at his house. I stopped at our office, found the client form Bernie had filled out the first day we met him, and jotted down his home address. When I checked my messages I heard the same strange clicking noise I had heard the day before and it crossed my mind that someone was tapping my phone. Phone tapping's tough but not impossible. I'd heard that if you hunted down the right catalogs you could order the equipment through the mail. I made a note in my Daytimer to get my phone checked on Monday. My computerized voicemail told me I had one message.

"Julie, this is Dalton. Looks like you were right about the tampons. Out of the three in Gloria Reynolds's purse, two of them had a deadly form of grayanatoxin in them. Call me."

I tried Dalton at the station and they said he was out. Next I called his home number but got his message machine. My watch said ten so I guessed Dalton had a hot date. I left a message.

"Hi, it's Julie. You can stop looking for Ricky Larson. If you check his medical records I'm pretty sure you'll find that it was his blood you found at the scene of Bernie's murder. I think Bernie altered his own personnel records so his blood profile matched Larson's. If you get this message in the next hour meet me at Bernie's house. Eleven-oh-two Carson Avenue, number five, in Brisbane. I know who Night Dancer is. At least I think I do."

I hung up and dialed Paoli's house, but no answer. Where could he be? I thought up several possibilities and didn't like any of them so I decided to stop thinking, but the Red Sea would part first. My mind swirled with thoughts about Night Dancer, about Paoli, about how I would nail a murderer, about how I would act when I next saw my boyfriend.

Bernie's address was about half an hour away from the office. Highway 101 was packed with cars, even at ten at night, and I wondered where everybody was going. Shouldn't they be home? But then, maybe they were all like me—out on the streets, up to things they probably shouldn't be. That's what makes life interesting.

I pulled off the freeway in Brisbane and stopped at a gas station for directions. When I arrived at Bernie's, the address turned out to be an apartment building, a two-story beige stucco block with the kind of nice landscaping and pool that made me think it had been converted to condos. Bernie's unit was on the first floor near the front on the west end of the building.

I walked up to his door and jiggled the knob. It was locked, no surprise. There wasn't anyone around, so I tried a window, but found it equally uncooperative. Even though the outside of the building was deserted I heard a television next door with the volume so high I learned all about the next day's weather. It was going to be cloudy. I saw lights on in some of the other units, which made breaking the window too risky, so I got an idea.

I loosened the bulb in one of the outdoor lights, throwing the outside of Bernie's place in darkness. Then I walked back to my car, unlocked it, opened the driver's door and pressed the switch that unlocked the other three doors. Then I relocked the driver's door, closed it, walked around to the passenger door and opened it. Bingo. The Toyota's alarm system had been triggered and the horn blared obnoxiously.

I knew how to set off the alarm this way because I had done it accidentally several times when I was unloading things. Luckily for me I never got around to having it fixed.

There are few things more annoying than a car alarm and few things louder, and as soon as the horn started blaring I ran around the side of Bernie's building and slipped out of view. I heard someone yell out their window, describing my Toyota in the most unflattering of terms. Peeking around the corner I saw a couple of people headed outside looking for the car's owner, ready for a lynching. Everybody knows that when a car alarm goes off there's no chance of there actually being a thief around. Car thieves are way too smart to set off car alarms.

While everyone was distracted by my shrieking Toyota, I took off my high heel and broke Bernie's window, the one on the side of the building facing a narrow alley and a fence. I always knew high heels were good for something. I put my shoe back on, walked casually out to my car, apologized profusely for the car alarm and turned it off.

After everyone was back inside and settled in front of their televisions I went back to Bernie's window, pulled out enough glass for safety, reached in and unlatched it, raised it and dragged up a planter to use for a stepping stool. Climbing into what turned out to be the kitchen, I stepped from the windowsill down into the sink, then slid onto the floor. My arm knocked into something, followed by a clattering of metal as it crashed downward. In the stream of moonlight coming through the window I saw the gleam of a kitchen knife. I picked it up and put it back on the counter.

I groped through a couple of rooms until my eyes adjusted to the darkness. Bernie's house didn't look like the house of a dead man. It was too neat and clean and personal. The place was small and it didn't take long for me to find his computer.

I sat down, switched it on and waited while the screen's glow sliced through the darkness. Since it was Bernie's home computer it had no password, and I got into the system easily, the keys flying beneath my fingers. It was after midnight Wisconsin time, but Janet was still awake and watching an old black and white movie with her boyfriend, she said. I told her what I was up to and she asked me to give her a minute to get her computer system ready. While I waited, I started checking through Bernie's files.

It bothered me that maybe a neighbor would hear the computer keys clicking in a dead man's condo, but there's no way to type silently, and I was too driven to stop. I went through two menus and found a group of files called Net, and as I searched through them I got a surprise. Buried amidst some innocuous letters were several copies of ErotikNet notes from Testy Tina and Looking for Love, the same ones Paoli had found on Jennifer's computer. My blood started racing. I thought I knew why Bernie had them, but I needed one more piece of information before I could be sure.

Janet came back on the line and said she was ready. I went through the same process I had gone through at Biotech. I got into Bernie's Net menus, created an E-mail on his ID and sent it to my computer at our office. Success.

"That's it," Janet said. "Whatever computer you're using, it's at the same physical address as Night Dancer's."

She paused. "So what are you going to do now?" Good question.

"Get out of here and go to the police," I said. I thanked her for her help and we hung up. Sliding down into Bernie's chair, I rested my elbow on the table and my forehead against my fist. It was hard for me to accept it, yet I knew it was true. Bernie was Night Dancer.

Janet had just helped me prove that he had sent the threatening notes to himself, and that one fact made at least some of the others fall into place for me. I closed my eyes and attempted to put the pieces together. When Bernie worked on people's computers at Biotech he must have liked to snoop around their files. That's how he found Kaufman's letters to the Saudis, how he found Jennifer's ErotikNet notes. At first he probably found Jennifer's electronic love life funny, but then it gave him an idea, a creative solution to a problem. That's why Jennifer's phrase *Punish me with your mouth* had ended up as one of Night Dancer's phrases. Bernie had used some of the verbiage from Testy Tina to help him create his make-believe stalker.

My body went stiff with disgust and anger. Bernie had sent the notes to himself from his home computer to set up the scenario for faking his murder, and he had used Paoli and me as his lackeys to corroborate the Night Dancer drama. Bernie wasn't dead. A slumped body, some blood on his shirt, all purposely cloaked in the darkness of the parking lot had fooled me completely. I had never questioned any of it because I had seen the blood, and the blood was real. But it had been Ricky Larson's blood and it was Larson's body that had been tossed in the Biotech incinerator.

There were still holes to be filled, but at least I knew how Bernie had done it. It was the why that now disturbed me. That first day we met Bernie he had seemed genuinely scared of something, a man frightened for his life. Those

247

emotions had been real. Nobody was that good an actor.

A hundred questions bounced around my cranium and I was too nervous, too jumpy to keep my thoughts straight. Focus, I told myself. Analyze the data. It was like examining different fragments of a software program. I had to correctly piece them together to figure out what the program accomplished, but my mind wasn't cooperating.

I closed my eyes again and concentrated on that night we had seen Bernie's body. That afternoon Bernie had insisted that Paoli stay late at Biotech. Bernie must have purposely suggested the meeting with Paoli to Jennifer so when I walked out to the parking lot that night I'd be alone. That part had been critical. Bernie knew that after I saw him I would run back into the office to call the police, leaving him time to make his escape. Bernie, despite his feigning death, must have been shocked when I came out with Paoli. It could have ruined his plan, only Paoli had gone back inside the office with me.

Bernie had access to the laboratory. He had access to Gloria's purse. Even if someone had discovered that Gloria had been murdered, they wouldn't suspect a dead man. He had killed her because she wanted to tell the world what Kaufman was doing, and that would have made Bernie's stock worthless.

My mind was muddled with so much information. I needed someone to talk to, someone to help me sort it all out. Anxious and excited and depressed all at once, I used Bernie's phone to call Paoli. No answer. Next I dialed Dalton. I got his message machine again.

"It's me again. Julie. I'm at Bernie's Kowolsky's house. Listen, Bernie sent the Night Dancer notes to himself. I'm not sure why. Not yet. And I'm pretty sure he willed his stock to Ricky Larson so he could take on Larson's identity."

It was then I realized that I was talking to a dead phone. The humming noise of Dalton's message machine was disturbingly silent. I heard a muffled squeak in the house. The sound was light, barely there, but I heard it, the same sound I had heard at Biotech, and I realized it was the sound of a crepe-soled shoe. Sitting up stiffly, I listened in the darkness. There was someone in the house.

I pressed and released the telephone's disconnect button, but still no dial tone. Had someone cut the phone wires? Dread filtered through my body. I shouldn't have come there alone. Dumb thing to do. I should have waited for Paoli, but I had been too jealous, too petty to ask him to come along. I hoped the mistake wouldn't be fatal.

If someone was in the house I assumed he or she had to have come through the front door since I would have heard anyone coming in the window. That made the window my escape route. Slowly, quietly, I pushed the chair back and stood up.

Just make it to the window, Julie, I told myself. But I didn't make it. Before I even got close to it, out of the darkness someone lunged at me.

18

A body slammed into me and something hard, a fist or an elbow, jammed into my solar plexus. With a gasp of shock and pain I hit the floor on my knees, the breath knocked out of me, and I waited for the follow-up blow I assumed was coming. But it didn't come.

As I gasped for air I looked frantically around me. Where was he? I saw a human form a few feet from me fumbling for something in the darkness. I looked for a gun or knife in his hand, but what I saw instead was the tip of a needle shining in the moonlight and at that moment it was more frightening than any weapon.

He came at me. I flipped onto my back, kicked him in the groin, feeling my narrow heel plant hard into him. He reeled backward. I lunged in the direction of the front door. A hand on my leg jerked me to the floor. I kicked again and this time felt my heel catch his jaw. He stumbled and slammed against the door, blocking my exit.

With that option gone I scrambled back toward the kitchen, but behind me I could hear his feet against the floor of the hallway. Then I remembered the knife. The knife should still be in the kitchen, but the kitchen seemed miles away. I felt something grab at the back of my sweater and I fell. He threw himself on top of me, his knees straddling my body. I tried to turn over but he held me down so tightly I could only twist my head.

I strained to see my attacker's face but he was wearing a nylon stocking over his head. With one hand he held my throat. The other hand, the one with the needle, jabbed at me wildly, missing. A drop of fluid hit my cheek. I could hear his heavy breathing, his grunts of frustration, and I sensed he was as afraid as I was.

Managing to roll on my side, I punched upward, my fingers curled like a claw. A searing pain shot through my fingers as the impact bent them backward. He howled and the grip on my throat loosened enough for me to scramble out from under him. I wanted to yell for help but my breath was trapped inside me.

I ran for the kitchen and went for the knife. As my fingers wrapped around the handle he fell onto my legs. I looked back but all I saw was the needle coming at me. My hand came up from my side and I swung the knife back at his head. He yelled with horror. I missed, but in dodging the knife he collapsed backward.

I jumped up, the knife still in my hand. He was sitting on the floor next to the kitchen counter breathing hard, his head down. Keeping the knife near his chest, I reached forward and tore the stocking off.

He looked up at me, his face filled with panic. At first I assumed it was because of the knife I had pointed at him. It wasn't. It was the needle that had planted itself in his arm when he fell.

"Call an ambulance. Please, call an ambulance," he muttered softly, his manner as innocently pleading as a child's, reminding me of the first day I met him. I just stood there.

"The phone's dead, Bernie."

"Go next door then. Please," he said. His tone was more begging now.

I knew I should go make the call. I didn't know what was in that needle, but from the look on Bernie's face I figured it wasn't vitamin C. He could die. But my body wouldn't move. Max had told me only a few days before that everyone had a dark side to their souls, and at that moment I found mine. Still holding out the knife, I felt it wobble in my hand. I wrapped my fingers more tightly around its handle.

"No," I said. "I'm not calling anyone. Not until we talk."

Bernie's face crumbled. "Please, I don't know how much got into my bloodstream. I need a doctor."

"I know what you did, Bernie. I just don't understand how you got Ricky Larson's blood on the pavement. You didn't kill him until later that night."

"Please help me, Julie. Call an ambulance."

"Tell me how you did it!" I screamed the words.

He was shaking all over now, with little fretful noises coming out of him. I wondered if Larson made the same kind of noises when Bernie killed him.

"Okay, okay. I told Ricky I could have his blood tested for HIV at Biotech, so he let me draw samples from him."

I pictured Larson trusting Bernie, letting him inject him with something lethal without realizing what was happening. And now here was Bernie looking at me with those despairing eyes. I felt so sick and disgusted and weary with the world.

"But why fake your death? It was so risky. You didn't have to."

Bernie's breathing was quickening and I saw tears in his eyes. "But I did. I did have to!" He spit the words out, crying hard now. "Kaufman said he was going to kill me. He was going to do it. He was following me around. Calling me and saying things. I was afraid. I'm afraid now, Julie. Use a neighbor's phone, Julie. I don't feel good."

"How did you know I was here?" I asked, but as soon as the words came out of my mouth I remembered the clicking sounds I had heard on my phone line. Bernie had been tapping my phone. He had heard me tell Dalton where I was going.

Bernie sat up on his knees, holding his arm close to his torso. "I'm begging you to call an ambulance. Do you hear me? I'm begging. I can pay you. I'll have lots of money. I know you want to help me, Julie. You wouldn't just stand there and let me die."

"How do you figure that, Bernie?"

"Because you're not that kind of person."

"I wouldn't be so sure of that if I were you. This job's changing me."

At that moment I heard knocks at the front door, then the sound of it bursting open. Dalton and Paoli ran into the kitchen, with Paoli still wearing his tux. I hadn't realized until then how handsome he looked in it.

"Go next door and call an ambulance," I told him. "Better hurry."

Once the danger was over the first words Bernie spoke were "I want a lawyer." At least that's what Dalton told me. The syringe contained thiopental sodium, a barbiturate used at Biotech to euthanize lab animals when they had outlived their usefulness. Personally, I thought Bernie had outlived *his* usefulness, but he had only gotten enough thiopental to make him sleepy. The dark side of my soul wished he had gotten more.

19

*T*he fascinating thing about technology is that it always ends up being used for things for which it was never intended. The Internet was developed for information exchange yet it was being used by people to explore the darkest recesses of their souls. Bernie had used it for sex, for murder, and ultimately as part of a plan to change his identity.

But like a lot of technical innovations, it had a glitch, at least for Bernie. Kaufman's biological warfare experiments became public during the police investigation and Biotech's stock never made it to the public auction block, effectively hitting the 'delete' key on Bernie's dreams of a new life, a new identity, and new wealth.

Both Morse and Kaufman were ousted from Biotech and apparently the new management recognized George's true genius because he finally got his own office. And as for Abdul, the last I heard he had found a new girlfriend via the personal ads in the *Bay Area Guardian*. The print medium seems a little archaic, but I guess whatever works.

Two days after the case was finished Paoli walked into the office armed with pastry and coffee from the Hard Drive. He said he wanted to have a celebration party, but I didn't feel like celebrating any event associated with murder. I picked out a doughnut anyway, just to be polite.

"So do you think Bernie had planned the whole scenario for months or did he improvise as he went along?" Paoli asked as he took a big bite of a jelly-filled.

"I know he had it planned at least two months ago, because that's when he started sending himself the Night Dancer notes. Kaufman kept threatening him. He was scared to death and wanted a way out, but at the same time keep the Biotech stock."

Paoli swallowed a bite, licking a little jelly off his lip. "But we know Ricky Larson was alive when we saw Bernie that night in the parking lot. Mamie said Larson was home watching TV. How did Bernie get Larson's blood on the pavement before he actually killed him?"

"Remember that Mamie said Bernie was helping Larson get an AIDS test?"

"Yes. So?"

"Leonard from the lab told the police this morning that two months ago Bernie had asked him how to draw blood from the lab animals and how to run blood scans. Bernie said it was to help him with his volunteer work at the AIDS center, so Leonard showed him how to do it. That's how he was able to get Larson's blood profile and put the information in his own personnel record. And when the police lab tested the blood on the pavement, it matched Bernie's blood profile. He must have drawn blood from Larson a few days before he killed him."

I saw Paoli go over to the window and peer out of it, looking downward at the shrubbery.

"What are you looking at?"

"Nothing. Keep talking. What were you about to say?"

"Just that Bernie knew we're security specialists, not networking experts. That's why he chose us. He didn't think we had the know-how to figure out where the Night Dancer notes were really coming from. He had already poisoned Gloria's tampons weeks before, so he assumed that after we thought he was dead, we'd drop the case and then he'd be free to leave town. Only we didn't drop the case. Bernie found out that we were still showing up at Biotech every day, so he tracked us to find out what we were doing."

I took a bite of doughnut and washed it down with some coffee. It bothered me a little that I had let my emotions get out of control on the Kowolsky case. When I had worked at ICI I had always kept them in check, but it was easier then. At a corporation you can keep your distance from things, wrapped in the cocoon of your office and your job title. But now all my old protection was missing, my emotions so much closer to the surface, and it disturbed me and satisfied me at the same time.

There was a knock at the door. It was Josh.

"I came to get paid," he said. I pulled a check out of my drawer and handed it to him. "Is the case over?" he asked.

"Yes. All over." I took a bite of doughnut.

"After what you told me about it, I've decided not to use ErotikNet any more. Too many weirdos."

Paoli walked over to my desk and sat on the edge of it. "Well then, now that you're not going to be using your alias anymore, can you tell us what it was?"

Josh looked sheepish. "Alone on Pluto," he said. "Silly, isn't it?"

As I choked on my doughnut I got an idea. I got up and walked around my desk.

"Listen, Josh, since you're not going to find love on the Net anymore, would you be interested in a blind date?" I asked him.

Josh brightened. "Sure. A friend of yours?"

I smiled and nodded. "Her name's Jennifer Bailey. I think she'd appreciate a nice guy like you." In my opinion a cockroach would be preferable to Kaufman, but I didn't say it out loud. "I can call her today if you'd like."

Joshua gushed with thanks before he left. Still sitting on my desk, Paoli twirled a pencil around his fingers and eyed me warily.

"You really think Joshua and Jennifer could be a match?" he asked.

"Why not? They're both nice people and they're both

lonely. Who can say when it comes to love?"

He swung himself off my desk. "Speaking of love, I want you to know that I've been thinking about that abbreviated discussion you and I had at Max's wedding, and I've decided that the idea of living together is out of the question."

My heart took a swan dive. "It is?"

"For now anyway. I mean, we haven't even known each other a year. It would be irresponsible to make a decision like that."

I was suddenly enveloped in a Maalox moment. Had Paoli fallen for Wayne Hansen's niece, that cheap trollop? I started to protest, but Paoli kept talking.

"I mean, you and I need to establish ourselves on a firmer footing. How do we know we can properly nurture a relationship when we haven't had anything to test our nurturing skills on?"

Nurturing skills? Were we going to adopt Wayne Hansen's niece? Paoli was up to something.

"What are you talking about?"

He grinned and walked out of the office. A few moments later he trotted back inside preceded by a large dog.

"This is Cosmos," he said proudly. "I got him at the pound."

"Obviously," I said, examining the pooch who was now sniffing my shoe. His curly hair was black tinged with gray, and he didn't resemble any particular breed I could think of. "You're not suggesting that you and I take care of this dog?"

Paoli dropped to his knees and muzzled Cosmos. "Why not, Julie? We can put his bed in your kitchen. I'll keep him on our off nights and he can come to the office during the day. It's an opportunity for us to grow as individuals and as a couple."

Cosmos pulled the leash out of Paoli's hand and wandered around the office, sniffing at everything.

"Paoli, we don't have time for a dog. Besides this one is

obviously untrained and possibly not too bright," I said as Cosmos turned over the trash can and began chewing paper. He then walked over to our first box of new Data9000 brochures. He sniffed it suspiciously.

"Although his judgment seems excellent," I added as Cosmos lifted his leg and moistened the cardboard box. I was liking this dog better. I decided to look at the bright side.

Cosmos was a much better playmate for Paoli than Wayne Hansen's niece.